THE FORENSIC SERIES

BLOOD EVIDENCE

AUGUSTINA VAN HOVEN

Cover designed by Elizabeth Mackey

Developmental Editing by Theresa Leigh

Copy Editing by Mary Marvella

Formatting by Kalie Gerwig : Good Girl Author Services

Proof read by Mary Marvella

Amazon eBook ISBN: 978-1-951534-23-3

Draft2Digital eBook ISBN: 978-1-951534-24-0

Print ISBN: 978-1-951534-25-7

For my husband Stuart. Without his help, this book would not have been written.

CONTENTS

THE FIRST VICTIM

Detective Sean Landers sketched an image of the body in his notebook. The crime scene photographers would accurately catalog the scene, but it always helped him focus his mind by making a drawing for his personal reference.

He walked around the king-size bed, noting the color of its quilt, a shiny thing, probably satin. Varying shades of green contrasted with a leaf pattern on its different panels. It was too feminine for his taste. The artwork above the headboard depicted a forest scene with deer drinking at the bank of a stream. Sean raised his eyebrows; every house in the state of Idaho seemed to have some version of this painting. He snorted. At least it wasn't Elvis on velvet. He directed his attention back to the victim, leaned over her and murmured, "Tell me your story."

The woman appeared to be in her mid-thirties, well-built and pretty. She lay with her hands, feet, and mouth bound in duct tape. Her unblinking eyes stared at him. His stomach clenched. It happened every time he was called to investigate a murder. When he worked in Los Angeles, he'd practically lived on antacids because of it.

"Detective?"

Sean looked up at the man who had spoken. "Yeah?" He recognized the queasy look on the young officer's face. "What is it?"

"Sir, the people from the forensic lab just arrived. Do you want me to send them up now?"

Sean turned his head towards the photographer just in time to catch a flash full in the face.

"Damn," he swore. Now he'd be seeing green spots for the next 20 minutes.

He rubbed his eyes. "Billy, you about finished?"

"I just need a couple more shots from this angle," the man replied.

"Sid?" he called to another man with a video camera documenting the broken items on the dresser.

"Almost. This is the last part of the room I need to shoot." Sid continued to record the turned over jewelry box and the costume jewelry scattered over the floor.

"Good," Sean nodded to the young officer. "send the lab boys up."

As the officer left the bedroom, Sean held up his notebook and scratched his chin with it, listening to the young man's feet echoing along the hall and down the stairs. He glanced back around the room. Something didn't feel right.

He hadn't worked on a murder since he left California four years ago. This area had its share of crime, but, oddly, murder wasn't very common. Of course, being a state in which nearly everyone hunted and owned firearms, finding a defenseless victim was not easy. He glanced at the woman on the bed. Someone had found one.

Sean wrote the date, April 8th, slipped the pencil into his coat pocket and pulled out a pen. The woman lay on her back in what was obviously the master bedroom. She wore a black nightgown, the long kind with skinny straps. It had a matching robe, currently lying in a pile on the other side of the bed. Angela Mercer, a beauty expert with her own business, failed to show up for a weekly standing hair appointment. Her client got worried and called nine-one-one.

The body had ligature marks around the neck, probably from the cord that lay next to the bed. It looked like the power cable to a laptop computer. He made a note to ask the lab boys about it. Angela's brown eyes stared blankly at the ceiling. The nightgown was pulled up on one side, exposing her well-shaped leg up to mid-thigh. Sean didn't think she'd been sexually assaulted, but that was something else to be determined.

The scene looked like a burglary gone bad, but something bothered him. It had the usual destruction, jewelry boxes overturned, drawers opened with some of their contents dumped on the floor. The wide open closet doors showed clothes piled on the ground, many still hooked on their hangers. Angela appeared to be a clothes horse. The perpetrator, Sean was relatively sure there was only one, must have been looking for a safe or a hidden box used to store money and other valuables. When they finished here, he'd question a friend or relative to find out what, if anything, was missing.

The entrance of the forensic team interrupted his thoughts. Cliff Bowman strode in, carrying what looked like a large tackle box. Bowman seemed uncomfortable in his white Tyvek suit. It looked like the man had grabbed a size too small from the crime scene trailer. The front zipper of the suit hung open from neck to navel. Bowman's large belly draped over the top and out through the opening of the unused zipper. Sean smiled to himself. Obviously, Cliff's latest diet wasn't working.

A few moments later, a woman came in. She carried a second tackle box. Her Tyvek suit was zipped up but fit her like a bedsheet. Sean nearly laughed.

Bowman glanced over his shoulder at the woman, then turned to Sean. "I don't think you've met my new partner.

This is Stephanie Webb. She transferred earlier this month from the Boise lab."

Stephanie stepped forward and nodded to him. She didn't offer to shake hands. Her own were encased in blue nitrile gloves. He nodded back and watched her closely as she walked through the room and stood against the wall near the bed.

Stephanie had a pleasant, pretty face. As for her build, well, he couldn't tell much with that baggy outfit. Cliff's voice brought him back to business. "Tim's here with the laser measure."

A uniformed state police officer came in carrying a case and a tripod.

Sean turned to face the fresh addition. "Hey, Tim, welcome to the party."

Tim frowned. "You know how I hate to do these. I mean, they made this equipment to measure and reconstruct auto accidents, not work crime scenes. They keep promising new equipment, but you know how that works. Boise gets first dibs on any new stuff. Can I get a hand with the tripod?"

Stephanie moved out from her place against the wall. "I'll help. There's nothing else we can do at the moment."

Tim nodded at her and handed it over.

The sound of stomping feet drew Sean's attention back to the stairs. Joseph Mackenzie, his partner, came into the room puffing like a bellows. He stood for a moment, leaning on the doorjamb, then reached into his pocket and pulled out a piece of nicotine gum.

"Mac, you find anything?"

Mac chewed for a moment then came further into the room. "I walked the perimeter with the deputies. It looks like the perp gained access to the house by breaking the small window in the back door of the garage."

When Mac took another step closer, Sean could smell the cigarette smoke clinging to his clothes. The man was a nicotine addict. Sean wouldn't be surprised if he pulled up Mac's shirt sleeve and found a nicotine patch as well. "Do we have any more information?"

Mac read from his notebook. "Angela Mercer was a divorcee, thirty-four years old and has a son." He looked up. "That would explain the room down the hall with all the super hero stuff in it. I don't know where the boy is. I have a deputy heading over to the ex-husband's house. I hope the boy is there and not out with friends. No kid should come home and find his mother like this."

"Is anyone canvasing the neighborhood?" Sean continued to write in his notebook.

"There are two deputies out there now. We don't have any more men available to work the scene. There's a three-car pileup on Highway 95, so we're spread rather thin today."

Sean nodded. That was constantly the problem with the department, not enough personnel. The sheriff's excuse for it - the budget didn't allow for the hiring of more officers. *Yeah, but there always seemed to be enough money for more equipment for the SWAT team and other high-profile things.* He took a deep breath. The sheriff's poor management skills and his love for the media spotlight had caused problems in previous cases because of a lack of proper equipment and personnel. Sean frowned. He'd have to announce he was running for county sheriff in a month. What would his partner Mac think? As soon as he announced, he'd be confined to a desk, he was sure of it. Sheriff Walter Sparks, referred to as little Bonaparte by the men in the department, behind his back, of course, did not like competition. Thank heavens there would be a budget meeting with the commissioners this afternoon, or that media hog would be here to pose for the cameras and look like he was leading the parade. Sean surveyed the room again. Sid was packing up the video camera. Cliff and Billy, the photographer, were chatting in the corner while Tim and the new girl carefully measured the room. It was a typical crime scene, a bunch of people standing around waiting for their turn to work while watching someone else process their piece of the puzzle.

He watched the new girl move the stick with the target while Tim measured the distance. She seemed friendly and had a pleasant smile. Tim said something, and she laughed.

The feeling of Déjà vu flashed through him. His late wife Peggy's laugh sounded exactly like that. *Easy sport. This is the wrong time to walk down that memory lane.* He ran his fingers through his hair. *Back to work.* He looked at his notes, then scanned the room again. When he worked in LA, his partners used to joke about him being psychic. He wasn't, of course, but he always had a sense about the killer and the crime scene, a sort of first impression. He'd tell his partner about it and, no matter how odd it was, in time, his impressions would prove right. The first thoughts that came to him when he walked into this room were the words "step one". He didn't know why, but he'd be willing to bet a month's salary this was no ordinary burglary. The killer was just getting started.

STEPHANIE

S tephanie slipped out the kitchen door and walked to the backyard gate. The media had shown up, much to everyone's chagrin, claiming the front sidewalk as their base of operations. A television crew was setting up on the other side of the house, and two print reporters with cameras hanging around their necks stood on the sidewalk chatting with each other. One sheriff's deputy, like a palace guardsman, watched everyone from the driveway, making sure only authorized personnel set foot on the property.

Her partner, Cliff, and most of the investigation team were still in the house, either working or talking to each other, not wanting to go outside. Nobody wanted to talk to the press. Unfortunately, her white Tyvek suit and tackle box were a dead giveaway that she was part of the investigation team. She stood by the side of the house, hoping for some sort of distraction so she could make her getaway. The opportunity came when Tim, the ISP officer she'd been helping, stepped out the front door with his equipment and headed to his car. He was immediately set upon like a gazelle at the lion's watering hole. His repeated "no comment" to every question shouted at him was her cue to move. She pulled off a glove as she walked to the investigator's crime trailer parked on the street in the other direction.

She quickly opened the zipper of her suit for some cool air. There were too many people in the victim's bedroom, and her Tyvek suit felt like her own personal sauna. *I'm going to need a shower before I meet my family at the game tonight.* She unlocked the trailer and swung the door open. Inside were the tools of the trade. She took great comfort in noting the presence of each item. Shovels, axes, and other digging tools, along with collection containers, extra gloves, Tyvek suits, evidence collection envelopes, and vests marked ISP Crime Lab. They equipped the trailer to handle evidence collection in a wide variety of locations, houses, fields, office buildings, industrial sites, and forests. This was her world now, a place where she fit in. *A place where I really matter.* She set down her tackle box and slipped the suit off, then stuffed it along with the gloves in a large trash bag for disposal. She closed her eyes and breathed in the cool air.

"Ah… Stephanie, was it?"

She turned to see the older detective walking up to her, followed by a young sheriff's deputy. They'd managed to get out quickly while the press was still harassing Tim.

"Yes, can I help you, sir?"

"Call me Mac, everybody else does. Ah… Deputy Clark has found something across the street. Can you grab some gloves and an evidence bag and come with us?"

She nodded. "Sure, give me a second." She turned and reached for the glove box sitting in the rack on the side wall of the truck to grab two clean nitrile gloves. The plastic evidence bags were stacked on the rack on the opposite side. Everything was neat and orderly, just the way she liked it. She grabbed a large bag and turned back to the men. "Okay, lead the way."

The street was L shaped with the victim's house on the outside of the elbow. Catty-cornered across the street was an open space between two houses. As she neared it, she could see two lines of compressed soil, the result of years of tire marks, worn into the dirt. It looked like a parking spot for an RV. The house next to it appeared unoccupied. A tall hedge of arborvitaes made a border between the space and the driveway. On the other side, a tall fence blocked the view of the house next door.

The three of them crossed the street. The young officer led the way until they reached the sidewalk. "I saw it lying on the ground when I canvased the neighborhood. I don't know if it has anything to do with the murder, but I thought I should report it and get it added to the evidence collection."

Stephanie stuck the evidence bag in her pocket so she could put on her gloves. On the ground lay a black stocking cap, the kind that could roll down and hide a face.

When Mac held up his hand, she stopped in her tracks. So did deputy Clark. The older man carefully walked around the area, looking at the ground. "The dirt is too compacted to leave a decent tire print. There's no way of knowing the last time someone parked here." He motioned for them to approach.

Stephanie kneeled beside the stocking cap. "It looks dry, so it can't have been here overnight. There's a chance it belongs to our perpetrator. Do you want a photo before I bag it as evidence?"

Mac scratched his chin. "Paul, go back to the house and fetch Billy. Let's have him snap a few shots of the area. It's probably nothing, but I'd rather have too much information than not enough."

Deputy Paul Clark left for the house. Stephanie straightened up. After looking around the area, she turned to the crime house. The same hedge that blocked the view of the house next door also blocked the view of the victim's house. Only the second story was visible from where she stood. She strolled to the sidewalk and looked at both sides of the street.

It seemed like a quiet suburban neighborhood. Most of the houses were split-level homes with well-maintained yards. There was evidence of children present in some homes. Basketball hoops above garage doors looked used. Toys littered lawns and bicycles sat in driveways. Several of the residents stood outside, watching the spectacle in their neighborhood.

She looked back at the RV parking space and then at the crime house again. She frowned. "Ah… Mac… I think the person who broke into the house and killed the lady parked here."

Mac turned and walked back to stand beside her. "You might be right. It's an easy spot to get in and out of, and it's partially hidden from view." He scratched his chin. "It'll be interesting to see what Sean thinks of it."

She frowned and turned to face him. "Your partner? I thought you were the senior detective on the scene."

"I've been with the department longer, but Sean has more experience with murder cases. He worked homicide in Los Angeles for several years." Mac reached into his pocket and pulled out a piece of nicotine gum.

She raised her eyebrows. *The man smells like a tobacco shop and he's chewing that kind of gum?* "Los Angeles to northern Idaho is quite a change. I got my degree at Long Beach State. I know how crowded and fast-paced life is in the LA area. It must have been an enormous culture shock for his family to move from there to here."

Mac raised an eyebrow. "Ah, Sean doesn't have a family. His wife died of cancer about five years ago, and they didn't have any kids. I know it's a much slower life style up here, but I got the feeling he moved so he wouldn't be surrounded by all the memories of her." He unwrapped the gum and started chewing.

She blinked. The handsome detective was a widower? She turned her back on the older man and looked at the crime house again, staring as if she could see through the walls. Sean had caught her attention from the moment Cliff introduced him. Handsome, sandy blonde hair with deep blue eyes. He was the kind of guy she'd love to date but never could attract. Good-looking guys didn't go for the nerdy girls. She scoffed. The detective probably already had a girlfriend or a list of women who wanted the position. She took a deep breath. She'd come back to the area to be close to her family. If it didn't work out again, she didn't need any anchors holding her here. As she stood lost in thought, Paul came out of the house, followed by Billy with his camera. The press tried to follow, but the deputy in the driveway stopped them.

When they reached the RV space, Mac instructed Billy on the shots he wanted. She got out of the way and watched Billy work. The sound of Sean's voice drew her attention back to the street. The detective and Cliff walked to the end of the driveway. Sean called to the reporters. "I have a brief statement to issue. This afternoon, the Kootenai County Sheriff's office responded to a request for a wellness check. An investigation is underway about what we found. There will be an official briefing offered later. We are not answering questions at this time. Thank you." He turned and strode toward the crime trailer as the reporters grumbled and shouted questions at him.

The coroner's van came down the street and stopped in front of the Mercer house. It took the officer in the driveway a moment to get the reporters out of the way so the van could back in. Two men got out of the vehicle and opened the back to remove the gurney. A print reporter took pictures while the television crew recorded the movements on video for the evening news.

Mac called her name. She turned to him. When he motioned for her to pick up the stocking cap, she quickly placed it in the evidence bag and handed it to him.

"Thank you, Stephanie. It was nice meeting you. I'm sure we will see more of each other in the future." Mac smiled.

Stephanie nodded. "Thank you, Mac. It was nice meeting you as well." She slipped off a glove and shook his hand before heading back to the trailer. She glanced toward Sean and saw him shaking hands with Cliff before he walked back to the house. Good, she wasn't ready to talk to him yet, but the thought of seeing him again made her smile.

QUESTIONS

Sean leaned back from the table, lifted his arms and stretched his back. He checked his watch. He and Mac had been working for two hours, logging in evidence from today's crime scene in the department's secure room. The tedious work required concentration. Filling out each line on the evidence envelopes accurately could make or break a case. There were strict rules on the handling of each type of evidence. Both prosecutors and defense attorneys would go over all of it. If there was an error, it could mean a guilty person being released back into society to commit more crimes.

"I'm starving. Do you want to order some takeout?"

Mac looked up from his paperwork. "I promised Karen I'd be home for dinner tonight, even if I'm late. She's making spaghetti. It's her grandmother's recipe. The sauce is absolutely amazing." He set down his pen. "You're welcome to come over. She always makes extra."

Sean hastily grabbed an evidence envelope. Mac invited him over for dinner regularly, but he never accepted. Eating with a family reminded him too much of what he had lost.

"No, thanks, Mac." Sean shrugged. "I'll just grab something on the way out. Besides, I don't have much time this evening. I'm supposed to have a Zoom call at eight about campaigning for sheriff. I'm being introduced to Sam Kestner. He's going to be my campaign manager."

Mac folded his hands. "Sean, I know you don't like the way little Bonaparte has handled the department, but do you really think running for sheriff is the best thing for you? I mean, you are a gifted detective with amazing intuition. The sheriff is an administrator. You'll be buried in paperwork and political meetings. You're going to hate it."

"Probably, but there have been too many problems with lack of resources for everyone except SWAT. If this keeps up, something will happen that causes serious problems for the entire department. No one wants to challenge little Bonaparte. Until he has a serious challenger, nothing will change." Sean took a deep breath.

"Okay." Mac nodded. "I agree with you. I'll help you any way I can."

"Thanks, Mac." He picked up his pen and listed the number and description of the item in the envelope on his evidence log. "Do we have any information from the medical examiner?"

Mac frowned and shifted in his chair. "The initial findings show she had sex, but there were no signs of force. We should have the complete report in a week or two. They got the duct tape off. Hopefully, it'll have some fingerprints on it." He reached out for another bag.

Sean bit his lip. "I wonder," he muttered.

"What did you say?"

Sean cleared his throat. "I was wondering about the ski mask you found in the empty lot. Do you think it's related?"

Mac continued writing. "The new girl at the lab, Stephanie, thought it was. When the officer took me to the spot where he found it, she came out with us. She suggested the murderer may have accidentally dropped it while trying to load his car and make his getaway. A jogger or a person walking their dog might have interrupted or seen him."

Sean rubbed his chin. "She may be right." Mac's sudden movement caused him to look up. Mac had an odd grin on his face.

"What?"

"I was just wondering what you thought of her?"

Sean shifted in his chair and remembered her laugh. He'd found the sound of it both comforting and upsetting. He closed his eyes. His memories of Peggy still haunted him. *Her face, her smile and the echo of her laugh when he told her a funny story.* He shook himself. Hearing the same sound from Stephanie made him feel an instant connection to her, one he really would like to explore farther. No way would he tell Mac that. "She seemed nice, very helpful. I really didn't get to talk to her."

Mac leaned back in his chair, smiling. "Tim said she had a great sense of humor.

"I thought she might. She had a great laugh."

Mac raised an eyebrow. "You listened to her laugh?"

"Now, Mac, don't get any ideas. I'm not looking for a date. I have a lot of work to do and a campaign coming up."

Mac smirked. "Who said anything about dating? I just find it interesting that you noticed her laugh. You normally only notice a woman's looks then go back to work."

"I'm not having this conversation. Let's get back to the case." Sean set down his pen and flexed his fingers. "What was your gut reaction to everything?

Mac shifted in his chair. "It looked like a break-and-entry where the burglar found the owner at home. Given the way the victim was dressed and the medical examiner's initial information, we know there was a man with her earlier. I think she was having a nap after her, ahh… other guest had left. The intruder likely surprised her. He strangled her and ransacked the place." Mac reached into his pocket for a piece of nicotine gum and looked over to Sean. "Why? What did you see?"

Sean bit his lower lip. "I saw exactly what you did. A burglar surprises a home owner, kills her and steals what he can carry away easily without drawing too much attention to himself." He stopped speaking for a few minutes. The only sound in the room was the hum from the electric clock on the wall. He raised his head and met his partner's eyes.

Mac looked down his nose at him and shook his head. "And?"

"What do you mean... and?"

Mac laughed. "With you, there is always an 'and'. I've worked with you long enough to know you have a sixth sense about crime scenes. What did you notice about the scene that makes you sound so skeptical?"

Sean shifted in his chair. "It felt wrong, like we were seeing what they meant us to see. Like the whole thing was planned and staged."

Mac raised his eyebrows. "Why would someone murder a woman to send a message?"

"That's the question I've been asking myself. I think we need to take a much closer look at Angela Mercer."

Mac nodded as Sean leaned forward, picking up another evidence bag.

———

Ray walked through the door of his basement apartment and swore. The bloody furnace was out again. His breath hung in the air like a cloud. "Great, now I can stand in front of the open refrigerator and get warm." The lights came on when he flipped the switch. Well, at least the power was still working. He pulled out his cell phone to call the building management company. The last time this happened, it took them six hours to even send a repairman, and he had to get a hotel room for the night. That had blown a hole through his budget. Hopefully, they would be faster this time. Now he was more prepared. The apartment had a small fireplace. Being mostly for show, it didn't put out a lot of heat, but it would help make the temperature bearable. He now had a package of presto logs waiting next to the fireplace for just such an emergency.

After stoking the fire, he walked over to the refrigerator and opened the door. *Yup, definitely warmer.* He quickly checked the freezer. The small freezer compartment gave just enough room for one person's needs. He moved the TV dinners stacked in the box's front and checked the contents in the back, a rack of blood vials, each carefully labeled, several clear freezer bags containing hair or skin scrapings, and a small stack of plastic storage containers. He set the TV dinners back in place, except for the one he planned to eat, and closed the door.

———

Stephanie hurried from the parking lot to the bleachers. She was late for the softball game. It would have been nice to just stay home and relax after a long day at work. Her sister had invited her, so she didn't want to disappoint Susan by not showing up. Even though she had to finish up at the crime scene, to her father, work was not an excuse to miss a sporting event. She sighed. Being born the only klutz in a family of athletes had not made for an easy childhood. She glanced over the field and saw her two older brothers and sister. Dennis stood on the pitcher's mound, staring down the batter. Douglas shifted on his feet behind first base, ready to tag the runner. Susan was in her usual position as shortstop. She didn't need to search the stands for her parents. They would be on the center bleacher about halfway up. It was their customary spot as the kids grew up.

This way, whoever was playing could always find them in the crowd.

She made her way along the row and sat down next to her mom. "Hi. Sorry I'm late."

"We're glad you could make it, sweetheart." Her mom patted her knee with a gloved hand.

"Yeah, you missed a great game so far. The teams are pretty evenly matched, so your brothers are giving them the switch each time they're in the outfield." Her dad grinned as he watched the pitch. Her brothers were identical twins except for one thing: Douglas was left-handed and Dennis was right.

By the time the game finished, Stephanie felt like a popsicle. Tired as she was, the invitation to join everyone at the local sports bar sounded great.

She sat at the table and watched the people in the room. Her family didn't trust her to carry any of the food. She could trip over her own two feet on a smooth linoleum floor. She actually had once and ended up wearing a pitcher of beer.

Her family wound their way through the crowd and back to the table. The twins each carried a large pizza. Her mom and sister had the drink pitchers, and her father held a plate of hot wings. How many times had she sat in a place like this after a game, part of the family but an outsider to the world of sports?

"Dig in everybody." Dennis set down a deep-dish pizza covered with meat and cheese.

"Great, I love the house special, and you got extra cheese, too." Her dad grabbed a large piece and slid it onto his plate.

Everyone attacked the food like a pack of wolves. That may be a cliché, but anyone who had ever seen her brothers eat would draw the same conclusion. Stephanie limited herself to a single slice of pizza and a glass of beer. Her siblings could burn off the calories with their sports, but she didn't get much exercise staring into a microscope.

The dinner and conversation were interrupted when a man walked up to the table and put his hand on Dennis' shoulder. "Great game. I didn't know you could pitch left-handed."

Everyone laughed. Douglas held up his beer glass in his left hand.

The man grinned. "Brilliant. Maybe we can use your brother on the campaign."

"Campaign?" Her father set down his slice of pizza. "What campaign?"

The man's eyes widened, and he frowned. "I'm sorry. I thought you told them."

Dennis grumbled. "If you'd waited another fifteen minutes, I would have."

"Mom, Dad, I'm going to run for county sheriff."

Douglas grinned. The twins always knew what the other one was doing, even if the rest of the family was clueless.

Her dad glanced from one son to the other. Her mom just looked confused. Susan sat there grinning. Obviously, her sister was in the know. Stephanie glanced back at her parents. For once, she wasn't the only family member in the dark.

Her father straightened in his chair. "Is the law firm aware of this?"

Dennis smiled. "This is Tom Oliver from my office. He's one of the firm's partners. Given the way things are in law enforcement these days, several people got together and decided they wanted a lawyer in the sheriff's position."

Tom Oliver held out his hand. "I'm pleased to meet you, sir. We felt they needed a talented lawyer in the sheriff's office, and we believe your son is the right man for the job."

Her dad shook Oliver's hand. "That's great. When does the campaign start?"

Dennis turned to his dad. "I have to get a campaign staff together and rent a space to use for a headquarters. Doug is going to be the campaign treasurer since it looks good to have a treasurer who's a CPA. Susan will help organize the campaign volunteers. As soon as we get everything in place, I'll announce. It will probably be next month."

Stephanie listened to the conversation, feeling, as usual, on the outside looking in.

Tom Oliver started rattling off details about the campaign and how to target different voter groups. In the middle of his speech, Dennis turned to her. "Stephanie, you know how to work spreadsheets. Could you do the data sorting that Tom is talking about?"

It took Stephanie a moment to realize her brother was actually addressing her. "I'm sorry. What sorts do you need?"

Tom smiled at her. "The county elections office has a list of all registered voters done in spreadsheet format. They also have voter history, so it is possible to find out which voters vote in the primary. Can you help with this?"

Suddenly Stephanie was in her element. She had a puzzle to be solved. She couldn't throw a ball or run without tripping, but give her a puzzle and she wouldn't surface until she'd figured it out. "Well, if the data is in column format with headers, it's an easy sort. Depending how the voting history is laid out, it's possible to determine who votes in all primaries or simply a primary in a presidential year. You mentioned election reports where the donors are listed as well as the candidate's expenses. I could pull the donor names of people who have contributed to a sheriff race in the past. These can be cross matched with voter lists and …." She looked up to see everyone at the table staring at her and Tom with a grin from ear to ear.

"Well, Dennis, I think we found your data miner and list manager."

"How about it, sis? Are you willing to work on my campaign?" Her brother gave her a smile.

She grinned back. "Sure, I think you'll make an excellent sheriff. When do I start?"

PLANS

Sean walked to his desk, rubbing his shirt with a handkerchief. Some politician he was going to make, since he couldn't even keep a shirt clean between his place and the office. He set the offending coffee cup with its loose lid down on his desk. He'd have to wear his suit jacket buttoned up for the rest of the day to cover the brown spot. *At least the weather is still cold. Nothing like sweat stains to add to the overall effect.*

He sat down and turned his computer on. He should have just enough time to check his messages and reports before Mac showed up.

Sean reached out and took the envelope from his in box. He glanced at the label and nodded. These were from the robbery of a warehouse, a case they'd gotten last month. He turned back to his computer. Voices in the hall warned him, Mac was on the way in.

Mac set his coffee and briefcase on his desk and looked at Sean. He grinned. "Nice shirt. Is that a new fashion style?"

"Smart ass. Who were you talking to in the hall?"

"Officer Clark. I have his notes from yesterday. All of Angela Mercer's neighbors mentioned that there was a man who came to the Mercer's house several times a week. He drove a silver car. One lady remembers the car very well and the man who drove it." He sat down and turned on his computer.

"Okay, I'll bite. Why does she remember him so well?"

"Apparently, he came around a corner too fast one time and nearly ran her over while she was walking her Shih Tzu."

Sean laughed. "Yeah, well, that would do it." He reached for his coffee cup, only to have the lid come loose again. He swore under his breath and tossed the lid in the trash. "Okay, I want to go through Clark's notes and see if anything else stands out, then interview the Shih Tzu lady." He rolled his eyes. Ten to one, he'd have dog hair all over his suit five minutes after they got to her house. He had to go home and change shirts. A coffee-stained shirt was one thing, but combined with dog hair, it would be too much.

"Before we talk to her, I need to swing by my place and pick up a clean shirt." He looked at his coffee cup and frowned. "I'm going to dump this. It's cold, anyway. You want to stop at a coffee shop? I'm buying."

Mac laughed. "I never say no to free food."

An hour later, Mac turned their car into the parking lot of a local coffeehouse. He parked in a space between two patrol cars. "Where does the law enforcement community's passion for high carb, sugar pastries come from, anyway?"

"I don't know, but I want an apple fritter and large latte. Let's get in there before the rest of the department cleans out this morning's entire batch of baked goods." Sean got out of the car and led the way in.

Forty-five minutes later, they slowly rounded the "L" shaped street passing Angela Mercer's house and turned into the driveway of her neighbor.

A knock on the door brought them face to face with Mrs. Ezekiel Mortenson, a stout woman with steel gray hair and gray eyes. A moment later, a small fur ball ran up to the door and started barking at them.

"Now, now, sweetheart, it's all right. These big men aren't going to hurt you." She bent down and picked up the dog then looked straight at Sean. "Are you two from the sheriff's department?"

"Yes, ma'am. I'm Detective Landers, and this is my partner, Detective Mackenzie. May we come in and ask you a few questions?" He reached into his pocket and pulled out his shield holder with credentials. She took it from him and read his name and badge number before handing it back.

"I guess so." She stepped back and opened the door farther to let them in.

The living room looked exactly as Sean expected it would, filled with comfortable furniture, old but still in good shape. There was a portrait over the fireplace of a man and woman. He was sure it was the late Ezekiel Mortenson along with his wife. Judging by the difference in the appearance of Mrs. Mortenson, he guessed the photo had been taken about fifteen years ago.

Mrs. Mortenson gestured for them to take a seat on the couch. She sat down in a recliner covered with a large afghan. Clearly, this was her customary seat in the house. Sean sat down on the overstuffed couch while Mac took his place on the other side. Thank heavens it wasn't a cramped love seat.

Mrs. Mortenson fussed with her dog, trying to calm him down. This gave Sean a few minutes to study the rest of the room. There was lots of clutter, knickknacks and doilies on all the flat surfaces. Besides the portrait, there were several paintings on the wall, all of them landscapes. He had to suppress a smile. One landscape had two deer drinking at a stream. *Yup, traditional Idaho decor.*

"Mrs. Mortenson, thank you for meeting with us. You told the officer who interviewed you that you could give us a good description of your neighbor, Angela Mercer's, frequent visitor."

Mrs. Mortenson shifted her position so the little dog rested partly on her thigh and wedged against the side of the chair. "Yes, I can tell you about him. He's been coming here for over a year. If you ask me, he's the reason for her divorce." She stroked the dog's head.

"Did he usually come in the daytime or evenings?" Mac asked. He pulled a small notebook out of his jacket pocket.

"I didn't notice the car until after I retired. Once I was home during the day, it was hard to miss. He came only during the day and stayed for an hour, sometimes two, but never more than that." The dog gave a small yelp, and she stroked him again.

Mac scratched his chin. "You said this man's visits led to Mrs. Mercer's divorce. Are you sure?"

"I can't be sure, but the car kept showing up about two months before her husband moved out and filed for divorce. My dog could tell right away something was up. He always did his business right by the car's tires."

Mac raised his eyebrows. "Her husband filed for divorce?" He scratched something in his notebook.

"Yes, it was in the papers under the legal announcements. If you want the details, you'll have to ask Angela's ex, Mitch Mercer." When she shifted in the chair, the dog yelped. "I'm sorry, baby. Mommy is sorry. Mommy loves her little prince." The dog yelped and tried to lick his mistress. "Yes, baby. You are Mommy's little Prince Albert."

Sean bit his tongue to keep from laughing. He glanced over at Mac, who looked like he was having a stroke.

Sean cleared his throat. "We plan to interview Mr. Mercer soon. In the meantime, is there anything else you can tell me about the visitor, like his appearance and the type of car he drove?"

"Wouldn't you rather have his name?

"You know who he is?" His eyebrows rose almost to his hairline.

"Well, of course I do. I'm not senile. He's David Turner, the county prosecutor.

Sean was certain his jaw was scraping the coffee table. He turned and looked at Mac, who wore an equally pole axed expression. This murder investigation just turned into a political hot potato.

———

Mac turned the corner and headed toward the highway. "How do you plan to proceed with this?"

Sean kept staring out the window in silence.

Mac waited a few more minutes before speaking again. "Ground control to Major Sean." He glanced over to see his partner leaning against the side window with his head buried in his hand. "Look, it could be worse. I know you have your own political race to run, but we just have to play this one completely by the book."

Sean turned his head and peered through his fingers. "Seriously, by the book? You do realize I am now between a rock and a very hard place." He ran his fingers through his hair. "I'm announcing a run for the sheriff's office in a few weeks, and I get to call the county prosecutor in for questioning as a murder suspect."

"Well, at least you can prove to the voters that you don't play favorites."

Sean snorted. "And make an enemy of an influential county official at the same time?" He shifted his position on his seat. "I don't doubt he is… I mean was having an affair with our victim, but I don't think he killed her. His affair is going to be exposed. It's only a matter of time before the press gets the story, and when they do, it will ruin his marriage and his political career. You can't run as the moral, law-and-order candidate and be shown to have feet of clay."

Mac rolled his eyes. "Okay, so what's the game plan?" He kept a smile off his face. Sean was upset. Who could blame him? The timing of everything was terrible, a high-profile murder case and a political campaign. Well, that combination went together like matches and gasoline.

Sean straightened up. "I want to call the prosecutor's office after we've interviewed the ex-husband and ask to speak to David Turner. If I can get him on the phone, I'll try to get him to meet us at a neutral location, maybe in the back room at a restaurant or something. I can't stop the press from finding out, but I can buy him some time before the story breaks."

———

Stephanie got up from the table and stretched her back. All the sitting and concentrating she'd been doing made her muscles stiff. As soon as she went home from the sports bar last night with the thumb drive of voter information, she sat down and started working. By one in the morning, she had several of the sorting parameters done and ready for the campaign to use. Her assignment wasn't tough, just time consuming. She stretched again. She should have the entire project finished by tonight. They'd given her a week to complete everything, but she wanted to impress her brother as well as help him. She glanced back at her stereo microscope. Marijuana analysis was one of her least favorite things to do, but, unfortunately, everyone had to do drug testing. It was the main staple of the lab.

Cliff wandered in from the breakroom chewing an apple. "The evidence officer from the sheriff's department just dropped off the evidence bags from yesterday's murder. Do you want to run tests today or wait till tomorrow?"

Stephanie ran a hand along her sore back. It was tempting to wait and do something easier until the end of her shift, but that wasn't her family's way. She wasn't the athlete her siblings were, but she didn't back down from a challenge, either.

"I'll go to the locker and sign out the stocking cap and run it for hair and fiber samples. I still have some paperwork to finish from yesterday, as well."

Cliff nodded. "I'm not done yet, either." He threw his apple core into the trash. "What did you think of Sean Landers, the lead detective?"

"He seemed nice and competent. Why?" His question made her suspicious.

"Oh, he's very good. He's like a dog with a bone when it comes to a case. He won't let go until he's figured it out." Cliff rubbed his chin. "I'd better get to my paperwork while I can still remember what happened." He turned and headed for his office.

Stephanie shifted on her feet. Detective Landers didn't let go of a problem. Well, she and the handsome detective had something in common then.

OBSERVING

Ray sat in the corner of the Bull Dog bar, a cheap watering hole near the state line. The bar had low lighting and 80s rock playing on the sound system. There were three televisions over the bar and two at the back of the room. The left front television and one of the back ones were tuned to a baseball game. The right front and the other back played an old comedy show. The remaining television displayed a cable news channel.

He'd nursed a single beer for the last two hours while observing his prey. Leaning back in his chair, he took another pull from his bottle then set the drink down. The seeds for this vengeance were sown during his fourth year in prison. He'd carefully watered and tended the plants ever since. The woman was the first step. Now he was preparing for step two.

William Curtis Spellman sat at a table across the room getting happily drunk on White Russians. Spellman, known as Billy to his friends, was the only son of former public defender, now private practice high-priced defense attorney, Curtis Roger Spellman. Billy wore dirty jeans and tennis shoes. His black tee shirt had a hole in the right side that was partially hidden by his flannel over shirt. All in all, Billy Spellman was a prime example of a waste of space and air.

Ray closed his eyes and thought back to the day he met the heartless bastard public defender Spellman.

————

The table under his elbows was cold. He folded his hands together and stared at the cuffs on his wrists and shook, making the chains that secured him to the table rattle. How in the hell had things gotten to this point?

His eyes jerked up when he heard the door unlocking. A middle-aged man in a crisp gray suit strode into the room. He had a briefcase in one hand and a file folder in the other. "Good afternoon. I'm your court-appointed attorney, Curtis Spellman. I've gone over your file, and I think I can get you a plea bargain for this. This is your first offence, but the county is cracking down on drug cases. The unfortunate part was the officer being injured when he opened the box. That's going to add time to the sentence. I'll try to get you four years, but it will more than likely be six."

"But I'm innocent. I didn't put that stuff in my trunk. I don't know how it got there."

Spellman snorted. "Surely you can come up with a better excuse than that. How did the stuff get into your locked car trunk if you didn't put it there?"

"The trunk doesn't lock. The lock broke over a year ago. If you want to open it, all you have to do is push down on the lid, and it will pop open." The chains rattled even louder as his hands shook and they banged against the desk.

"Listen, kid, I can't sell a half ass story like that to the prosecutor or the judge. The friend who was with you when you got arrested is a blithering idiot and not a credible witness. You haven't got a leg to stand on. Now plead guilty. I'll try to get you a good deal. If this thing goes to court, you're looking at ten years." He opened his briefcase and tossed the file in.

Ray laid his hands on the table to stop them from shaking. He straightened up in the chair and looked the attorney in the eyes. "I will not plead guilty to something I didn't do. I don't even know exactly what was in the trunk, let alone where to get that kind of stuff. I'm innocent, and I expect you to defend me."

Spellman closed the briefcase and picked it up. "Whatever. You want to flush away ten years of your life for being stubborn and stupid. Go ahead. I told you about your case, but you're choosing not to listen. See you in court." He turned and left the room.

———

Mensa candidate Billy was beginning to slur his words while his two drinking companions were only a few sips behind him. Ray shook his head. Apparently, no one thought to have a designated driver. Perhaps Billy's faith in his father's ability to defend him against any charges had caused him to be reckless. Most likely, it was the fact that he wasn't the brightest crayon in the box. Ray debated on stealing their car keys. The way this idiot was acting, he'd get himself killed before Ray could send his father a message. Billy had a history of drug abuse. His father had put him through rehab twice. Apparently, he had turned to alcohol. The inability to stay in college and his father's continued efforts to bail out his son made Billy the perfect tool to use against the attorney.

Ray held up his beer bottle in a silent salute to the drunken fool. Billy came to this dive at least twice a week after work. During the day, he worked at a tire store fixing flats, and every evening he was out somewhere drinking or gambling. The guy practically had 'loser' tattooed on his forehead, but he had a father who cared about him. It was probably the attorney's only endearing quality.

Ray straightened up in his chair. It wouldn't be tonight, too many witnesses, and it didn't send the right message. Perhaps tomorrow or next week, it didn't really matter. It would be soon, and Curtis Spellman would have someone precious taken from him just like his sloppy job of defense had taken someone precious from Ray. Ray took another sip from his bottle. He was a patient man. Ten years in prison had taught him to be. He drained the rest of his beer and placed a tip on the table for the server.

The bill for attorney Spellman's lack of interest and incompetence in defending a frightened and innocent man was about to come due, complete with ten years of compound interest.

———

Sean was in early the next day and busy at his computer typing up his notes on the Mercer murder when an officer brought in a few follow-up reports. After flipping through them, Sean got up and stretched, then went out into the hall to search for his partner. Mac was great to work with and a clever investigator, but the man was a total social butterfly. He found Mac a few minutes later with two other officers, chatting about last night's baseball game.

"Mac, we have to go. We got a credit card case to follow up, and the suspect is currently in custody."

Mac rolled his eyes. "Wonderful. Why does work always interrupt a good sports discussion?"

"I don't know. Why don't you write out a complaint and send it to little Bonaparte? I'm sure he will want to take immediate action about this appalling situation."

Mac gave him a dirty look.

"Right, I'll get the car." He left Mac to finish up the conversation while he went out to the motor pool.

Twenty minutes later, they were heading to an apartment complex off Lancaster Road to interview Ms. Sarah Bell. Mac was driving, and he still looked annoyed. "So, what's the lowdown on this case?"

"Ms. Bell shares an apartment with Ms. Francis Greene. When the mail arrived yesterday, Ms. Bell noticed several extra charges on her credit card. She confronted her roommate about it, and Ms. Greene confessed to borrowing her card without permission. This didn't go over very well, so Ms. Bell called the Sheriff's office. Ms. Greene was arrested and is currently a guest at our holding facility." Sean shuffled through the papers on his clipboard.

"Hmm, it's safe to assume that Ms. Greene will need to find a new place to live as soon as we release her." Mac stopped at the light.

"I'd say that would be a safe bet." He looked up from his papers. "I'll interview Ms. Bell while you go over the bill and make a note of any local merchants where Greene purchased items. We'll check the stores and see if they can confirm the sale and the sales associate can recognize Ms. Greene from a photo in a photo lineup." He held up a picture taken by the arresting officer. "After that, we'll hurry back to the jail and interview the suspect before she's released on bail.

"Wonderful. That's going to take us a couple of hours. I'm going to need another coffee and a donut before we interview the merchants."

Sean snorted. "Absolutely. I wouldn't want you to succumb for lack of sustenance."

"Smart ass, what other cases do we have to follow up on?" Mac grumbled as he turned onto a side street and pulled up in front of one of the apartment blocks.

Sean flipped the pages on his clipboard again. "We have another auto burglary report near Athol. It sounds like the same suspects from the other two reports we did last week. This car had a nice Nikon camera in a bag on the backseat and a collection of jazz CDs in a case on the floor, all of which were missing. Then last but not least, somebody blew up one of those group mailboxes on Government Way and sprayed graffiti all over the back of it. So, I hope you didn't have any special plans, because we're going to be running around all day." He opened the door and got out.

Mac turned off the engine. "Wonderful, there's nowhere good to eat near Athol." He opened his door and got out. "After we finish with the jail interview, let's head up to Spirit Lake and grab one of those juicy burgers from that restaurant on Main Street."

Sean leaned on the roof of the car. "I'm always amazed at how your stomach runs your life."

"Hey, life is short. I like to eat, so I might as well enjoy my meals. And you get to benefit, as well. I know you like a good burger." He closed the door and pressed the key fob to lock it.

Sean laughed. "Yes, but I'm not obsessing about lunch at 9:15 in the morning."

THE EX-HUSBAND

Mac pulled up in the parking lot of Silver Star Realty. Most of the parking spaces were occupied. "Looks like a busy office. What do we know about this place?"

Sean snorted. "They don't deal exclusively in buying or selling real estate. They have a thriving business in finding affordable rental homes and apartments for working-class people who aren't eligible for housing assistance but make too little to qualify for a mortgage. It's a growing problem in this area. The average wages are low and stagnant. These people have jobs but can't afford a thousand dollars or more per month on rent. It's a great service they provide. Otherwise, these people need to move to another area or quit their jobs to qualify for help."

Mac slid the car into an open parking space. "Wow, impressive use of Google."

Sean grinned. "Thank you. I thought it wise to know as much as I could about where he works before we end up questioning his co-workers. I'm not so sure we'll find Mitchell Mercer at work, given the circumstances."

"If it was me, I'd want to get away somewhere like a

friend or relative's house. Someplace where I can grieve but also have help with all the funeral arrangements. It surprised me that Angela Mercer didn't have any close relatives. I guess her ex-husband will have to handle it. After all, she is the mother of his son." Mac killed the engine. "Ready?"

Sean grabbed his notebook and exited the car. "That's why I don't expect him to be here. I do want to get as much as I can out of his secretary, or assistant or whoever. I expect we'll be talking to him in a day or so."

The two men strode into the building. The office was indeed busy. Cubicles lined the side walls, each one either filled with agents on the phone or dealing with clients in person. The back wall had four enclosed offices, while the center of the room held copy machines and computers. Immediately in front of Sean sat a reception desk occupied by a very pretty young woman talking on the phone.

Sean noted the number of people in the room. Mac pulled out his detective's shield and clipped it to his suit pocket. Sean smiled. This was a sure sign that Mac was impatient. People tended to move more quickly when they realized this was an official visit. It worked. The receptionist glanced up, her eyebrows raised and her eyes wide. She quickly brought her call to an end.

"Officers, what can I do for you?"

Sean noted her hands shook. "Good morning, I'm Detective Landers, and this is Detective Mackenzie. We're here to see Mitchell Mercer or his assistant."

The color drained from her face as she punched a button on her phone and picked up the receiver. "Mitch, there are two detectives here to see you."

Sean turned to his partner. Mac looked surprised. *What is Mercer doing at work?*

When a door to one of the back offices opened. A man wearing dress slacks and a sweater over a button-down shirt stepped out. He raised his hand, beckoning them to come to his office. Sean's eyebrows rose. The man didn't look like he was grieving at all. Mitchell Mercer closed the door as soon as they entered the room. Sean introduced himself and his partner while noting the lack of personal photos in the office. He looked Mercer in the eyes. "We are sorry for your loss, but I'm afraid we need to ask you some questions."

Mercer didn't look surprised. He merely nodded, turned and headed back to his desk. Mac narrowed his eyes, a movement that told Sean his partner had formed an instant dislike for the man.

Sean took a chair in front of the desk, but Mac leaned against the door.

Mitch Mercer sat at his desk, playing with a pen. "I knew I'd get questioned sooner or later."

Sean opened his notebook. "Mr. Mercer, can you tell us where you were on Tuesday morning?"

Mercer shifted in his chair. "I was holding a seminar with several owners of rental properties in the county. The receptionist can give you a copy of the flyer and the attendance sheet. We had thirty people there for a six-hour seminar and luncheon."

Sean glanced at Mac.

Mac nodded and stepped away from the door. "Mr. Mercer, can you think of anyone who might have had a disagreement with your ex-wife or may have threatened her?"

Mercer looked genuinely shocked. "What? She was killed by a burglar wasn't she?" He looked from Mac to Sean. "Are you saying someone targeted her?"

"We can't say. It's early in the investigation, so we are just looking at all possibilities and following the information." Sean shifted in his chair. "Do you know of anyone who might have bothered her or been angry with her?"

"Look, Angela and I may not have had the best marriage, but she was a good person. Everybody loved her.

She was a great mother. I can't think of anyone who would want to hurt her." He got up and started pacing the room. "This has been very hard on my son. He hasn't spoken to anyone since he found out about his mother. He's at my sister's right now. As soon as your department gives me the okay, I will move his furniture and other stuff to her house permanently."

Mac interrupted. "Your son isn't going to live with you?"

Mercer shook his head. "I work long hours and travel a lot. He's better off at my sister's. She has three kids, and Michael fits in well with her family. She can offer him a stable home." He paused for a moment. "I thought this was an unfortunate tragedy of being in the wrong place at the wrong time." He stopped and looked directly at Sean. "Gentleman, don't try to make it something more. My son is already traumatized. Please don't add to it."

"Sir, I can promise you the investigation will be thorough, which means we'll be following the evidence. My job is to get to the truth, and I will." Sean closed his notebook. "Mac, do you have any other questions?"

"We understand you filed for divorce. Can you tell us more about the issues involved?"

"Angela and I should have divorced a long time ago. I have a wandering eye, and she finally had enough of it. I know she had someone else, and I'm glad she found him. I hope he treated her better than I did." He looked down at the blotter on his desk.

"Why did you file for divorce instead of her filing?" Mac kept writing in his notebook.

"She didn't have the courage to file, so I did. It was better for both of us." He sighed.

Mac looked up from his notebook. "I think we have enough for now."

Sean turned back to Mercer. "Thank you for your time. And again, sorry for your loss."

Sean and Mac stepped out of the room and nearly bumped into the receptionist, who stood by the door.

She held out a flyer and a list of names. "Here, this is where Mitch was at the time his ex-wife was killed, and here is a list of people who saw him there."

Sean took it from her and smiled. "Thank you, Miss… ah?"

"Chrissy, Chrissy Palmer." She nodded at Sean, turned, and went into Mercer's office.

When Sean got back in the car, he laughed. Mac got in and closed the door. "What's so funny?"

"Mercer is having an affair with his receptionist."

"Now I like him even less. The man is going to let his sister raise his son? I understand why Angela Mercer found another man. That guy's a shmuck." Mac started the car. "He's not our guy, but I think we should pin it on him anyway, just on principle."

Sean laughed. "We can't go arresting everyone you don't like. We're low on jail space, as it is." Sean opened his notebook. "We learned something about Angela Mercer's life, and we eliminated a suspect. I'm ready to talk to David Turner to get the other side of this. I'll try to get a hold of him tomorrow."

———

Stephanie returned from lunch feeling full and ready for a nap. Unfortunately, there was more work to be done today. She went to the file and pulled out ten marijuana cases to analyze. That would fill her dance card for the afternoon and not leave her too drained for an evening at the gym with her sister. She shook her head. Only Susan would think that a night of sweating on a treadmill and lifting free weights was a great way for two distant sisters to get to know each other again. Stephanie scoffed. *This will be a great night for Susan, the high school gym teacher, to show off her toned muscles and athletic skill while I trip on the treadmill and drop a ten-pound weight on my foot. Why can't we just go out for a drink like normal people?*

She grabbed her papers and headed down the hall to give them to Evelyn, the evidence technician. It was necessary to maintain the chain of custody of every piece of evidence the lab had to analyze for a case. Only evidence technicians enter the vault and return with the evidence envelopes. The technicians complete the paperwork and signs the evidence out to the criminalist working the case.

Stephanie took the evidence envelopes back to her workstation and powered up her tablet. She grabbed the first envelope and scanned the barcode so that the case would pop up in the evidence program. She clicked the tab button on the computer and it brought up the analysis worksheet. The investigating officer had initialed and sealed each envelope. The envelopes had to be opened without affecting the officer's seal. She did this carefully and pulled out a baggie full of green plant material. She placed a small dish on the balance and then tared it before weighing the evidence. The next step was to look at the plant material under a stereomicroscope and see if she could find little bear claw shaped hairs on the leaves. This was one of the signs that it was marijuana. She placed a small amount of the evidence in a test tube with the case number marked on the side and then reweighed to see how much was left. The rest she placed back in the baggie that she labeled with the date, her initials, and the case number. She then placed it back in the evidence envelope and resealed with her own tape. The test tube went into a slot on a rack. She leaned back in her chair and took a deep breath. *One sample started. Nine more to go.*

Three hours later, she finally finished her work. She closed her eyes and stretched her back. An evening at the gym to work out the stiffness actually sounded good. After a couple of minutes, she wandered off to the break room to grab another cup of coffee.

Most people thought forensic scientists were like the people in the television show *CSI*, running around playing the detective and arresting officer. The truth was that most of them were lab rats having to deal with the evidence and analyzing it. It wasn't as sexy as the television show, but it required brains and attention to detail.

THE CAMPAIGN

Samuel Kestner's insurance agency conference room was crowded. Sean's campaign team sat around a small table, taking notes about Sam's campaign plan as he revealed the details. Sean started doodling in the margin of his notebook. All of this campaign strategizing made him cross-eyed. Why couldn't he just talk to people and tell them about the problems in the department and what he planned to do to fix them? That's all they really needed to know. Apparently, there was a lot involved in actually getting that message out.

"Sean," Sam added another point to his list on the whiteboard. "We are going to have to start dialing for dollars as soon as you've announced. I put together a budget for the campaign, and I'll let you know how much you need to raise each week to do all the things necessary to win."

He winced then nodded. Calling up people and asking for money had to be the worst part of a campaign. He didn't like it, so he wasn't very good at it. That was salesmen's work, and he was no salesmen. Every year, when they had to sell tickets to the sheriff's appreciation dinner, he just bought ten tickets and gave them away. He had offered to fund his own campaign, but Sam squashed that idea immediately. Apparently, it was important to have people invest in a campaign, which made it feel like some sort of Ponzi scheme. Sam said it looked good on election financial reports to have money coming from lots of contributors because it showed broad support. Also, Sam said, "Even the little old lady who sends only a dollar gives you her vote along with it."

There were eight other people in the room, each having an important role in the campaign, and most of them were unknown to him. All of them were people Sam had worked with in other elections who had agreed to work on Sean's bid for sheriff. He liked the idea of having experienced people at the helm. Volunteers would come from other sheriff's personnel, along with their wives. Little Bonaparte was very unpopular among his own people, as well as some members of the community who objected to the way Walter Sparks handled the department.

Sam opened his briefcase, pulled out a stack of folders, and handed out a packet to everyone in the room. The first thing in it was a calendar marking all the distinct steps of the campaign and the date they had to be completed marked in red. It looked like someone had bled on the pages.

His eyes landed on the first deadline, announcing his candidacy in two weeks. "Sam, is this an accurate calendar or just a sample to set one up?"

Sam laughed. "It is an accurate calendar, and, yes, you have to announce in two weeks. Your announcement must be made before Sparks makes his. He is announcing next month."

Sean's stomach turned over. *Am I making a mistake?*

———

Sean turned the steering wheel and entered his street. His mind kept running in circles like a hamster in a wheel.

Thoughts bounced around about lists, fundraisers, yard signs, and pamphlets, all of which made him want to run away screaming, except this is what had to be done to win an election and give the community the law enforcement they truly needed. He slid his fingers through his hair. Announcing his candidacy in two weeks seemed crazy, but Sam had explained the reasons for it. He really wanted more time to prepare, but there wasn't any. There were also rumors that a lawyer was planning to run. All of this gave him a headache.

The car's headlights lit up the driveway and the garage door. He should go straight to bed, but it would be useless with all the thoughts running through his mind, each one trying to push aside the others. He needed sleep, but he had to clear his head first. The best way to do that was to make his body more tired than his mind. Twenty minutes later, he was back in his car, dressed in his workout clothes and heading toward the gym.

———

Stephanie pulled on the strap of her new exercise clothes.

"Will you stop fussing with that?" Susan rolled her eyes.

"It feels like a second skin, and I look ridiculous." Stephanie stopped at the entrance to the Complete Fitness Gym. She'd been cautious when her sister wanted to take her to the gym for a workout. Just us two girls, she'd said. Well, it sounded like an olive branch to reconnect. But standing here in this skin tight outfit about to make a fool of herself in front of a bunch of strangers, well, it might be time to revisit her thought paradigm.

Susan grabbed her arm. "No way, sis, you're going in, and I'm going to teach you how to use the machines. You can do it. You just need a bit of practice and confidence. Now, come on." Susan opened the door and gave her a small push.

———

Stephanie plodded along on the treadmill while Susan ran on the machine next to her. Stephanie shook her head. *We look like the tortoise and the hare.* Of all her siblings, she was the closest to Susan. She admired her sister, who was pretty and athletic like the rest of her family. When she was little, she'd wanted to grow up just like her, but she didn't have Susan's coordination or skill. Stephanie pulled her earbuds out and rubbed her ears.

Susan glanced over. "See, I told you it wasn't hard. You're doing great."

"I feel like I should be jogging instead of walking on this thing."

Susan stopped running and turned off her machine. "Steph, this isn't a competition. This is just exercise. I don't care if you run or walk. You're my sister, and I'm thrilled that you're home again." She stepped off the machine and reached for a towel, to wipe the sweat from her face. "What were you listening to?"

"It's a lecture on insect infestation in a decaying corpse. You can estimate how long a person has been dead by which types of insects are nibbling on him." Stephanie turned off the machine and stepped off.

Susan shook her head. "You are a geek to the core. Come on, I'll show you another machine."

———

Sean closed the locker. A run on the treadmill and some weight lifting should work out the stress and tension. He entered the gym and headed to the treadmills, only to find them all occupied. *Oh well, I guess it's weights first.* The gym was very busy this evening. When he reached the free weights, two women were picking up the five- and ten-pound hand weights. One woman had a very nice feminine shape, full and ripe breasts, a narrow waist and round hips, while the other one was clearly an athlete. The shapely one looked up at him and turned the color of a ripe tomato.

"Ah… Detective Landers, I… ah."

It took Sean a minute to place her. He smiled. She looked a lot better in her workout clothes than she did in that baggy Tyvek suit. In fact, she looked very enticing. "Oh, yes, I remember you, the new scientist from the forensic department. Hello." He held out his hand to shake hers. She just stood there, turning an alarming shade of purple. The other woman took his hand instead.

"Hi, I'm Susan Webb. So, you know my sister Stephanie from work?"

"Yes, we met the other day at a crime scene."

The woman had a such a firm grip he had to pull his hand out of her grasp. *The two women may be sisters, but they are nothing alike.*

He turned to Stephanie. "I know these aren't office hours, but I've been going over my notes on the Mercer case, and I wondered if you have had a chance to look at any of the evidence we sent over."

The transition on Stephanie's face was amazing. The high color vanished, and her eyes brightened. Sean almost smiled, but didn't in case it embarrassed her.

"I took a quick look at the samples. I noticed two types of hair from the evidence at the scene. One hair may be similar to those in the stocking cap we found. I need to do a more thorough examination. I can call you with more information late tomorrow if you're in a hurry." Her hand slid down her exercise clothes like she was looking for a pocket. The skin tight outfit had no place for pockets.

He felt the eyes of the sister boring into him. This was awkward. There were several questions he needed to ask, but this wasn't the time or place. "Can we meet for lunch, instead? I have a few questions and concerns."

Stephanie looked shocked, and her sister kept moving her head back and forth like she was watching a tennis rally. He wanted to laugh. It took a moment before Stephanie answered. When she did, the word came out like a whisper. "Okay."

"Good. How's Thursday at that sports bar near the lab? I can meet you there at one o'clock. That should give you time to run some more tests." He ran his fingers through his hair.

The sister finally spoke. "She'll be there. Nice to meet you, Detective. Now, if you'll excuse us, we need to get back to our workout." She grabbed Stephanie's arm and led her away.

Stephanie turned her head and looked back at him. "I'll see you Thursday."

———

Ray woke up gasping for breath and soaked in sweat. He sprang from the bed and placed his back to the wall, fists in the air, waiting for the punch that didn't come. It took him a few minutes to realize he wasn't in prison. He slid down the wall and closed his eyes, letting his heart rate and breathing slow down to normal.

When he regained control, he got up and returned to the bed. Something had triggered the dream. It had been a long time since he'd dreamed about the beatings during his first year in prison. He sniffed the pillow. Lavender. He hadn't noticed it when he'd washed the sheets at the laundry mat. It was late the last time he'd washed clothes. When he got there, he discovered he'd forgotten the detergent again. That left him only one option, buy the cheap soap from the vending machine. He didn't read the ingredients on the box but just dumped the contents in and started the washer.

During the third month in prison, they transferred him to

a different cell block. No matter how much he kept to himself, the bullies sought him out as fresh meat for their taunting. The enforcer for the white supremacists wore an herb salve on his forearm to help with a nasty burn. It smelled of lavender. Even now, he could feel the man's arm around his throat. He gasped for air as the man slowly choked him. The beating he got after the choking resulted in two weeks in the infirmary. It was a miracle no bones were broken. He rubbed his elbow. It still ached when the weather turned cold. He clenched his fists. There was nothing to do but strip the sheets off the bed and try to sleep on the mattress under just the blankets.

He lay down on the bed again, but his mind kept running like a dog chasing his tail. All the conflicting memories, the betrayal that led to his arrest, the people and the system that failed him, losing his mother, and his years in prison. Prison, the thoughts of his first year there sent a shiver down his spine. How many times was he beaten or harassed into giving up food… and other things until the day Declan Bishop took pity and brought him into his gang. A man alone is an orphan. A man who is part of a gang has protection and support.

Once he belonged to a group, he discovered there were more benefits than safety. Other members of the gang had some rather unique skills. The old comment about learning how to be a better criminal in prison was true, and he proved to be a very talented student. He snorted. The problem was he hadn't been a criminal when he was sent up the river.

He rolled over on his side and took a deep breath. Ten years they stole from him, his best years. Ten years and the potential of what he could have been… destroyed. Why? He snarled. "Jealousy because of a girl."

THE PROSECUTOR

Sean picked at his slice of apple pie while Mac stirred his coffee. David Turner hadn't shown up for their 10:00 meeting by 10:20. The diner wasn't crowded at this hour, but the lunch rush would start in about forty minutes.

"Do you think he's still coming?" Mac grabbed his fork and stabbed the cinnamon roll in front of him.

"I don't know. I couldn't tell him what the meeting was about in case someone was listening or recording the call. I only told him I needed to see him and it was important. If he doesn't show up, then we have no choice but to question him at his office." He shifted in his chair and looked out the window, scanning the parking lot.

"How long do you think it will be before the press starts asking more questions?" Mac asked through a mouth full of roll.

"No telling. Did you read the story in this morning's paper?"

"Yes. They managed to write an accurate account, as far as it went. I'm sure Turner read it, as well, and probably knows what this meeting is about. You'd think he'd welcome the bone you've thrown him by wanting to meet with him privately." Mac took another bite of cinnamon roll, managing to get a smear of glaze on his chin.

"That's not necessarily true. I didn't give any details about why I needed to see him. For all he knows, we want to meet about the jewelry store robbery from last month." Sean checked his watch.

Mac snorted. "You're kidding, right? The man is not an idiot, and you have a reputation for digging down to the truth. He knows darn well why you want to speak to him. The question is, does he want to speak to you?"

Sean checked his watch again. "If he isn't here in fifteen minutes, I'm going to call his office. Do you think it's possible he may have called in sick?"

"I doubt that. If he's around his family all day, they would know he's upset and not coughing or puking. I'd never be able to fake an illness in front of my wife." He took another bite of his cinnamon roll and continued speaking with his mouth full. "You want to make a bet on how long it takes before the press digs up the story?"

Sean laughed. "That depends on which reporter gets curious and starts digging. He could get lucky. They could miss it, but a prosecutor having an affair... hmm... no, he's been in office long enough to have pissed off a few people. Somebody has to have noticed his habit of disappearing for an hour or so during the day. Remember, according to Mrs. Mortenson, the affair's been going on for about a year." He ran his fork through the rest of his apple pie. "I'm sure somebody knows or suspects. All a reporter has to do is talk to Mrs. Mortenson. If the poor bastard is really unlucky, he'll draw the attention of the guy with the moose column."

Mac choked on his coffee. He grabbed a napkin and rubbed coffee droplets off his lapel. "I wouldn't wish Jeff Olsen on anyone. The man is vicious as a wolverine and as tactful as a sledgehammer. He would be a great investigative reporter, except he has his own agenda and doesn't let details like the truth get in the way of whatever issue he's trying to push." His eyes narrowed. "I think that's Turner pulling into the parking lot. That's the kind of car Mrs. Mortenson described."

Sean turned and shifted his position to see what Mac was looking at. David Turner stepped out of a silver Mercedes. The man looked terrible, even at this distance. Sean and Mac glanced at each other. This was going to be a delicate meeting.

David walked up to their table and looked at Sean. "Thank you for your discretion."

Mac raised his eyebrows.

David pulled out one of the empty chairs at the table and sat down. "I know you two have figured out my connection with your latest case. I've seen your work on enough cases to know you're the best detective team in the county because you know how to connect the dots."

When a waitress approached, he stopped speaking. She offered him a menu, but he declined it. He ordered coffee and a slice of peach pie. When the waitress left, he turned to Sean. "It isn't or wasn't like it sounds. I loved Angela. My wife and I have been living separate lives for several years."

Sean studied the man's appearance. David's eyes looked lifeless, and there were dark circles underneath them. The man's tie hung loose and askew.

"We are planning to file for divorce next year after the election. Leslie wants to move back to Philadelphia. Her father is getting older, and she is an only child. She will inherit several apartment buildings when he passes away. He wants her to take over the management now while he's still alive to teach her the ropes."

The waitress arrived with David's order. He thanked her and took a sip of the coffee. He set down the cup, sloshing some of the liquid over the side. "Angela and I planned to get married." He stared at the table.

Mac discretely slid an extra napkin across to him.

Sean looked up at David. "We have to ask. Can you account for your whereabouts on Tuesday morning?"

David blinked and looked up. It took him a few minutes to speak. "I was with Angela from eight fifteen until about nine thirty." He made a choking sound and quickly picked up the coffee cup. He took a few swallows. "I went straight to the office so I could pick up my notes and go over them before the budget meeting with the county commissioners at eleven." He stared at his coffee cup. "If I had stayed with her longer, I could have saved her." His voice broke on the last word.

Sean caught Mac's eye and nodded. The man wasn't the murderer. You could not fake grief like that. That brought them back to the possibility of someone targeting Angela specifically or looking for vengeance. After speaking to Mitch Mercer, vengeance against him wasn't the likely motive. That left someone with a hatred of Turner.

Mac shifted in his chair. "Have you ever noticed anyone near her house, someone who seemed out of place in the neighborhood?

David shook his head. "No."

Sean picked up his fork. "Did you have a regular meeting schedule, something that someone who was following you or her would have noticed?"

David looked up. "What?"

Mac turned to look at Sean, as well.

"I was just wondering if someone could have planned this rather than just a random break in."

David's breathing rate increased. "I can't think of anyone who would want to hurt Angela. She was the nicest person…" He broke off and buried his face in his hands.

Sean exchanged glances with Mac. Clearly, they weren't going to get anything useful out of him today. Best thing to do was leave him alone for a week and let some of the shock wear off. Sean knew from experience that the grief would always be there, but time helped one cope with the reality of the loss.

"We're going to need to speak with your wife. How can we get a hold of her?" Mac pulled out a pen and his notebook.

David placed his hands on the table. "What? Oh, yes, Leslie works as a controller for a construction company." He pulled out his phone and opened his contact list. "Here is her number and the name of her company."

Mac wrote in his book then looked up. "You didn't answer the question about your meetings with Angela Mercer. Did you have a regular, scheduled routine, or were your meetings random?"

David buried his face in his hands again. "It was scheduled, every Tuesday and Thursday around eight fifteen. Oh, God, was she killed because of me?"

Sean looked at his partner. Mac nodded. Sean bit his lip. It looked like his initial impression was playing out. Time to change the subject and help David regain his composure.

"Do either of you know why Jeff Olsen's column is called 'Moose Droppings'? I mean, the guy is a hack, but I would think he'd want a more dignified title for his weekly offering of swill?"

Mac glanced at David, then turned to Sean and answered. "Several years ago when Olsen first started writing for the local paper, someone wrote a letter to the editor slamming his reporting of a political event. The writer compared Jeff's column to a pile of moose crap. The ownership of the paper had just changed over, and the new editor didn't like Olsen very much. He wanted to fire him, but since Olsen was a shirttail relation to the new owner, he couldn't. So, the next time Jeff's column appeared in the paper, there was a sketch of a moose chewing some long grass while standing in a stream. It was titled "Moose Droppings". Jeff was furious, but so many people called in saying they liked the name that it stuck. The column has been around so long now that most people don't know the story and think it's just a quaint local name. From what I've heard, he still hates it, but since it's become his brand, he can't get rid of it."

David picked up his fork and took a bite of peach pie. He still looked bad, but at least had a better grip on himself.

"I should get back to the office. I'll think about your questions and get back to you if I can come up with anything else that might be relevant. Again, thank you both for your discretion." He wiped his mouth with the napkin and reached into his pocket to pull out a twenty-dollar bill. He dropped it on the table, nodded to both men, and left the restaurant.

Mac shook his head. "Poor bastard is mourning and has to hide it from everyone."

———

Stephanie carefully set the cup of hot cocoa down on the coffee table before returning to the kitchen for cookies. Everything was ready for her relaxing evening. A large bowl of popcorn sat next to the remote control. It was movie night, and she'd picked one of her favorite romance films to watch. She enjoyed seeing someone else getting a happily ever after, even though it seemed to keep passing her by. There was always hope.

She sat down on her favorite spot on the couch and pulled her thick velour robe around her nightgown. Two furry bunny slippers smiled up from her feet. Everything was perfect, or at least it would have been if Susan hadn't dropped off another thumb drive full of campaign data to cross match and sort. The thumb drive was an unexpected curve ball, but she would not let it completely throw her game. Her dad always said that you had to be ready to improvise if the play book wasn't working. So, the movie would play in the background while she sorted.

This really was a snapshot of her life, home alone, watching TV or a movie and having some sort of geeky project to work on. She'd hoped moving back to her hometown would change that but apparently not. She started her laptop as the movie's opening theme music played. The data on the screen surprised her. It was a donors list for current sheriff, Walter Sparks. A word file gave her the instructions to match up these names with the all the election reports the man had filed since he first ran for election, who donated, when they donated, and how much they gave. She smiled. This wasn't such a bad task, so she should have it completed before the movie hero and heroine went on the sleigh ride.

With a final click to save her work, she powered down her laptop and leaned back on the couch. Now it was time to enjoy the movie. She loved Christmas romance films. Every holiday season found her glued to the television, watching one after the other. Why couldn't she meet a handsome stranger who just came into town? Maybe moving back home would introduce her to someone new, since there was no old boyfriend here to reconnect to.

All during high school, she was either buried in her schoolbooks or experimenting in the chemistry lab. Her older athletic siblings had left quite a mark at the school. Most people had no idea she was related to them. The couple on the screen were drinking hot cocoa and talking to the town mayor. She reached for her own cup, which still sat on the coffee table.

Actually, she had met a handsome man who was new to town. At least he wasn't here when she left to attend college. Detective Sean Landers had grabbed her attention the moment she saw him. *Tomorrow I'm going to meet him for lunch.* Her hand started to shake so badly she almost spilled the cocoa. Why on earth had she agreed to meet him? He was out of her league, and she knew it. It was the case. That's really what he was interested in. She had to remember that so she wouldn't make a fool of herself tomorrow.

When I get to the lab in the morning, I'll review all the data and take notes. That would give us something to discuss while we eat. That brought up another problem. What was she going to wear? Her biggest fear was dribbling something on her shirt and wearing a stain for the rest of the day. Maybe she should bring a bib. *Relax, Stephanie, you're overthinking this. Sit back and enjoy your movie.* She snuggled back into the couch cushions and pretended that she and Sean were the couple on the screen.

LUNCH

S tephanie gathered her notes and slipped them into a small file folder. She grabbed a legal tablet and placed it in the file, as well. If he wanted to discuss anything or had specific questions, she could take notes. The only way she was going to make it through this lunch without embarrassing herself was to treat it like a business meeting. Watching the movie last night and thinking of Sean had been a big mistake. All night long, she dreamed of the handsome detective.

She made sure to dress professionally, wearing the navy blue pant suit she usually wore when she had to testify in court. She added a lace-trimmed top under the jacket along with a pair of low-heeled navy dress shoes. She almost never wore high heels because it was too easy to trip and fall. She glanced up at the clock. Great, she was going to be late.

The parking lot looked full, but she managed to find a parking spot. When she turned off the engine, she checked her makeup in the rearview mirror and closed her eyes. *Relax Stephanie. It's just a friendly business meeting, not a grilling by an aggressive defense attorney.*

———

Sean walked into the sports bar and checked his watch. It was five minutes after one. He hoped Stephanie had gotten there early and snagged a table. The place was noisy and nearly full. It had two main seating areas and a back room that could be closed for private parties but was currently open. He wandered through the areas, seeing several people he knew, and nodded greetings as he walked by. After a complete tour of the place didn't turn up the forensic scientist, he made his way to a free booth with a view of the front door. At least he'd be able to see her the moment she walked in. As he sat down, a waitress came up and handed him a menu.

"Would you like to hear today's specials?"

He smiled at her. "In a few minutes. I am waiting for someone to join me."

"Okay, can I get you something to drink while you're waiting?"

"I'll have one of your hand mixed lemonades and a glass of water."

"Would you like it plain or flavored? We have strawberry, raspberry, or mango."

"Strawberry, please."

She nodded and left the table.

Sean pulled out his phone and checked the time. She was ten minutes late. Had something happened at the lab that detained her? He closed his eyes and visualized her as she looked that night at the gym. She was painfully shy. That was obvious. He remembered how she reacted when he asked about the evidence. She literally came alive. Her comfort zone was her work. That was something he could easily relate to. His own comfort zone was his work, or, more accurately, his work was his refuge from the past. He shook his head. *No point in going down that road.*

The waitress returned quickly with a glass of water and

his drink. He turned his attention to the video screens that lined the wall, focusing in on one that showed the highlights from last night's baseball game. Each time the door opened, he glanced up. There was still no sign of her. Was he being stood up? He pulled out his phone to check the time and see if he had any messages. When she finally walked through the door, he almost missed her.

Sean stood up and waved at her. She wore a momentary look of panic, but she closed her eyes, took a deep breath, and walked to his booth.

"It's Stephanie, right?"

She smiled and sat down. "Yes, Stephanie Webb. How are you, Detective Landers?"

He grinned at her. "Call me Sean."

Their waitress walked up and interrupted the awkward moment. She set a glass of water in front of Stephanie. "Would you like to hear the specials now?"

Sean looked at Stephanie. "Do you like burgers?"

She nodded.

He turned to the waitress. "Give us two of the All-American Burgers with fries. Stephanie, what would you like to drink? Lunch is on me."

Steph glanced at his drink. "I'll have what he's having."

When the waitress left, there was an awkward silence. Sean cleared his throat. "Thanks for meeting me. I know it isn't protocol, but I need to know anything you might have found in the evidence we sent over. I… I have a feeling about this one." He ended lamely and took a sip of his drink.

Stephanie smiled. "Mac told me about your special abilities with crime scenes."

Now it was his turn to feel uncomfortable. "I wouldn't call it a special ability. I just get a feeling about the scene, and it usually proves to be accurate."

"I would say that was a special ability. Mac seems to be quite impressed with it, as well. I'm curious. What did you sense at the Mercer house?" She tilted her head and looked at him.

He felt uncomfortable talking about this with a stranger. It was bad enough with his partners, but at least they were around him long enough to know he wasn't a freak.

He leaned forward and stared at the table. He didn't want to answer, but he couldn't leave her question hanging there. Since she worked for the lab, they were bound to meet at more crime scenes, so she'd find out eventually. He sighed. "The first impression I had was the words 'step one'. The crime scene felt off, like it was staged rather than real." He looked up into her eyes, expecting to see surprise or skepticism. Instead, he found understanding and interest. He hadn't anticipated that.

The waitress returned and placed Stephanie's drink on the table. Stephanie took a sip. "Oh, this is good." She set down the glass. "You asked me here to answer some questions. What would you like to know?"

He took another sip of his own drink. "What have you found out so far?"

"I don't have much to tell you yet. We sent the duct tape to the fingerprint lab. It will take a few weeks before we know if we have anything. Even then, unless the perpetrator is in the system, we won't be able to give you a name. The blood and hair samples are at the DNA lab, and it will take at least a month before we know anything there. Do you know when you'll get the coroner's report?"

Sean frowned. "In another two weeks. We're interviewing right now. It's all I have to work with until I get some lab results. That's why I asked you here today. Is there anything you noticed in the evidence that you can tell me about?"

She hastily picked up her glass again and took a large swallow. Sean observed her. He knew the look of someone who had information, but was unsure if it could be told. He decided not to press her too hard. *Let her feel comfortable with me.* Experience had taught him people are more forthcoming if they are allowed to draw their own conclusions in their own time.

When the waitress arrived with their food, Sean welcomed the distraction. He reached immediately for the ketchup bottle and baptized his burger, then made a pool among his fries.

Stephanie laughed. "My brothers drown their food like that." She shifted in her seat. "There is one thing I can mention to you… unofficially, of course."

He set down the ketchup and gave her his full attention.

"The stocking cap that the deputy found near the house, well, the hair inside definitely belonged to a person of African origin."

Sean nodded and stared at his fries. He was relatively sure Angela Mercer was targeted, and the perpetrator covered up the attack with the burglary. *If someone is targeted, it is usually because they know something or have something that someone else wants.* That was not the case for Angela Mercer. He was pretty sure someone killed her not because of who she was but who she was in relation to the two men in her life. After his interviews with Mitch Mercer and David Turner, he was sure it was David. The question was who and why. The sound of someone clearing their throat brought him back to his surroundings.

"I'm sorry, did you say something?" He hastily picked up a fry.

"You're trying to figure out something about the case."

He frowned.

She smiled. "My brother Douglas gets the same look on his face when he's working on an accounting problem."

He chuckled. "Is he an older brother or a younger one?"

She reached for the ketchup. "All my siblings are older than I am. You met Susan the other day. She's a high school physical education teacher and coach's girls' basketball. She's the middle child. My twin brothers are the oldest. Dennis is an attorney, and Douglas is a CPA." She put ketchup on her burger and took a bite.

They ate in silence for a while. Stephanie finally broke it. "Do you have any family in the area?"

Sean wiped his mouth with a napkin. "I don't have any family living anywhere. Not really. I'm an only child, and my parents are both gone. There are some extended family members but no one I'm close to." He wasn't about to mention his late wife, Peggy.

Stephanie frowned. "I'm sorry. I can't imagine not having any family. I don't always get along with mine, but it's a comfort knowing they're there."

"My folks have been gone for a long time. My mom passed away when I was sixteen, and my father died in a car accident shortly after I started the police academy."

There was another awkward silence while they ate their meal. When he'd finished his hamburger, Sean spoke again. "So why did you decide to become a forensic scientist?"

Stephanie set down her burger and smiled. "I've always loved science and puzzles. When I was a freshman in college, I took an aptitude test to help determine what I'd be good at. The results showed that I'd make a good forensic scientist. I've always been very good at math and chemistry. It took me longer to get through school than my siblings. They each got some sort of sports scholarship, while I had to pay my own way. I'm the oddball in the family. I'm not very good at sports. My father swears they mixed me up at the hospital. He might be right. My entire family is very athletic except me."

"I can't believe you're not athletic. I saw you at the gym the other day." He grabbed a fry and dipped it in the ketchup pool.

"You weren't there earlier to see Susan and me on the treadmills. She was running like she was in a marathon. I was doing everything I could to keep from falling off the machine." She picked up her burger again and took a bite.

He laughed. "You mean you don't do sports at all, not even bowling?"

She shook her head. "All I can do is roll gutter balls and try not to break a toe when I drop the thing."

He smiled. "What did you do when your siblings were playing sports?"

"Sit in the bleachers and watch."

"That must've been boring. Did you play video games or read a book while they were playing?" He grabbed another fry.

"Oh, no, that was not allowed. Sports are practically a religion with my father. When you come to a game, you have to give it your full attention just like in church. Doing something else while someone was playing is disrespectful and not tolerated." She picked up one of her fries.

"Couldn't you stay home?" Her shyness was beginning to make sense to him.

She looked down at her plate. "My father wouldn't allow it. Any time one of my siblings was in a game, the entire family would come to cheer them on. The only exception was if I was ill, and I mean seriously ill. A cold or a headache was not an acceptable excuse."

"It sounds like you had a tough upbringing." He finished his fries and picked up his drink.

"It was hard being the ugly duckling of the family, but my siblings were always supportive of me. My sister came to my chess championships, even though my father wouldn't. My brothers always helped me when I had trouble with my car and made sure that my dates behaved. I lived away from home for several years while I was going through college and when I was first hired by the state crime lab. I had an opportunity a few months ago to transfer to the lab here. I took it to be close to my siblings again." She pushed her plate away and grabbed her purse, which sat on the floor. "Thank you very much for lunch. I'm sorry I couldn't give you more information about the case. I'll let you know if I find something else. I really have to get back to the lab since we're buried in drug cases right now." She stood up. "Thank you again for lunch." She held out her hand, and he shook it.

"Thank you for meeting me. I'm sure we'll run into each other again soon. In this business, it's inevitable."

She smiled and walked out of the restaurant.

He watched her go. There was something about the shy scientist that aroused his curiosity and other things. He hadn't felt that way in a long time.

REASONS

Ray stood shivering next to his car at the gas station. A wind gust whipped rain into his face. What a miserable night to be outside. His back and arms ached, partially from the cold and partially from the long day's work. He glanced over his shoulder at the meter on the gas pump. Time to get home before he ended up soaked to the skin. The pump stopped, and he hurriedly secured the nozzle and his gas cap before heading into the convenience store. He grabbed a few items and made his way to the cash register. At the counter, he stopped to pick up the paper. No more stories about the murder, but another letter to the editor demanding more police patrols through neighborhoods. The paper shook in his hand. All his research, all the time watching her house, planning out every detail, and the cops still hadn't made the connection. He thought for sure they would have figured it out by now. Every day he checked the headlines, looking for the story about the murder victim and her affair with the prosecutor, but each day he was disappointed. It was like Declan Bishop told him in prison. *The entire system is corrupt, and there is only justice for those who could pay for it.* He snorted. That was so true. He had been poor, innocent, and found no justice. Now he would make them all pay. If the system was trying to circle the wagons and protect one of their own, then he would have to break through the barrier of silence. He glanced at the paper's table of contents and found the spot where it mentioned the column "Moose Droppings".

The wicked grin on his face must have startled the cashier because the man stepped back when Ray set down his purchases. Ray ignored him and pulled out his wallet. "Pump six needs to be added to my bill."

The clerk nodded and hurriedly rang up his items and placed them in a bag.

Ray grabbed his groceries, nodded at the cashier, and went back out into the rain.

Declan had told him that a man who wanted justice had to prime the pump to get it. He smiled. An anonymous phone call and a nudge in the right direction should get the ball rolling. He got back in the car. In order for him to get justice, the guilty parties had to pay. He started the engine and turned on the windshield wipers. All of this started twelve years ago while he was sitting in his car.

———

TWELVE YEARS AGO.

Ray surfed through the channels on the radio but couldn't find a song to match his mood. Getting the job at the electronics store was going to change everything, and he couldn't wait to tell Amber about it. The job meant he'd make enough money over the summer to attend technical school in the fall. He shoved a CD into the player, and loud rock and roll blared from the speakers in the back. The subwoofer in the trunk beat out the baseline. He glanced at the clock on the dash. Amber wouldn't be off work for another two hours. Great, there'd be time to stop by Jimmy's and see if he wanted to get a burger.

The burger place wasn't that busy at this hour. Ray ordered the double with cheese, bacon, and all the trimmings. He reached for the ketchup cup and noticed that Jimmy kept looking out the window. "Are you expecting someone?" He reached for a fry.

"Yeah, I told Vince where we were going. He said he might stop by." Jimmy took a large bite of his burger and chewed.

"Your big brother doesn't want to hang out with us. He runs around with those tough guys and the druggies. I really don't want to eat with him." Ray grabbed another fry and dipped it into a cup of ketchup.

"Don't worry. I think he just wanted to come here and annoy me." Jimmy quickly grabbed his drink and took a sip.

"What is it with you? You're twitching in your chair like you're sitting on a cactus." Ray wrinkled his forehead. Something didn't feel right.

Jimmy shook his head. "Everything is fine. I guess he changed his mind about coming." He concentrated on his food for a few minutes, only glancing out the window two more times. The last time, he seemed to see something he liked because his shoulders relaxed and he quit squirming.

Ray looked out the window, trying to figure out what Jimmy saw, but the angle of his chair and the bushes in the landscaping obstructed his vision.

Twenty minutes later, they piled back into Ray's car. "Drop me off at my house before you pick up Amber." Jimmy fiddled with the dial on the radio.

Ray pulled out onto the road. "I don't have time to take you home. Amber gets off work in fifteen minutes. I'll drop you off after we pick her up."

Jimmy shifted in his seat and glanced at the side mirror.

Ray didn't pay much attention to him. Instead, he pushed

the radio button to his favorite channel and turned up the sound. With music blaring from the speakers, he started singing along. They traveled down the road for several blocks. Jimmy suddenly stiffened in the seat. The motion startled Ray, so he looked over at his friend. "What's wrong?" Lights started flashing red and blue in the rear-view mirror. "Shit. What are they pulling me over for? I'm not speeding, and the music isn't that loud?"

A second police car pulled up behind the first. Both officers got out of their cars at the same time. Ray watched their movement through the side mirror. "What the..? One has his hand on his gun, and the other one is... oh crap, he's bringing out a dog."

The lead officer shouted. "Get out of the car with your hands up."

"Jimmy, they think we're someone else, a robber or something." He turned to his friend and saw sweat running down his face. "Oh shit, you don't have any of your brother's dope on you, do you?"

Jimmy shook his head. He looked like he was having a stroke.

"Jimmy, relax. As long as we stay cool, they'll figure out their mistake and let us go."

Ray unlocked his door and slowly got out of the car.

"Put your hands in the air and step away from the car." The officer held one hand out, while the other still rested on his gun.

The second officer walked up with the dog, a large black and tan German Sheppard. When he walked the dog up to the car, the animal started sniffing the vehicle, lingering at the trunk. It barked and scratched at the bumper.

"Hey, be careful of my paint job," Ray said to the officer.

"Quiet, keep your hands up."

The officer with the dog looked up. "Open the trunk."

Ray frowned. "It doesn't lock any more. All you have to do is push down on it and it will pop open."

The officer next to him didn't look thrilled. Ray glanced over the car at Jimmy. His friend looked pale, and a sheen of sweat covered his forehead. What the hell was wrong with Jimmy? His thoughts were interrupted by the arrival of another officer.

The new cop got out of his car and strode over. He nodded at the officer with the dog. "Need any help?"

"Yeah, back up Bill, while I put Ginger back in the car."

The new cop walked up. "Do you want me to check the truck?"

"Yes. The kid says if you push down on the top, it will open."

The new officer followed the instructions, and the trunk sprang open. He leaned over and looked inside.

"There's a grubby box in here." He reached in and tried to lift the lid. Something caught, so he had to pull hard to make it open. There was the sound of breaking glass. The officer screamed. The second officer ran up from his car and pulled the injured man away from the trunk.

The officer appeared to be splashed with acid. There were burn marks on his face and hands. There were holes in his uniform where the acid had burned through the material.

Ray leaned over and lost his lunch on the asphalt.

———

Ray pulled out of the gas station lot and onto the road. He was only twenty minutes away from his apartment, and there wasn't much traffic this evening. Most people were snuggled up at home and out of this wet weather. He snorted. Hopefully, the heat wasn't out at his place again. He turned the wipers on high. It was raining the day he got a visitor at the prison. He'd never had a visitor before, and it changed everything.

———

SIX YEARS AGO.

Ray lay on his bunk reading a comic book he'd borrowed from one of the members of Declan Bishop's gang. He didn't even look up when the prison guard came into his space. The guards mostly left him alone since he'd joined up with Bishop. He wasn't an enforcer or a troublemaker. He was just a quiet, ordinary guy with powerful friends. It didn't really register when the guard said he had a visitor. Nobody visited him… ever.

"Tisdale, I said you have a visitor. Now get moving. I have to escort you to the visitor's room." The guard looked impatient.

He frowned. "Who is it?"

"I don't know. It's some guy in his thirties. That's all I know. Now, come on." He turned and led the way to the visitor's room.

The visitor's room was a square white room with ten small tables, each with two chairs facing each other across the table. Three officers stood against the walls to make sure no one broke the rules of no touching and no items given to the inmates. Nine of the tables were already full, mostly with inmates meeting their girlfriends or spouses. At the remaining table sat a tall, thin man with dark brown hair.

Ray frowned. The man looked vaguely familiar. He walked over to the table and sat down. "You wanted to see me?"

"Yes, I'm not sure if you remember me. I'm Les Wyler. I used to hang out with Vince Morgan."

The light went on. "Oh yeah, you were the one who used

to get him… ah… yeah, I remember you. What are you doing here?"

Les cleared his throat, looked around the room, then faced Ray again. "I went to rehab a couple of months ago. I'm on a twelve-step program. One of the twelve steps is to apologize to the people we have wronged and try to make amends." He cleared his throat again and stared at the table. "I'm not sure you know why you are here." He looked up and waved a hand.

"I'm here because somebody put drug stuff in the trunk of my car." Ray's nostrils flared, and he cracked his knuckles.

"That's why I'm here, to tell you what happened and why." Les shifted in his chair and leaned forward. He lowered his voice to make it harder for anyone to listen in. "You had a girlfriend before you got arrested didn't you?"

Ray frowned again. "Yeah, Amber Ricci. She left me right after I got arrested."

"I know, and that was the whole reason for the drug paraphernalia in your trunk."

Ray started to shake. "You're not making any sense."

"Jimmy Morgan wanted your girlfriend."

Ray froze in place. His eyes went wide, and his mouth fell open. Images of Amber and Jimmy flashed through his mind. He remembered how Jimmy would watch her sometimes, but she didn't pay the slightest attention to him. That never stopped Jimmy. He always commented on how pretty she was or how good she looked in her jeans. He slammed his hand on his thigh. How could he have been so stupid?

Les cleared his throat. "I'm sorry."

Ray looked up. "So, Jimmy set me up to get a shot at Amber?

"I'm afraid that's right. He just wanted you to be in trouble, though not really hurt you. He figured when Amber's parents found out, they'd forbid her from seeing you." Les scratched his chin. "It worked. They wouldn't allow her to go to your trial or visit you while you were in the county jail."

Ray leaned back in his chair. "I thought that might be the case." Some of the pain in his chest lightened up. She didn't just dump him. Her dad had stopped her from seeing him and supporting him. He looked up at Les. "Did she ever go out with Jimmy?"

"They got married about a year after you were sent to prison. They divorced a couple of months ago. Amber has sole custody of their daughter." Les set his hands on the table.

Ray slammed his fist on his leg again. He looked around the room, wanting to pound something else, especially the messenger.

Les pulled his hands from the table and leaned back in his chair.

When Ray finally got himself under control, he looked at the man sitting in front of him. "So, you came all the way here to tell me that my best friend stabbed me in the back in order to take my girlfriend?"

Les shifted in his chair. "Not exactly, but you needed to know why it happened in order to understand how things went wrong."

"How things went wrong? I'd say it started with having a snake for a best friend." Ray frowned and scratched his chin.

"Jimmy didn't want you to end up in prison. He just wanted you out of the way so he could get to Amber. As long as you were around, she only saw him as your best friend. She really liked you."

Ray snorted. "Well, she's got a great way of showing it. She runs off and marries the guy who put me in prison."

"Like I said, it wasn't supposed to go that far. Let me tell you the rest of the story." Les sat up straighter. "Jimmy went to his brother, Vince, and told him he wanted some weed put in the back of your car. Not much, but enough to get you arrested for possession, but not for selling. Vince, of course, came to me. The problem was at the time all the weed I had was already spoken for. But I had an old boxed meth lab that I needed to get rid of. I told Vince I'd put that in your trunk instead."

Ray reached out and grabbed the table edges with both hands. If this idiot didn't shut up soon, he was going to start swinging, and he wouldn't stop until the guards pulled them apart.

Les scooted back in his chair. "Look, you shouldn't have gotten nailed for the box. When the forensics came back, they would've shown fingerprints on the box and on the stuff inside, but none of them yours. And with the fact that your trunk didn't lock and anyone could have access to it, well, a competent defense attorney would've gotten you off. If that cop hadn't tried to play Mr. Macho, he never would have disturbed the acid and gotten sprayed with it." He slowly stood up. "I only came here to tell you what happened so you know the truth. You should try to get another attorney and see if you can get them to open the case. Jimmy probably wouldn't testify, but Amber might. And I'd be willing to tell them my part to help make amends. You should have enough information to get yourself a lesser sentence if they won't clear you entirely. Good luck man, you got a raw deal, and I'm sorry about my part in it." He walked away from the table and out the visitor's door.

THE NEXT STEP

Sean shifted from one foot to the other and checked his watch. The dial read nine fifty. Thank heavens there was a chilly wind blowing this morning, or he'd be breaking out in a nervous sweat. In ten more minutes, he'd announce his candidacy for sheriff from the front of the county administration building. They set a microphone up on the front steps.

When a hand came down on his shoulder, he nearly jumped out of his skin. "Sweet Bernadette, Mac, you scared the crap out of me."

Mac grinned. "I hope not. It would show in that blue suit."

"What are you doing here, anyway? Aren't you supposed to be on duty?"

"I'm on my lunch hour. Where else would I be? I'm your partner, and I'm here to support you in whatever idiocy you try to achieve."

Sean snorted. "Thanks for the vote of confidence. Aren't you worried Little Bonaparte will get wind of this and give you grief?"

"For one thing, he's in Boise for the state sheriff's conference. Nice timing, by the way. And for another, I'm already going to catch grief from him because I'm your partner. I might as well own up to it now and make the most of the call to his office questioning my loyalty to the department."

Their conversation was interrupted by the arrival of a van from one of the television news channels. Sean recognized the anchor of the six o'clock news when he stepped out of the passenger seat. A quick glance at his watch told him he only had four minutes left before his announcement.

Mac pulled a piece of nicotine gum out of his pocket and popped it into his mouth. "Nice crowd. Where did they all come from?"

"Sam, my campaign manager, had volunteers making phone calls and getting people to come to the announcement. That's him in the dark blue jacket, handing out yard signs." He pointed to a man of medium build with a thick crop of white hair.

"Do you know any of these people?"

Sean rubbed his chin. "Some of them. There are several wives of fellow deputies in the crowd. Sam did a lot of calling in the department. We need a show of support from the deputies, but they can't turn up here in uniform."

Mac smiled. "So, the wives are here instead, brilliant." He fell silent as Sam walked up to them.

"Ready, Sean, it's time."

Sean nodded and strode over to the microphone. He cleared his throat.

"I want to thank everyone for showing up on this windy day. My name is Sean Landers, and I am running for County Sheriff." Sean shifted his position and scanned the crowd.

"I decided to run because the county taxpayers can't afford another increase in their property taxes. Elected officials need to be good stewards of the monies they receive. For several years, the sheriff's department has been over funding one division at the cost of its most important responsibilities, training, retention of its deputies and the county jail. Crime has been increasing in our area, and many times the department is too low on personnel to adequately protect the public. The new officers we hire and train leave the department after only a year's service to work for other departments just over the border for higher wages and better benefits. This costs the taxpayers a great deal in training and service." He stopped for a moment to scan the crowd and judge their reaction.

"I believe that the safety of the people in this county should be the priority of the sheriff's department. If elected, I promise to make this my focus and to reorganize the department to reflect this belief." He stopped and cleared his throat.

"I will do an audit of the jail and look for cost-effective ways to handle the overcrowding problem. And I will make sure the deputies who serve this county are well trained and equipped to ensure this department will live up to its motto of 'to protect and serve'. Are there any questions?"

A woman from a small independent paper held up her hand. "Does this mean you're going to eliminate the SWAT program?"

"No, but I will not keep it as the main division of the department. The sheriff's deputies respond to far more auto accidents and burglary calls than mob riots or major crimes."

There was laughter from some people in the crowd.

Sean smiled. "It is better management to concentrate on the most common needs of the community than to spend resources on flashy equipment that may never be used."

The question and answers session went on for another ten minutes. Sean handled himself well with the crowd applauding several of his answers. When Sam gave him the high sign, Sean began his closing.

"Again, I want to thank all of you for braving this brisk wind and coming out to hear my announcement. This is a large county, and the sheriff's department handles…"

"Excuse me, Detective Landers." Jeff Olsen elbowed his way through the crowd.

Oh crap, not this guy.

Olsen stopped in front of Sean and stood close enough that the audience could hear his words over the microphone. "If the sheriff's department is so concerned about protecting the good citizens of this county, then why have you not brought in the county prosecutor, David Turner, for questioning as a suspect in the Angela Mercer murder? After all, Mrs. Mercer was his mistress."

――――――

Tom Oliver stood in front of the coffee tray in the conference room of Terwilliger, Pace and Holmes, PA pouring coffee into two monogrammed mugs. Dennis Webb leaned back in his chair and stretched his legs. "So, there's a detective announcing for sheriff today. When am I supposed to announce? I mean, I don't want to be the last guy to jump into this race."

Tom handed Dennis a mug and sat down in one of the posh leather chairs. "Relax, you will announce in another week. And you won't be the last one, Walter Sparks will be." He took a sip from his mug.

"How do you know that?"

"It's called opposition research, and it's part of my job to know this kind of thing." Tom stood up. "There are some great cookies over here." He picked up the tray and brought it to the table.

Dennis leaned forward and grabbed one. "I take it we have someone at the announcement taking notes?" He took a huge bite.

Tom laughed. "Notes? The guy's recording the whole thing. I want to know the detective's speaking style and presentation, as well as what he has to say." He helped himself to a couple of cookies. "Our guy should be here any minute. The announcement was only supposed to last twenty minutes, half an hour at the most."

"Do we know much about this, detective? Do you think he will be a threat to my campaign?" Dennis picked up his coffee mug.

"We are still doing opposition research. Your sister works in the law enforcement community. Does she know him?"

Susan walked into the room. "Do I know who?"

Both men turned to her. Tom spoke. "Not you, the other one. The detective who announced today. Do you know if Stephanie has much to do with the sheriff's department?"

"Of course she does. The forensic lab gets called out to a lot of crime scenes. Now whether she knows the guy who's announcing today, well, I'm not sure. I'd have to ask her. What's his name?" Susan sat down at the table and grabbed a cookie. She was about to take a bite when Tom spoke.

"His name is Sean Landers."

Susan almost dropped her cookie. "Oh, she knows him all right. She had lunch with him a couple of weeks ago."

Dennis sat up straight in his chair. "What? She's not dating him, is she?"

She played with the cookie. "Not that I know of, but then she really doesn't talk a lot about her work or her personal life."

"How do you know about their lunch?" Tom set down his coffee mug and leaned forward.

"I was at the gym with her, and we ran into him. He asked her out to lunch right in front of me. Can I have some coffee?"

Tom got up and poured her a cup. He leaned over the table and set it down in front of her. He was about to ask her for more details when the door opened.

A man rushed into the room. "Tom, you will not believe what happened at the announcement." He held up his iPhone.

"Aaron, sit down. Dennis, this is Aaron Jeffries. He's a friend of mine who agreed to cover the announcements of all the other candidates running for sheriff. Aaron, this is my candidate, Dennis Webb and his sister, Susan." There were nods all around the table. Tom sat down and leaned back in his chair. He reached out and picked up his coffee. "Okay, what happened?"

Aaron grinned and hit the play button.

"Holy crap." Tom nearly dropped his cup.

Dennis stood up. "What?"

Susan clamped her hand over her mouth.

———

Blinking lights and electronic sounds surrounded Ray. People were everywhere in the Indian Casino, gambling and drinking. He sat on a stool in front of a slot machine. A beer rested in the drink holder, his finger perched on the play button, but his attention was on a machine in a nearby row.

Billy Spellman stared at his machine, mindlessly pushing the button, watching all the digital pictures change in front of him. Three nights a week he had come to the casino to blow his cash. Ray shook his head. *The guy's father must be giving him a hell of an allowance.*

Ray watched the waitress set another white Russian next to Billy and take the cash he handed her. *What a life, getting drunk and throwing away money on a slot machine. Clearly, Billy has some serious issues. Well, not for long.*

He'd have to time it perfectly. With all the people moving around, especially the ones with wheelchairs or scooters, he could make it work. The opportunity came a few minutes later in the form of a very heavy woman with a walker. Ray got up and took a step toward Billy's chair. *Wait a moment. Now.* He walked over to Billy and had to leap aside to make room for the woman. He bumped Billy's arm, sending his drink to the floor.

"I'm so sorry."

Billy looked angry as he shook droplets of liquor from his hand. "Yah, well, that was a full drink."

"I'm sorry. Let me get you a fresh one. What was it?"

Billy wiped his hand on his jeans. "A white Russian."

Ray waved his hand, and a waitress came up. "Hello. Can I get a white Russian and a towel? We've had a bit of an accident."

"Yes, sir."

Ray reached into his pocket and palmed the small squeeze bottle. The waitress returned quickly. She handed Billy the towel and held out the drink to Ray. He handed her a twenty-dollar bill. "Keep the change."

"Thank you, sir."

He took the drink from her, and turned his back, carefully putting his other hand over the glass, and squeezed. Billy was too busy drying off his hands to notice.

"Here's your drink, and, again, I'm sorry."

Billy took the glass. "It's okay. You've made it right."

Ray nodded at him and walked away.

It took another half an hour before Billy got up and headed for the exit, his face flushed and a trickle of sweat running down his cheek. He walked out the main doors and went straight for his car.

Ray had parked a few spaces over from Billy. When the man stumbled past, Ray got out with the rag covered with chloroform held tightly in his gloved hand. The combination of alcohol and the drug rendered Billy weak as a child. Ray easily held him while the chloroform did its work. Ray didn't worry about being seen. The parking lot was fairly dark, and he had disabled the nearest surveillance camera with an air rifle before heading into the casino.

Once he had Billy's limp body resting in the driver's seat, he slipped into the passenger side and reached into his pocket to pull the small eye glasses case that contained heroin, a needle, a spoon, and a lighter. After rolling up Billy's sleeve and putting a rubber tourniquet around his arm, he opened the eye glasses case. With a few minutes of work, the hypodermic was loaded. It took a moment to find the vein and insert the needle.

Ray's mother had died while he was locked up in prison. Now Defense Attorney Curtis Spellman was paid back for that crime in full.

POLITICS & BEER

S tephanie walked into the conference room at Dennis' firm. The fifteen people in the room already stood around in groups or sat at the table talking. All eight seats around the table were taken, and there was only one seat left along the wall. She made her way over to it and sat down. She wanted to get to the meeting early but was delayed at work again, as usual.

Tom Oliver sat at the head of the table. He stood up and tapped his empty coffee cup with a spoon to get everyone's attention. "I'd like to get this meeting started. We have a lot to cover this evening."

It took a few minutes for the room to come to order. Stephanie glanced at all the faces. These were the key people in her brother's campaign for sheriff. Dennis and Douglas sat on either side of Tom. Susan was next to Dennis and Aaron Jeffries was on her other side. The rest of the people in the room she didn't know. It had surprised her when Tom called and invited her to the meeting. She'd done more work on the lists, but all of it was done at home. One of her siblings would drop off a thumb drive at her office or her apartment and she would do the work then email it to Tom. There didn't seem to be any reason for her to sit in on a strategy meeting.

"First, I'd like to thank everyone for showing up this evening. I realize there is a key baseball game on tonight, but there are some things we have to go over before our candidate announces, and this was the best night to hold the meeting. So, I hope you're all recording the game. I am. You really can't work with Dennis without being into sports in a major way." That brought a laugh from the room. Tom opened a bottle of water and took a sip. "Tonight, we are going to hear reports on where we are and what still needs to be done. First, we are going to hear from Jacob Knight, the keeper of the campaign schedule."

An older gentleman with a receding hairline stood up at the far end of the table. He went through all the planning stages listed on the calendar and summed up where all the different parts of the campaign should be at this point in time. Stephanie sat in her chair taking notes. This was the first time she was hearing the overall campaign strategy. After Jacob sat down, each member around the table explained their part of the campaign and how far along they were compared to the schedule. Like any organization, some people were up-to-date while others were behind.

After everyone had spoken, Tom stood up again. "As most of you know, we've already had the first candidate announce a few days ago. Dennis will announce in a week, and I expect Walter Sparks to announce his re-election bid a week or so later. There may be one other person getting into the race, but we haven't been able to confirm it yet. We will continue the campaign with the idea that it will be Dennis, Sparks, and the detective."

At the word detective, Stephanie lifted her eyes from her notepad, only to discover her three siblings and Tom staring at her. Her heart beat faster, and her cheeks felt warmer. Tom smirked. "Stephanie, what can you tell us about detective Sean Landers?"

Stephanie glanced from Tom to her brothers and then her sister, who gave her an encouraging smile. "Why do you need to know about Sean?"

"For those of you who don't know, this is Stephanie Webb, Dennis' youngest sister. She has been doing all of our data mining on the county voting lists and the election reports of previous sheriff's candidates and their donors. She is a forensic scientist with the state crime lab and works with the detective."

Stephanie almost fell off of her chair. *Sean was running for sheriff? He never mentioned anything about it. Of course, why would he?* Obviously, she really didn't know him that well. She didn't take the local paper and paid no attention to the evening news. She did not know who had announced. *Wonderful.* Now she was sitting in the hot seat. "I don't know what information you're looking for on Detective Landers."

Dennis spoke up. "Sis, we want to get an idea of what type of person he is. Is he quiet? Is he a hothead? Is he well-liked in the department? I need to get a feeling for what type of person I'm running against."

"I don't know him very well, but from what I've seen, he is well liked and respected by the other officers. He's extremely detailed, and even though he's not the most senior detective on the force, the others defer to him. I know he came up here from Los Angeles and is very experienced in homicide investigations." She shifted on her chair, wishing there was a hole in the ground she could crawl into. The last thing she wanted was to be the center of attention in this room.

Tom spoke up. "Were you there during the investigation of the Mercer murder?"

"Yes, my partner and I were called in, but I can't really talk about an ongoing crime investigation." She knew what they were driving at. Cliff had told her about Angela Mercer being the mistress of the county prosecutor. She did not know who Sean and Mac had interviewed so far in the case, but she was sure Sean would not use the prosecutor's predicament for his own gain.

Tom nodded. "I know you can't comment on the case, but does detective Landers strike you as the type of person who would cover up the indiscretions of his fellow officers or elected officials?"

She didn't like the tone of this meeting at all. Sure, she wanted her brother to win the election, and she liked the idea of him being sheriff, but she did not want the detective's integrity questioned. She might not know Sean well, but she knew he was a good and honorable man. "No, I don't think he'd sweep anything under the carpet, if that's what you mean. But he is very professional and would not comment on an ongoing investigation, no matter where it led."

Tom frowned. "He sounds like an actual law and order candidate, and he is going to have insight into the department that we don't have. Dennis, we are going to have to take his candidacy seriously."

Dennis nodded and bit his lip. "We need to do more opposition research on him. Why does a detective with lots of homicide experience move from Los Angeles to this area where homicides are rare? Did he have problems in Los Angeles? Was he asked to leave? I'm sure he took a pay cut to work here. There has to be a reason."

Stephanie got a sick feeling in her stomach. She didn't know much about politics, but she had seen campaigns where the candidates tore into each other. She didn't want to be a part of that. She loved her brother, but she didn't want him to hurt Sean.

———

Stephanie sat at the table at The Dugout sports bar, waiting for the rest of her family to return with the food. This evening had been another night of freezing in bleachers while watching the twins and Susan play a softball game. They'd won tonight again, so her entire family was in a festive mood, everyone except her. She was still bothered by the fact that her brother and Sean were both running for the sheriff's position. No one outside of Dennis' campaign committee knew yet that he was going to run. He would announce on Tuesday, and then the entire world would know. She didn't know how she was supposed to react the next time she saw the detective. This was going to create a very awkward work relationship for her. She was also upset that it would destroy any chance of getting to know the detective better. Her family would expect her to be loyal to her brother, especially her father. He would consider it fraternizing or giving aid and comfort to the enemy. She was already the odd duck in the family, and this could ostracize her even more.

The meal went, as usual, with the twins and Susan reliving the highlights of the game along with commentary from her father and mother. She sat quietly at the table, nibbling at her slice of pizza. She didn't have much of an appetite this evening, but no one at the table seemed to notice. The talk around the table changed to the campaign. She got up and headed to the restroom. When she finished washing her hands, she stared into the mirror. The entire point of coming home was to get back together with her family. She hoped now that everyone was older she would be accepted for who she was and respected for her own accomplishments. Instead, it felt like nothing had changed. She was still the odd child, attached to the group, but not really part of it. Maybe it had been a mistake to come home.

She walked out of the bathroom and nearly ran into Mac. "Hey, Mac, what are you doing here?"

"I was about to ask you the same thing. Come over to our

group. There are a couple of people I'd like to introduce you to." He pointed toward the bar.

Stephanie nodded and followed him. She'd need to get back to her family soon, but it would be nice to sit at a table where people actually talked to her. She arrived to find three men and two women sitting at a high-top table near the end of the bar. One of the men was Sean. Her face felt warm.

"Look who I found," Mac said as he walked up to the table.

Sean turned around and spotted her. "Stephanie, it's good to see you again."

Her heart beat faster.

"Stephanie, I'd like to introduce you to two other sheriff's detectives and their wives. This is Dean Cope and his wife Sharon, and this is Frank Beach and his wife Paula. Everyone, this is Stephanie Webb from the forensic lab."

There were greetings all around the table. Sean grabbed an empty chair from an adjacent table and set it next to his. "Here, Stephanie, have a seat."

She smiled and carefully stepped up on the foot rail to sit in the chair. *Please, don't let me fall.*

Mac signaled the waitress, who brought another glass. He filled the glass from the pitcher of beer on the table. A few minutes later, the group was laughing at Mac doing an impersonation of little Bonaparte.

———

Susan emptied her glass of beer and looked around. Stephanie hadn't returned from the bathroom, so she was beginning to worry. Her sister had been too quiet during dinner, and now she was missing. She glanced at the rest of her family. Her father and brothers were talking about the campaign, and her mother was listening while she finished her pizza. None of them seem to notice that Stephanie was still gone. She was about to get up and go look for her sister when her father pointed toward the bar. "What is Stephanie doing over there with those people?"

The whole family turned to see Stephanie laughing with a group of people around a high-top table. Susan couldn't remember the last time she'd seen Stephanie enjoying herself like that.

Dennis clunked down his glass of beer. "Who's the guy she's sitting next to? I can't see him from this angle."

Her father frowned. "I don't know. I don't recognize him."

Susan shook her head. "Those are some people she works with."

Her father scowled. "We came here to celebrate your game. She should be here with her family, not running off to some other table."

Susan stared at her father. "Seriously, Dad, you're saying she should be here with us? We've all been ignoring her. She's been missing from our table for over half an hour. Did any of you even notice she was gone?"

"I will not tolerate disloyalty to the family. Go over there and bring her back here." Her father threw his napkin down on the table.

Susan snorted. "Disloyal to the family? You mean the family that ignores her and never gives her credit for any of her achievements? Dad, you're driving her away. She moved back here to be closer to us, but you still treat her like you did when she was in school."

Dennis leaned forward to get a better view of his youngest sister. "Who is she sitting next to?"

Susan gave him a wicked grin. "She's sitting next to Sean Landers."

WALTER

Mac slipped into a parking space at their favorite coffee shop. "I mean, it was nice to run into Stephanie last night. She evened out the table."

Sean snorted. "How could she even out the table? Your wife wasn't there."

"Yeah, I know. Both kids have colds, and Karen felt like she was coming down with something. She told me to go without her. She just wanted to have a long soak in a hot tub and read a book." Mac got out of the car.

"So, you took the opportunity to cut and run?" Sean shut his door.

"Damn straight. When Karen doesn't feel well, it's best to stay out of her way."

"Smart man, no wonder you're still happily married." Sean held the shop door open.

"I'm hungry today. I want a blueberry muffin and a strawberry Danish." Mac walked up to the counter and ordered. Loaded with enough carbs for three men and coffee, Sean and Mac headed for their car.

Sean chuckled. "Between your wife's cooking and this

place, I'm surprised you still fit behind the wheel of a vehicle."

Mac pulled the car out of the coffee shop parking lot. "So, what do we know about Leslie Turner?"

Sean took a sip of his coffee and put it in the cup holder. He was balancing a Danish on top of his file folder in his lap, trying hard not to spill either on the floor. "David and Leslie Turner have been married for a little over eight years. They don't have any children. She works as a controller for a local construction company. She's very active in a couple of local charities. From all outside appearances, they seem to be a perfect couple."

Mac snorted. "They say looks can be deceiving."

Sean grinned. "Well, we need to rule her out as a suspect. I want to hear her side of the story about their marriage and see if she really is as indifferent to her husband's affair as he implied. After all, she may not overtly react to having her husband sleeping with another woman, but she could've done something behind his back."

"What, like hiring a hitman to take out the other woman?" Mac took a bite of his Danish while maneuvering the car one-handed down the street.

"It wouldn't be the first time something like that's happened. I worked on a case in LA where the wife was having an affair with the family accountant, and the husband hired a hitman to take out the bean counter. The hitman went to the accountant's house to shoot him, only to find he was with the wife at that very moment. The guy apparently wasn't too good a shot because he missed the accountant and got the wife. Oddly enough, it was the accountant who help crack the case. When we went over the financial records, there were two cash withdrawals from the family's savings account, fifteen thousand each. That was the money the husband used to pay the hitman. The husband and hitman are both doing a twenty-five-year stretch in prison, the wife is dead, and the accountant is still running a thriving business."

Mac laughed. "Well, that didn't go according to plan. I don't think Leslie Turner had Angela Mercer killed. David had no reason to lie to us that day at the restaurant. He was genuinely upset and grateful for the bone you threw him." Mac pulled into the parking lot of Weatherly Construction.

"I don't expect to find anything, either, but I have to cross her off my list." Sean took the last bite of his Danish, opened the glove compartment and pulled out a handy wipe. He handed it to Mac and grabbed another one for himself. "No one likes to shake hands with someone with sticky fingers."

The construction company was located in an old house converted to a business office. They went through the front door and found themselves in what used to be the living room, but now served as the waiting and reception area. Leslie Turner sat behind a desk, working on a computer. She looked up when they walked in.

Mac had his shield displayed on the chest pocket of his jacket. She immediately stopped typing. "Oh, you're here already." She stood up and walked around the desk.

Leslie Turner, a tall woman with a slim build, had nicely styled blonde hair. She dressed like she should be the receptionist at an expensive law firm rather than a bookkeeper for a local construction company.

How much of her appearance was paid for by her husband's salary or by her father's money?

"This way, gentlemen, we can have a more private conversation in the conference room. She led them into a large room and closed the door. The conference room had a long table with eight chairs. A conference phone sat in the center of the table, and there was a large flat screen TV on top of a media credenza.

Sean noted the cleanliness and professional appearance of the room. He wondered about the firm's clients. Clearly, they

didn't build standard houses for a middle-class neighborhood.

Leslie pulled out a chair and sat down. Sean and Mac
joined her.

"Mrs. Turner, we are investigating the murder of Angela
Mercer. Can you tell us where you were that day?" Sean
pulled out his notepad.

"I was at work from nine o'clock until eleven-thirty. I had
a luncheon planning meeting for an event to raise money for
breast cancer research. The meeting lasted until two. I came
back to work and left at five. I met some friends for drinks
and got home around eight. I didn't kill Angela, and I'm sorry
she's dead. It completely devastated David."

Sean leaned back in this chair, and Mac raised his
eyebrows.

Leslie looked at each of them and smiled. "I know you
think it's crazy that I'm concerned about my husband's
mistress, but, gentlemen, since you've already spoken to
David, you know we were planning on getting a divorce. We
are only staying together until after his re-election."

She cleared her throat. "I met David in my junior year of
college. My roommate was from Coeur d'Alene, and I went
home with her during Easter break rather than going back to
my father. We had a great week of parties and going out on
her parents' boat. It was unusually warm that spring, so a lot
of the parties were around somebody's pool. David showed
up at one of those pool parties. He'd just gotten a job in the
prosecutor's office. He was very handsome. I guess I didn't
really see beyond that. I never finished school. We got
married, instead." She shifted in her chair.

Sean jotted down a few notes. This woman was very cool
and businesslike, even though she was talking about her own
marriage. David's affair with the cheerful and friendly hair-
dresser made a lot more sense.

"The first few years were great, but as time went on, we

discovered we wanted different things. The old county prosecutor had to resign for health reasons, and David got appointed to fill the position. We tried to make it work because of his office, but our problems continued. Then came his election, and we had to keep up appearances. He won. I still wasn't very happy, and my father wanted me to come home, but David wanted to keep trying to make it work. Things got worse, and then I had an affair. David forgave me, but I don't think he ever really trusted me again. Not too long after that, he met Angela. Oddly enough, it was at one of my charity events. It was amazing to see the two of them together. It was love at first sight. I was a little jealous, but David is a good man and deserves to be happy. We agreed to stay married until after his re-election, then I'd go back to my dad for the holidays, and we'd file for divorce in January. Once it was final, he planned to marry her. I know this sounds strange. I really like David. We are very good friends. We were just not meant to be married."

Sean closed his notebook. "Thank you for your time. We'll contact you if we have any more questions.

———

Walter Sparks flung his pen across the room. "I don't care if Human Resources says I can't fire him. I want his ass thrown out of the building, and I want it now."

Burt Toliver shook his head. "Walter, think about it. He's an experienced detective with a very impressive case resolution rate. He's well liked in the department. If you fire him, you'll have a mutiny on your hands, not to mention how it will look to the press. You are running for re-election. You can't fire your opponent just because he's challenging you."

"More's the pity, but you're right. Still, it doesn't mean I can't think about it." Walter stomped over to his desk and sat down in his executive chair.

Even after six years of working with Walter as undersheriff, the sheriff's pettiness still surprised Burt. Sparks couldn't handle anyone challenging him and his authority. The man really deserved the nickname of little Bonaparte.

"Burt, I have to do something to him. I can't let this challenge go unpunished." Walter picked up a stapler and started playing with it. "Maybe I should cut back on his cases and give him all the small ones. I don't want him showing off."

"I don't think that's a good idea. I think you should do the opposite, load him up with cases. He's going to have to campaign when he's not at work, so overload him and wear him out." Burt sat down in the guest chair.

Walter scratched his chin before grinning. "I like that idea. You have a devious mind. We can give him and his partner all the heavy cases that come in and most of the nuisance ones. Keep him running from place to place and make sure he has to work overtime."

Burt leaned back in his chair. When Walter had someone else in his sights, then Burt's job was so much easier. Little Bonaparte would spend most of his time in his office plotting and making Sean Landers' life hell, and Burt could go about actually running the department. The man owed his position to Burt, but he was too arrogant to realize it.

When the phone on Walter's desk rang, he reached over to answer it. "Sheriff Sparks here." He straightened up in his chair. "One moment, Chairman Blackwater, let me put you on speaker. I have my undersheriff, Burt Toliver, here with me."

Walter pushed a button on his phone and hung up the handset. A deep voice sounded in the room. "As I said before, Sheriff, I am requesting your assistance with the investigation of a death in the casino parking lot. We don't suspect foul play. It looks like an overdose, but we ran the plates on the car and… well, let's just say I want this case handled strictly by the book with no mistakes."

Walter leaned forward and put his elbows on the desk. "Okay, I'll bite. Who is the stiff?"

"The car came back as registered to William Curtis Spellman."

"Oh, crap." Burt leaned forward in his chair. "That's the son of Curt Spellman, the defense attorney." He shook his head. "Curt's been bailing that kid out of trouble since he was old enough to walk. Are you sure it's an overdose?"

"It looks like it. They found him dead in his car with a needle still in his arm."

Walter rubbed his hands together. "While it may look that way, I think you're going to have to be very careful. Let's handle this as a crime scene investigation until we have definitive proof it isn't. That way, if Curt Spellman gets a bee under his bonnet and wants to take the death of the son out on somebody, we will have covered all the bases and not left anything he could poke holes in. The last thing you want is that man on your ass. He's not the most expensive defense attorney in the area for nothing. Tell you what, just to make sure that this is handled properly, I'll put my number one detective team on it. Expect them at the crime scene within the hour. Make sure the site is secure, and don't touch anything. Did you get a search warrant for the car?"

"Yes, we did."

"Good. Spellman will ask about that. I'll put a call in for the forensics people to meet us out there. We'll make sure no stone is left unturned."

"Thank you, Sheriff Sparks. I appreciate your help. Good bye."

Walter hit the speaker button on his phone then looked up and grinned. "Well, it looks like Detective Landers has his first nuisance case. No matter how good and complete the investigation is, Spellman's going to pitch a fit." He chuckled.

"Are you going to call him, or are you going to his office?" Burt shifted his position in his chair, getting ready to stand.

"I need to stay as far away from him as possible so I don't say something I'll regret. You'd better tell him, and when you do, only mention the Indians want help with a body in a car at the casino. Don't tell him anything else. I want to give him an opportunity to step in it."

Burt got up and nodded to Walter as he left the room. He had a feeling that this wasn't going to end up as a win for Walter.

THE SECOND VICTIM

"Look, Mother, I will not apologize for leaving the family and having drinks with my friends. How long did it take before any of you noticed I was missing?" Stephanie sat at her desk, fuming. The dirty looks she'd received from her father and brothers when she returned to the family table still hurt and angered her. If it wasn't for Susan leading her away and talking her off the ledge, she would have turned right around and offered to work on Sean's campaign.

"Your absence really upset your father and brother, especially since you were sitting next to his opponent in the election."

This was the first time that her mother had called her in months, and this was the reason she was calling? Her brother didn't trust her anymore to work on his campaign.

"Fine, if Dennis and Dad don't want me to work on the campaign anymore, they can simply leave me alone and find someone else to stay up all night sorting and compiling their spreadsheets." She held the phone away from her ear while her mother made excuses to justify her brother's position.

"Mom, I moved back here to be closer to the family, but

I'm beginning to see that the family isn't interested in being closer to me."

"Now, honey, that's not true. We want you to be with us."

She rolled her eyes. "Yes, Mom, I show up at everyone's games and then sit through dinner listening to everyone relive the experience while I'm completely ignored. I'm finally making new friends through my work, and you're practically calling me a traitor to the family."

There were more denials and excuses from her mother, but she'd had enough. "Mom, this really isn't the time to discuss this. I have to get back to work." She heard Cliff coming down the hall. "Mom, I really have to go. Let Dennis know that if he doesn't feel comfortable with me talking to his opponent, then I will no longer be a part of his campaign." She picked up an eraser and threw it across the room. "Tell Dennis that I am insulted that he thinks so little of me. I would never do anything to jeopardize his campaign, but, apparently, he doesn't trust me. Now I have to go, Mother. Goodbye." She hung up quickly before her mother could start another round of excuses. She wanted to talk to Susan and see what her sister had to say. A tear ran down her face. As much as she loved her family and tried to be a part of it, it was clear she would never fit in.

"Stephanie." Cliff stuck his head in the door to her office. "Grab your coat. We just got a call."

She quickly rubbed her eyes. "Where is it?"

"At the casino, I'll meet you at the car." He walked on and disappeared down the hall.

———

As soon as they pulled into the far end of the parking lot, the circus became visible. They'd taped off a section in roughly the middle of the large parking lot. In the center of the area sat a white Honda Civic.

A sheriff's deputy waved their vehicle in. Stephanie looked around. "I thought the tribal police had jurisdiction here?"

"They do, but they called the sheriff's department and requested help under their mutual response agreement." Cliff pulled into a parking space and cut the engine.

"They said it was an apparent overdose, so I'm not really sure why we've been called in." He unlocked the car and opened the door.

Stephanie got out and stood next to the vehicle. "Let's find out why we're here before we suit up. I don't want to get all decked out and then have someone change their mind."

"Yeah, I agree. I'll go find out what's going on. You stay here. This may end up being a drive around the county for nothing." Cliff closed his door and walked over to a sheriff's officer.

She spotted Sean standing near a tribal police car talking to an officer and spun around. Her face felt warm. Maybe Cliff could deal with Sean, and she could talk to Mac. She'd had fun last night, but things were going to get very awkward when Dennis announced his candidacy on Tuesday. It was sure to put a damper on any conversations between her and the handsome detective.

She sighed. What was she going to say to him now? There wasn't any new information to tell him about the Mercer murder. Everything was still being processed by specialized departments in the forensic lab, and she really didn't want to talk about last night. She'd have to tell him about Dennis at some point, but not right now. Maybe after their work here was done. With any luck, he'd be too busy to talk to her until after this scene was processed.

She turned around just in time to see him look in her direction. She frowned. Her luck didn't hold. He'd spotted her. She wanted to wave and walk away, but he motioned her to come and join him. Well, at least she'd find out why they wanted a forensics team here.

Taking a quick look around to see where Cliff had gone and seeing him still talking to a sheriff's deputy, she shrugged and walked over to Sean. He seemed pleased to see her.

"Hello, Stephanie. Do you know Officer Daryl Garry with the tribal police?"

She held out her hand. "No, I've never worked with the tribal police before." She turned to the officer. "Pleased to meet you. I'm Stephanie Webb with the state crime lab."

They shook hands.

"Can either of you tell me why the lab was called out?" With the wind picking up, a leaf blew past her.

Officer Garry answered, "We found a dead body in a car."

Stephanie frowned.

Sean smiled at her. "We have what looks like an overdose." He paused.

She looked at his face. "But?"

He nodded. "Yeah, but the victim is William Spellman, son of defense attorney Curtis Spellman."

Stephanie's eyes went wide. She hadn't been back here very long, but she'd heard Dennis talk about the man. Nobody wanted to go up against him in court. He was smart, thorough, and an excellent litigator.

"I know this situation will be gone over with a fine-tooth comb. Curt Spellman will tear the reports apart, and God help anyone who screws up. That is why the tribal police called us in. They don't want to handle this hot potato." Sean nodded to Officer Garry.

Garry smiled back. "Better safe than sorry. Excuse me. I need to talk to one of my colleagues." He left them and walked across the parking lot.

Stephanie wrinkled her brow. "So why bring forensics in?"

"The sheriff called you in. Everyone is walking on eggshells on this one. I was going to cancel the call, but when

Mac and I got here, we asked for the footage from the parking lot surveillance camera. We found it was disabled about an hour before the victim died." Sean ran his fingers through his hair.

Stephanie frowned and bit her lip.

Sean nodded. "Yeah, I know. I don't believe in coincidences, either."

"What's been done so far?"

"I told everyone to treat it like a crime scene. Billy and Sid, you met them at the Mercer house, are taking photos and video of everything. The tribal police tell me they didn't touch a thing, but I can't be sure." He ran his fingers through his hair again.

"How did they find out who the victim was?"

"The tribal police ran the car's plates. As soon as the name came back, they called us in. Curt Spellman has quite a reputation." A gust of wind blew a strand of hair into his face.

"I know. My brother's an attorney. He got to watch one of his colleagues go against Spellman in court. He said it was brutal, like watching a Cuisinart in slow motion." She pulled her coat tight around herself. The wind was getting worse.

Sean rolled his eyes. "That's why I want this thing covered from every angle. I don't want to be the next guy on the chopping block."

"What do you want us to look for?" She glanced at the car that was the center of attention.

"I'm not sure. Collect everything: hair, fibers, even the trash in the car. I'm having them pull the internal casino tapes. I want to see if he spoke to anyone and especially if anyone followed him out."

While Stephanie watched, the coroner's van pulled up. Once the photos of the crime scene were completed, they would remove the body and she and Cliff could collect evidence. Two officers walked over and stood near them. Sean pointed toward her car, and she nodded. They walked towards it, and when they were well out of earshot of any other people, he continued. "I know William Spellman had a drug problem in the past. That was one of the first things we looked up when we found out who the victim was. We know Curt has had his son in rehab. It even made the papers. That Moose Droppings guy did the story."

Mac walked up and interrupted them. "I have ordered a copy of the internal surveillance. Even though you asked for a two-hour window, there's a lot of footage. This is going to take us at least a day to go through to see if there is anything relevant." He turned. "Hi Stephanie, it's nice to see you again."

She nodded at him.

He pulled out a piece of nicotine gum and started chewing. "Sean, we need to get this scene under some kind of cover. We're going to have rain in an hour. I've asked for a tent. They are bringing one up from the golf course. It should be big enough to cover everything and give us moving room. I expect we're all going to be here for a couple of hours."

Cliff came over and joined the group. "Are we having a caucus? I vote for calling it an overdose and going home." He stood there in a light windbreaker and was obviously cold.

"Sorry, Cliff, we're working it as a crime scene. You guys will need to suit up. It looks like they're finished with the cameras. Once the body is removed, Mac and I will fingerprint the doors and the interior, and then it's your turn."

Cliff frowned. "Peachy, come on, Steph, I don't want to be changing in the rain."

———

Sean walked back to the crime scene with Mac behind him. The coroner's assistants pulled a gurney with a body bag lying open on top of it from the back of the van. One man strode over to the car and stuck his head inside. He pulled it back out. "We are going to have to remove the needle from his arm. It's most likely going to fall out during transport and it could stick out through the body bag."

Sean turned to Mac. "Get an evidence collection container from Stephanie so we can safely secure the needle."

"Okay."

As soon as Mac left, Sean addressed the coroner's assistants. "I am treating this as a murder investigation and not an overdose. Please handle the body accordingly."

Both men nodded their understanding.

Mac returned with the needle safe and a small tackle box. He wore a pair of nitrile gloves. He carefully removed the needle and placed it in the safe. With the needle secure and marked as evidence, the coroner's assistants removed the body.

After they were out of earshot, Mac leaned over. "Too bad Stephanie has to get into a Tyvek suit; it obscures the view of those nice legs and great ass."

"I'm going to tell your wife."

"Hey, just because I have a car of my own doesn't mean I can't admire any of the other ones." He grinned. The wind whipped some leaves past his face. "We'd better get the tent up soon, or we are going to have a problem with contamination of the scene. You really think this was a murder and not an accidental overdose?"

Sean nodded. "Yes, I do. Billy Spellman has a history of drug and alcohol abuse, and he's been in rehab twice. Now granted, his last stint was two years ago, but he had a DUI last year. He has an addictive personality. I wouldn't be surprised if he's been smoking pot regularly since they legalized it in Washington. With his drug history, it wouldn't be that hard for him to score some heroin. I mean, he would know where to go to buy some. What doesn't make sense is the overdose? He's used before. He would know how much to shoot. Unless there is something wrong with the drug itself, cut with something poisonous or a far purer quality than he was used to, he shouldn't be dead. Also, why here? I mean, why shoot up in a casino parking lot? Did he meet his supplier here? Did he win or lose at the slot machines? We'll have to wait for the coroner's report and the toxicology test to get some answers." Sean adjusted the collar of his coat against the cold. "It's the camera that really bothers me."

"What did you sense when you saw the body?" Mac shivered.

Sean looked him in the eyes. "Revenge."

"Do you think this is step two?"

Sean nodded.

Mac frowned. He picked up the tackle box from where he'd set it down and opened the lid. Sean pulled nitrile gloves out of his coat pocket and slipped them on.

The two of them were still finger printing the car's doors, steering wheel, dash, and trunk when Cliff and Stephanie returned.

Six men crossed the parking lot and headed to the car. Two of them pulled a large rolling cart covered in white material and metal poles. Mac looked up toward the approaching men. "I'd better go deal with this and ensure the integrity of the area. Can you finish without me?"

"Sure, we're almost done, anyway. Let's get that tent up. We'll have a more private area in which to work." Sean glanced over at the crowd forming along the crime scene tape. This was way too public.

THE PARKING LOT

J eff Olsen pulled a stocking cap out of his coat pocket and put it on. The wind was picking up, and, judging by the sky, it would be raining soon. The entire crime scene didn't make sense. One of his contacts on the casino staff said some guy overdosed in the parking lot. So why was the sheriff's department here, along with the forensic lab? Obviously, this was more than an accidental overdose.

A man walked up and stood next to him. He was a bit too close. Jeff wanted to move, but this vantage point was too good to leave.

"Do you know what's going on?" the man asked.

Jeff glanced over at him. He wore aviator sunglasses and a black hoodie over most of his face. Only a wisp of sandy brown hair stuck out. He was clearly some local and not a member of a rival paper.

"It's supposed to be an overdose, but the cops are treating it like a murder scene." Jeff stuck his hands in his pockets to keep warm.

"Thanks," the man said and walked away.

Jeff frowned. *Odd*.

He went back to watching detectives Landers and McKenzie processing the door handles for fingerprints. Over by the crime trailer, the forensic team was suiting up. Why did they think this was a murder scene? He had to find out.

The opportunity came when the men with the tent showed up. He took advantage of the temporary chaos as they set up the polls and prepared to secure the area against the weather. He walked along the police tape until the tribal police and sheriff's officers were distracted then slipped under the tape. It took only a minute to cross the distance and get close enough to the car. When he was as near as he dared get, he stopped and pulled out his cell phone. He took several shots of the vehicle and made sure he got a clean shot of the license plate. He managed to get back under the police tape without being noticed. Behind him, the men were pulling the canvas over the polls. In a few minutes, the car disappeared inside a large white tent. At this point, he didn't care. He had everything he needed. He had to get back to his car and get the plate run. Maybe the name of the owner would explain something.

———

Sean was relieved when the tent was up. It kept the wind away and stopped the leaves and dirt from landing all over the car and flying into his face. The tent was a good forty feet wide and used for special parties out at the golf course. It gave them plenty of workspace. The men had put up the tent around some of the police cars, which was very nice. He smiled. They could stay dry as well as have a more secure site. He finished collecting the fingerprints. Now Stephanie and Cliff were up at bat. This would give him a little time to gather his thoughts about what he'd learned so far and what other things he needed to learn from the crime scene.

———

Stephanie frowned when she saw the inside of the car. It wasn't in the best shape. The car seats were well worn, and there were cracks in the dashboard. Billy Spellman wasn't the cleanest of car owners. There was trash on the floor, the front seat, and in the back. The car was a tour of all the fast-food places in the area and liberally sprinkled with candy wrappers.

"I'll take the front seat. You take the back," she said to Cliff.

He nodded and opened the back door.

The first thing she did was place the hype kit in a plastic evidence container. After that, she packed most of the trash in a large evidence bag, except for the two beer cans she found at the bottom of the pile. Those she placed in their own separate bags in case they needed to run tests on the remaining contents.

When Cliff emerged from the backseat, he had a similar collection of items, along with one rather ripe sweatshirt and a porn magazine. A close examination of the car seats didn't turn up anything except some hairs on the headrest of the driver's seat. They were most likely Billy's. An examination of the glove box turned up something interesting. Besides the owner's manual and the car registration, there was a small bag of pills. A search of the trunk didn't turn up anything except a spare tire, the jack, and a crowbar.

Mac collected the evidence bags and placed them in the trunk of his patrol car.

Stephanie walked up to Sean. He was leaning against one of the tribal squad cars. "We've collected everything that was in the car. Most of it was trash except for one small package of pills, which may prove to be something. Is there anything else you need from us?"

Sean took a deep breath. "I think that will do. Mac and I

will get everything logged in and send it over to you some-time tomorrow."

She nodded. "How much longer will you be here?"

"Not much longer. I want to check out the parking lot camera before the weather gets too bad. You'd better get changed before you leave the tent. It's only drizzling now, but it's promising a good downpour. I'll call you tomorrow. Thanks for all your hard work. Goodnight." She smiled at him and wished him good night before heading back over to Cliff.

———

Sean watched Stephanie and Cliff get out of their Tyvek suits. He nodded and made up his mind to ask her out to dinner. He walked over to his car and pulled out his raincoat before leaving the tent.

Sean looked up at the broken parking lot camera and stared. The rain was still little more than a drizzle. He was going to get soaked, but there was no help for it. He should have brought a hat. Another wind gust sent more leaves in his direction. He needed to get his questions answered. How does a camera break, or, more accurately, how would you break an outdoor camera if you needed to? He took a step closer to the camera pole. It wasn't possible to find out what had happened to the thing by staring up at it. Several rain drops ran down his cheek. He glanced around for one of the tribal cops. Time to get some answers and see if his gut feeling was right again.

It took a while, but they finally brought him a ladder. One of the maintenance people held it for him while he climbed up to the light. The camera lens had a small hole in it. Someone had shot it. He was sure it wasn't done with a bullet. A gun shot would have been loud and drawn unwanted attention to the person with the gun. Whoever did this used some sort of air gun. He climbed back down. He was pretty sure Billy Spellman was murdered. It wasn't a spur-of-the-moment thing. Whoever did this had planned it out carefully. He glanced back at the car. Was Billy Spellman the target, like revenge for a bad drug deal, or was he someone's way to get back at his father?

"Are you staying up there to look for sails on the horizon or because you don't have enough sense to come in from the rain?" Mac stood at the bottom of the ladder.

"Get a tribal officer over here. We need that camera carefully removed and placed into evidence. Someone shot it with a pellet or air gun. I want the camera and the projectile analyzed. I also want the video from the other cameras on this side of the building."

Mac shook his head. "Oh crap. That means you think…"

"Yup, I think this was a murder."

———

Sean made his way down the ladder, being careful not to slip. When he reached the bottom, he motioned for Mac to follow. They walked back to the tent and stepped inside. On the far side of the tent, away from the victim's car, two sheriff's officers were talking to the tribal police. Apparently, the casino had sent out a rolling cart with coffee and some cookies, and the police gathered around it.

Sean pulled a handkerchief out of his pocket and ran it over his face to get rid of some of the water. "This is definitely a crime scene."

Mac frowned. "Great, looks like we pulled the short straw again."

"No, we didn't pull the short straw. Sparks handed it to us. We need to get inside the casino and find the manager. I want to talk to the servers and other workers who were on the floor last night and see if any of them remember Spellman. If we can find out from some of the casino employees where Spellman was on the floor, we could limit our search perimeter and save ourselves a ton of time."

"Okay, let's talk to the floor supervisor and see who was working last night."

———

One of the tribal officers gave them directions to the security area. They ran out of the tent and headed for the closest door to the casino. Outside, the promised downpour had finally arrived. They both stood in the entryway and shook their coats to remove as many of the droplets as possible before entering the warm building. The artificial lights were bright, and the room was filled with the sounds of the slot machines. The casino was packed, despite the crime scene in the parking lot. Sean shook his head. Casinos were an interesting cross mixture of society. The clientele ranged from the young and the healthy all the way to the old and barely mobile. Some people came to have a few drinks and watch the flickering lights while they played the slot machines. Others came here hoping to win big while they spent their car payments and the rent money chasing after a fantasy.

Sean wove his way through the narrow aisles between the rows of slot machines. Older folks with walkers or those little mobility scooters blocked the way several times. Servers worked the room, filling drink orders and removing empty glasses. Like all casinos, there wasn't a clock in sight, and it was very easy to lose track of time here. This was the first time he'd been to an Indian casino. He'd been to plenty of casinos in Vegas with his wife years ago. The only difference between them, as far as he could tell, was the Indian casino was cleaner.

When they reached the security office, they were introduced by the head of the tribal police to John Halperin, the head of security, and Eddie Long, the floor supervisor. Unfortunately, last night was the end of the weekly shift for that group of workers. They would have to be questioned at home. The tribal police would handle the initial interviews, since it was their jurisdiction. When they found staff members who actually remembered Spellman, then he and Mac would be called back to question them further. With any luck, they could narrow down the video search areas and times.

In the meantime, they talked to Halperin and found out about the various cameras and the angles they were set at in order to observe the casino floor. By the time they headed back to their car, Sean was exhausted. He needed a good night's sleep. In the morning, he would be able to attack this case with a clear head. Unfortunately, it would still be hours before he saw his bed. The evidence needed to be logged in and his initial reports finished before he could go home.

———

Mac leaned back in his chair and stretched his arms above his head. "I have never seen so many hamburger wrappers and chicken nugget boxes that weren't in the dumpster behind a fast-food place. Did this kid ever make a home-cooked meal?"

"I doubt the guy even owned a pan. The only appliance in his kitchen that's seen any work is probably the microwave." Sean listed his current envelope on the evidence log. "I'm starving. Do you want to get some food delivered? I can't leave the building until I fill my incident report out. I don't know when Sparks is going to give Spellman the bad news, but I want to make sure my paperwork is all in order before I go home tonight, just in case."

Mac yawned and scratched his nose. "I agree. We'll get enough crap about this case no matter what we do. I'd rather not add to the load by having our paperwork in late. I wouldn't mind Thai food. What do you think?"

"That works for me. I have a menu from the restaurant on my desk." He stood up and put his envelope in the evidence cart. "Looks like we're done here. I'll turn this in. Why don't you go back to the office and order dinner? I want the same thing I ordered the last time. It should have a star next to it on the menu."

Mac added his final envelope to the cart and left the room.

By the time Sean got back to his desk, Mac had already ordered dinner and was busy typing on his computer.

As soon as Sean sat down, Mac leaned over. "Heads up, Officer Clark was just in here. He said he saw Spellman come into the building, and they escorted him to Spark's office. We may end up with a visit tonight."

"Wonderful, with our luck the food will arrive just before Spellman bursts through the door demanding to know what we're doing." Sean closed his eyes and took a deep breath. No use worrying about things he couldn't control. Spellman was going to live up to his reputation, so he would just have to roll with the punches.

Forty-five minutes later, Officer Clark came in carrying two bags from the Thai restaurant. "You're safe to eat these tonight. Spellman left the building fifteen minutes ago, and little Bonaparte left five minutes after that. The officer on duty in the lobby said he could hear Spellman's voice through the walls of Spark's office. Spellman is grief stricken, and he's also angry. I hope you guys can catch who did this quickly."

THE DAY AFTER

Ray sat on the couch in his tiny apartment, nursing a bottle of whiskey. Planning a murder wasn't a difficult thing to do. You simply went over each detail again and again until you were sure there were no holes in the plan. Executing, well, that was another matter. To knowingly snuff out a man's life took detachment and single-mindedness. Now he sat with his bottle, dealing with the aftermath and trying to get his blood circulating again.

He was justified in his actions. Declan Bishop had told him so. He smiled at the thought of his mentor, a short and muscular man who ruled his gang in the prison with an iron fist. Declan had shown him the passage in the Bible where it spoke about an eye for an eye and a tooth for a tooth. God understood revenge. Declan always said the system was rigged. It had captured Ray, chewed him over, and spat him out. Now that he was free again, he had a right to take from those who had stolen so much from him.

He leaned back in his chair. Curtis Spellman had refused to listen to a scared and innocent kid. His lack of interest in his client and his nonexistent defense had cost Ray more than just the time he spent in prison. It had cost him his future and potential. It had also cost him his mother. Incarcerated during the final years of her life, he couldn't help her or visit during the cancer treatments. Even worse, he wasn't at her side when she took her final breath. The pain of it was still an opened wound. He'd never forgive himself for not being there, and he would never forgive Curtis Spellman for being one of the reasons that he wasn't. Now Spellman had someone he cared about taken from him. It didn't make up for Ray's loss, but the ledger was closer to being balanced.

Tilting the bottle back, Ray took another gulp. The liquid burned in his throat. Johnny Walker was Declan's favorite and now a reminder of his time behind bars. A copy of the local paper lay open on the wooden box he used as a coffee table. The story of the Mercer murder finally made the news yesterday. The Moose Droppings guy wasn't much of a reporter, but he took good notes. He copied down everything word for word. Now, David Turner was publicly humiliated and his entire re-election campaign turned into a dumpster fire. If the article was true, he had lost not just a mistress but the love of his life. He knew Declan would be proud of him. His revenge against the prosecutor was complete. The man had put his political ambitions ahead of the quest for justice, and it had cost him everything. As soon as the papers reported the story about Billy, he could tick Curtis Spellman off his list as well. He set the bottle down on the end table, two down and two to go. It was time to get ready for bed. There were three corpses in the cooler at work, and they needed to be ready for their funerals this weekend. It would be a busy few days, but he welcomed the distraction.

———

Stephanie made it home just before dark. She needed to take a long soak in the bath, but she didn't have that kind of time. She was cold, and her clothes were damp. The last thing she needed was to catch something. A good shower, as hot as she could stand it, would be the best bet. Dropping her purse and coat on a chair, she headed down the hall.

Steam filled the bathroom, so she couldn't see anything in the mirror. She'd have to wait a bit before combing the tangles out of her hair. After making a cup of hot cocoa and microwaving a pot pie, she sat down on the sofa and turned on the TV. Hopefully, she could catch one of the news shows and see what they were reporting about the crime scene before going to bed. She'd missed the early news. Now she'd have to wait until 10 o'clock for the next report.

She surfed through the channels and found a romance movie. This brought it all back. What was she going to do about Sean? She really liked him, and the more time she spent with him, the deeper her feelings grew. Even more surprising, he seemed to like her, too. What was he going to do when he found out Dennis was running for sheriff against him? It wasn't going to be easy, and she did not know how to phrase it, but she had to tell him soon. If she waited too long and he heard it from someone else first, he would feel betrayed. She didn't want to lose him before they'd actually began. Maybe she should call him tomorrow and ask him out for lunch. Making her confession in a neutral and public place may help the situation. She shook her head. There really wasn't a good way to explain this.

The movie played on, but she really wasn't paying attention. She was at a fork in the road, and she knew it. By leaving her brother's campaign and telling Sean about Dennis running, she was choosing sides between her family and Sean. Susan would understand, Dennis and Douglas would probably forgive her eventually, but her father, well, he never would. She'd no longer be welcome in her parents' home. Could Sean be worth it? She wrapped her arms around herself and stared at her slippers. There was no way of predicting the future. Once she crossed this bridge, there would be no going back.

She glanced up at the television. The heroine was making a choice between staying with the hero or taking her dream job in another city.

She grabbed a tissue and blew her nose. She would have to move out-of-state if things didn't work out with Sean. It would be too difficult seeing him at all the different crime scenes and being isolated from her parents.

———

Sean arrived at the forensic lab around ten thirty in the morning. He was carrying a large box full of evidence envelopes from the casino crime scene and had a bit of trouble getting in the door. Evelyn, one of the evidence technicians at the front desk, came out and held it open for him.

"Thank you. The last thing I wanted to do was drop this." He set the box down on the counter.

"Good morning, Detective. Where is the evidence officer this morning?" She sat down at the computer and printed out the evidence list already entered in the system by the evidence officer.

"I thought I'd better bring this one in myself. It's a sensitive case, so I want to make sure everything goes by the book." He ran his fingers through his hair.

Evelyn grinned. "We know. Cliff told us about the connection to Curtis Spellman. Everyone is walking on eggshells around this one."

"Yes, they are. The sheriff informed Mr. Spellman last night. I'm not sure what happened, but I heard Spark's looked a rather pale afterwards."

Evelyn chuckled and started going down the list, making sure each item was present, labeled with the case number, the crime scene location, the officer's name, and the description of the item. She made sure the envelopes were properly sealed and signed by Sean before signing the chain of custody line. She attached a label with the laboratory's case number and bar code. When she finished, she loaded the envelopes onto a rolling cart and took everything to the evidence safe. It was absolutely crucial that there were no breaks in the chain of custody.

This process took a while and gave Sean a chance to think about what to say to Stephanie. The last woman he had asked out to dinner was his late wife, Peggy. He snorted. That was twelve years ago. He was definitely out of practice.

When Evelyn returned, Sean cleared his throat and got to the main reason he wanted to bring the evidence over personally. "Is Stephanie available?"

"Let me check." She tapped a button on her desk phone. "Stephanie, are you able to speak to Detective Landers right now?"

He waited while Evelyn listened to the answer.

"Do you want her to come up here, or do you want to speak to her in her office?"

"I'd rather speak to her in her office." He started feeling butterflies in his stomach.

"Follow me." Evelyn led the way down the hall and around the corner. Stephanie was sitting at her desk, working on her computer. She looked up when they entered.He smiled at her and turned to Evelyn. "Thank you."

Evelyn nodded and left the room.

"Good morning, Sean. You get any sleep last night?" Stephanie leaned back in her chair and returned his smile.

"Not much, I'm afraid. It took a while to catalog all the evidence. I just dropped it off. I'm not sure what's going to happen with the case, but everyone is expecting trouble with Spellman."

"That's what we're hearing, too."

"I think we have a little breathing room. He was quite

upset when Sparks informed him. I imagine when the shock of it fades a bit, he'll start looking for someone, anyone, to blame. All indications were that his son was a screwup and a loser, but Billy was still his son, and he loved him." Sean sat down in the guest chair.

"That is the hard truth about our business. The victim is always the son or daughter of someone." She shifted her position. "Why did you drop the evidence off yourself? Are you making sure there is no question about the chain of custody?"

He smiled. "That's part of it." He glanced down at the floor before looking back up at her face. "I wanted to ask you out to dinner tomorrow night, and I thought it would be better to do it in person rather than over the phone."

She hesitated for a minute and nodded. "I'd love to go."

He grinned. "Perfect. I'll pick you up at seven o'clock. We are going someplace nice." He pulled out his business card and grabbed a pen from the container on her desk. He wrote on the back and handed it to her. "Here is my cell number. Text me your address, and I'll see you tomorrow."

She pushed her chair back, but he held up his hand. "Don't get up. I'll see myself out. I'm looking forward to dinner."

———

Ray pulled the steam mop out of the broom closet before checking the floor. The boss liked everything clean in the preparation room. They'd processed the last body this afternoon, a teenager who died in a car accident. Ray reached into his pocket and pulled out his earbuds. He tapped his phone to bring up his cleaning playlist. The opening tones of Danse Macabre sounded in his ears. He flipped the switch and turned on the steam mop. It was always his job to clean up the room and make sure the floors and all the surface areas were shining when they finished the day's work. When the room was clean, he could clock out and go home.

He slipped his time card back in the rack and picked up his lunch pail. A frozen TV dinner didn't sound very appetizing for tonight's meal. Picking up some barbequed chicken on the way home wouldn't break the bank. His mouth watered at the thought. He deserved a good meal, especially after the other day. Chicken with mashed potatoes and gravy along with an ear of corn weren't gourmet food, but compared to some meals he ate in prison, they were a feast fit for a king. He might splurge even more and add a slice of apple pie for dessert. Maybe there was something good to watch on television tonight.

A quick glance at the calendar showed he needed to be in tomorrow at 9:00. Good, this would allow him to sleep in tomorrow. He usually had to be at work by 7:00. He checked his pants pocket. Yes, the hair and blood samples he'd collected today were still there and sealed in their containers. When he got home, he'd add them to the others in his freezer. He'd start researching the history of the people they had belonged to tomorrow. Tonight was a night to relax and forget about everything for a while. He smiled and nodded before heading to the door.

THE DATE

S ean checked his image in the hallway mirror. He wore a blue sports jacket, navy slacks and a white shirt, with a navy tie. He frowned. *I'm not wearing my good suit, but I still look like I'm about to testify in court.* This wasn't going right. It had been a long time since he'd taken a woman out on a date, so he was as nervous as a teenager. He loosened the knot on his tie and pulled it over his head, then undid the top button of his shirt. He still looked too formal. After loosening the second button, he closed his eyes. *Sean, you're a grown man and you've already broken bread with her twice. There is no need to panic. It's going to be a pleasant evening. Now leave before you're late.* He opened his eyes and turned without looking at his reflection, grabbed the keys out of the bowl on the hall table, and left the house.

———

Half of Stephanie's closet lay spread out on her bed. The yellow dress made her look like she was pregnant. Her little black dress was too short. For a date night, the green dress was too frumpy. The three skirts and blouses she tried on made her look like an accountant or librarian from an old black-and-white movie. The two pants suit she had were too harsh and professional. That's why she wore them to court when she had to testify. She looked at the state of her bedroom and frowned. At this rate, she'd still be in her underwear when he knocked on the door.

She finally settled on a simple blue dress with puff sleeves, belted waist, and a skirt that ended just below her knees. It took her a few minutes to dig through the back of her closet and locate the matching shoes. A little touch up to her makeup and a darker shade of lipstick, and she was ready. Well, at least she was dressed.

She closed her eyes. "Please, God, don't let me embarrass myself tonight by tripping over my own two feet or spilling my dinner on my dress. Let us have a pleasant evening together before I break the news about Dennis. I don't know how he's going to react, but I want to have at least some pleasant memories of this date before he walks away."

A knock at the door interrupted her prayer. The butterflies in her stomach were practicing acrobatics as she walked down the hall and opened the door. Sean stood on her door-mat. His smile made the butterflies calm down.

"You look beautiful, Stephanie."

———

The drive to the restaurant was awkward. Soft rock played on the radio while they drove. Sean had opened the car door for her. None of her previous dates had ever done that. He was handsome and smart, a real gentleman, the perfect date. She closed her eyes. In an hour or so, she'd have to tell him about Dennis. He'd probably leave her at the restaurant. She'd only have the happy memories of this date to haunt her and make her wonder what might've been.

Sean drove up to the front entrance of the resort and let

the valet park his car. The restaurant was on the top floor with a fantastic view of the lake. The hostess seated them at a table with a view that included the boardwalk around the marina, currently lit with thousands of white lights. A small crystal bud vase containing a pink rose, asparagus fern, and baby's breath sat in the center of the table.

A waiter offered them menus while a second man brought them glasses with ice. He filled them with water, then left. The waiter talked about the chef's specials for the evening. They both decided on the surf and turf with baked brie for an appetizer.

"I hope you like this place," Sean said as he pointed out the window. "I came here once, about a year ago, for a retirement dinner. The food was excellent, and I really liked the view. It's the perfect place for a proper first date." He smiled at her.

"I've never been here before. My brothers have many times. Dennis' law firm holds their quarterly meetings here. I know Douglas likes to bring his high-end clients here for lunch. You're right about the view. It's beautiful." She was getting nervous. The small talk was getting smaller. She needed to find a topic that he'd be interested in, something besides police work, that is. The appearance of the wine steward pushing a cart interrupted her thoughts.

"Good evening. I understand you're both having the surf and turf. I have some wine suggestions."

Sean smiled at her. "Do you have a preference?"

"I'm afraid I don't know much about wines." She looked down at the table.

Sean laughed. "I'm no connoisseur, either. I just know what I like." He turned to the wine steward. "What do you suggest?"

"I suggest a good Pinot Noir. The flavor will complement the steak but not overpower the lobster. I have a sample for you to taste." The man poured a small amount into two glasses and placed them on the table.

Stephanie sipped hers. The taste was pleasant. Sean drank his and smiled.

When he looked at her, she nodded. He addressed the steward. "We'll take a bottle of it."

The steward grabbed a fresh bottle from his cart and opened it before pouring each of them a full glass and setting the bottle on the table. "Thank you, sir. Enjoy your dinner."

After a few moments of silence, Stephanie had to speak. "I hear you were a homicide detective in Los Angeles. How did you end up here in northern Idaho?"

Sean took a sip of wine before he answered. "Los Angeles has a lot more crime than this area. I got tired of all the violence."

A server arrived with their brie, interrupting their conversation.

Stephanie frowned and quickly grabbed her own wine-glass. His statement didn't really fit with his personality. Was he distracted because of a problem at work? Maybe there was something going on with the election.

When the server left, Sean shifted in his chair. "That's not the actual answer."

Stephanie's stomach clenched. Something unpleasant was coming.

Sean picked up his fork and ran it over his napkin before putting his hand on the table. "I liked my job in LA. It was hard work, and there were a lot of horrible things I saw, but I enjoyed looking for clues and putting all the puzzle pieces together to catch the guilty party. I was married then." He looked up at her face.

She kept her expression neutral.

"Peggy was my rock and my refuge. She taught third grade in a private school. She loved children, and they loved her." He closed his eyes. His expression changed.

She knew he was seeing his wife again in memory.

"We always wanted kids, but we were never blessed. She went to a specialist to find out what was wrong. They discovered cancer, ovarian cancer. She fought hard to conquer it, but, in the end, it claimed her. When she died, she took a large part of me with her. The best part, actually." He sat quietly for a moment, staring down at the table. "I couldn't stay in LA anymore. Everywhere I turned, there was something that reminded me of her: a restaurant, a store, a community event. The only hiding place I had was work, and it started to bury me." He stopped and looked down at the table. "I'm sorry. This isn't the tone I want to set for our first date."

Stephanie reached across the table and touched his hand. "Never apologize for saying what you feel. My family does nothing but hide their feelings. I want to be with someone who is honest about what he thinks and feels. Please, tell me more."

He looked at her face and saw the compassion in her eyes. More of the wall around his heart crumbled away. He smiled at her and nodded.

"Peggy was my sanctuary. No matter what horror or brutality I saw, when I went home to her, I left it outside the door. I would not allow the dark side of life to pollute our home. She enabled me to get away from everything and not be weighed down by it. After she was gone, I had nowhere to find peace. I couldn't live there anymore. I put the house up for sale and applied to law enforcement agencies in other states. I got offers but settled on this area. It was the right choice. I've been able to heal here and learn to live without Peggy."

Stephanie squeezed his hand. "I'm so sorry, Sean." The tears welled up in her eyes.

They sat quietly, holding one another's hands while the baked brie grew cold.

He looked up. "I've never told anyone that story before.

Mac knows I lost my wife to cancer, but I never really told him the reason I moved here."

She stroked his hand.

A server interrupted their silence, bringing them a basket of bread and a bowl of butter balls.

She had to tell him. Before the dinner went any further, she had to tell him. "Sean, I have something to say and I'm not sure how you will react." She let go of his hands.

He frowned. "Okay, that sounds ominous."

"It's not about you, at least not directly. It's about me." She cleared her throat. "I know you are running for sheriff. I heard about your announcement." She lowered her eyes and stared at her wineglass. "My brother Dennis is going to run for that position as well. He's announcing on Tuesday." She looked at his face. "I helped him on his campaign with his mailing lists and data mining, but I'm not working for him anymore. The night that I met all of you at the sports bar, I was with my family. They'd been ignoring me all night, as usual. So, when I ran into Mac, I was happy to go join your group for a while. My family wanted to know who I was sitting with. Susan told them. My father was furious. I told my family they would not manipulate me, so I resigned from Dennis' campaign." Her voice quivered. "I wanted you to know that I'm not spying on you for him. I'm going to remain neutral in all of this from here on out. If you don't want to see me or talk to me anymore, I will understand." Her eyes dropped back down to her wineglass. "I hope that doesn't happen." She picked up her napkin and squeezed it in her hand. "I really like you. I'd like to get to know you better. I... I... ah." A tear trickled down her cheek. She dabbed at it.

He reached across the table and took her hand. "Stephanie, please, don't cry. I'm not mad or upset. I knew there was a lawyer who might be running. Plus, they call it a race for a reason. There are others who want the position, and I expected to have to work for it. The current sheriff is plan-

ning on re-running, as well. He just hasn't announced it yet."
He leaned forward. "Listen, I don't want to come between
you and your family, but I want to see you again." He smiled
at her.

At that moment, their waiter arrived with their dinner. It
took a few minutes to get things sorted and for them to enjoy
the first bites.

Stephanie broke the silence. "I want to see you again, too."
She looked down at her plate. "You aren't really getting
between me and my family. I've been the unwanted child in
the family all my life. My father is obsessed with sports. He's
not a gambler or anything, he just loves watching games. My
brothers and my sister are all talented athletes. My dad is so
proud of them and brags about them to everyone. I'm not
sure he has ever told anyone I exist unless he has to. My
siblings have always stood up for me, but my mother always
defers to my father. I've recently realized that this will never
change. I have to learn to live with it. I love my family, especially my brothers and sister, but I'm never going to have a
good relationship with my father. I'm done trying to win his
love and attention. I need to be myself and make my own
decisions. If he doesn't approve, well, then so be it."

Sean reached across the table and took her hand. "I think
you're amazing."

She blushed, looked up, and smiled at him. "Thank you."
*I think this man is the first person who actually sees me and listens
to me.*

They went back to eating their dinner.

After a few minutes, Stephanie spoke again. "Isn't it going
to be hard to do all the campaigning that's necessary to win
when you have two major murder cases going on? Especially
the second one with its added pressure?" She looked around
to make sure no one at the tables nearest to them was listening. "I mean, with the victim's father scrutinizing everything
that is being done. We are making doubly sure that every-

thing done in the lab is by the book and all the paperwork is in order."

Sean chuckled. "You sound like Mac. He asks me that at least twice a day. I don't know whether he's worried I'll lose or afraid I'll win."

The evening lightened up considerably after that. The food tasted better, and the conversation flowed more naturally. They soon discussed the murder at the Indian Casino again.

"It's way too early to tell if this is a case of someone wanting to get even with Billy for some drug deal, or perhaps he owed someone a lot of money. It's also possible that someone wanted to get even with his father for something and Billy was the way of exacting their revenge. I need to see the casino surveillance footage and interview the casino staff. It will take eight to ten weeks to get the tox report back. Right now, all we have is a murder victim in the morgue and no idea why he's there." Sean picked up his glass and took another sip of wine. "This steak is delicious. How is yours?"

She smiled. "It's excellent. I really like this wine, too. The wine steward made the perfect selection."

A short time later, their waiter showed up again, asking if they would like to see the dessert menu. Sean glanced at Stephanie, but she shook her head. He nodded before turning to the waiter. "No, thank you. We're both full from the meal. I would like the bill now."

"Very good, sir." The waiter left them to finish their meals.

––––––

Sean opened the door and offered her his hand to help her out of the car. She accepted with a smile. He held her hand as they walked to her door. She glanced at the neighboring apartments to make sure no one had their curtains open.

When they stopped in front of the door, they turned to face each other.

"I really enjoyed our dinner and getting to know you better. I hope we can do this again soon." He reached up and brushed a strand of hair from her face.

She smiled. Butterflies were doing somersaults in her stomach. "I enjoyed dinner, too. And, yes, I'd like to see you again."

"We can try to meet someplace after work next week." He smiled at her. "I should say goodnight. I have court in the morning." He ran his hand along her cheek. "Would it be too forward of me to give you a goodnight kiss on our first date?"

She nodded, not wanting to speak, fearing that her voice would tremble.

He lifted his other hand and cupped her face. He slowly leaned in and brushed her lips with his. A shiver ran down her spine. She reached up and slipped her arms around his neck. They kissed again. *Oh, I am definitely going out with this man again.*

OBSERVATIONS

Ray stood in front of the grave, staring at the headstone and the flowers he had just laid in front of it. The lettering on the headstone blurred as the tears welled up in his eyes and slowly trickled down his face. This was the last resting place for his mother.

It had been just the two of them since he was five years old. His father, the drunken brute, was in a car accident. This time, his blood alcohol level was nearly double the legal limit. He sideswiped two cars before losing control of his own vehicle and crashing into a house. A twelve-year-old boy who lived there ended up with a broken leg plus scrapes and bruises when a wall collapsed. His mother divorced his father shortly after he went to prison. There was peace in their household after that, and he never saw his father again.

The wind picked up and blew a lock of hair into his face. "I'm sorry I wasn't there when you needed me, Mom." He rubbed a hand over his cheeks. He couldn't speak for a while as the grief washed over him.

When he finally dried his eyes, he stared at her marker again. They chiseled the date of her birth in the hard stone along with the date of her death. It was the second date that held his attention. The grief gave way to anger. Anger against fate. Anger against the system. Anger against the people who betrayed him, and anger at his own ignorance and inability to stop what happened to him. He stared at the date, August 5th. The anniversary was coming up. It would be the perfect day. Jimmy Morgan started all of this misery. It would be perfect justice for him to pay for his crime on that significant date.

He cleared his throat. "I'll be back here as soon as I can. I miss you, Mom, and I love you." He bent down, kissed two of his fingers, and placed them up against the cold stone. He stayed in that position for a short time before getting up and returning to his car.

———

Sean arrived at his desk irritated. His alarm didn't go off, or, actually, to be more accurate, he forgot to set it. The sound of the garbage truck woke him up at 7:45. He called Mac, only to get his voicemail. After leaving a message that he'd be half an hour late to the office, he hurried to get a quick shower.

The sheriff's station was busy, as usual. Little Bonaparte had an early budget meeting with the county commissioners, which is a splendid thing. At least the sheriff couldn't pester him for the rest of the morning.

His stomach growled. There wasn't time to pick up breakfast on the way in. Hopefully, he and Mac could make an excuse to leave the office and pick up something. His hopes were squished as soon as he got to his desk. An envelope containing a thumb drive copy of the casino security footage sat on his computer keyboard. *Wonderful, hours of footage showing people gambling and drinking, not something I want to handle on an empty stomach.* He seriously considered ordering a food delivery when Mac walked through the door carrying a cupholder with two large coffees and a bag that gave off the mouthwatering smell of bacon.

"Hey, you got here earlier than I thought you would." Mac set his burden down on Sean's desk. "I got a heads-up last night that the thumb drive was coming. When you called and left your message, I knew you'd be hungry when you got here." He reached down and pulled a coffee out of the holder and set it on the desk.

"Thanks, Mac." Sean grabbed the coffee while Mac opened the bag and placed two breakfast sandwiches and a couple of Danishes on the table.

"Did the casino security give you any idea about what was on the drive?" Sean picked up his sandwich.

"No. I'm sure they watched the footage, but they want us to draw our own conclusions." Mac took the other sandwich.

Sean snorted. "Draw our own conclusions or keep their hands clean if Curtis Spellman raises a stink?" He unwrapped the sandwich and took a bite.

"Yeah, there's a lot of cover your backside going on with this case." He claimed the other Danish.

Mac walked over to his desk and grabbed his chair. "This videotape is going to take hours, so we should get started." He rolled his chair over to Sean's desk.

Sean turned his computer on, and they organized their food while it booted up. When they were ready, Sean put in the drive and brought up the video program. He took notes as he watched it play. It took quite a while before they found the footage where Billy Spellman entered the casino and sat down at a machine. They watched him play and drink for two hours before a man bumped his hand and spilled his drink.

Sean sat up straight in his chair. "Back up the video and play that part again. Slow down the playing speed." He picked up his notepad and pen. Mac slid the keyboard over and tapped on the keys. The video rewound and showed a man walk toward Billy. The man had to step aside to avoid being run over by a heavyset woman with a walker.

"Stop the video." Sean leaned forward and stared at the scene. "Did that look planned to you?"

"You mean you think the guy waited until he saw someone who would force him to bump into Billy?"

"Yes. I think he did. Do we have another camera angle for this scene?" Sean wrote in his notepad.

"I'm not sure. I'll mark the timestamp of this footage and we can see if it matches up the something further along on the drive." Mac got up and went to his desk to grab his own pen and notebook.

They backed up the tape and continued watching it at a slower speed.

"Notice how we never see the man's face. It's like he knows where the cameras are pointing. His jacket is loose fitting and the colors are rather bland, a light brown windbreaker and jeans. Nothing that would stand out. I think we are looking at our killer." Sean made more notes. "The baseball cap obscures most of his hair, so we can't really see how it's cut or if it's the same color all the way around."

They watched more of the scene. The man bumped Billy's hand, and the drink spilled.

"Billy can see the man's face, but he isn't reacting like its someone he knows." Sean pointed at the screen with his pen. "The man signals the waitress. Note the time stamp."

Mac wrote in his notebook.

"We are going to need to interview the waitress and see if she can give us more details about the man." He wrote more notes in his book before starting up the tape again.

"Okay, so the guy talks to the waitress. She leaves and returns a few minutes later with a fresh drink and a towel. He pays her while Billy is drying himself. He hands Billy the drink and leaves."

Mac shook his head. "Sean, this doesn't look that suspicious to me. It just looks like an accident."

"It feels wrong to me. Let's watch the scene again from the moment where he bumps Billy's hand until he leaves. I know it's going to take more time, but I want to look at this frame by frame." Sean picked up his coffee.

They watched it again until the point where the waitress handed the man the drink. They watched him turn his back to the waitress and hold his hand over the glass while Billy was still mopping things up with the towel.

Sean sat bolt upright. "There. Look at his hand. He could have put something into the drink."

Mac shook his head. "I don't know. It's possible, but the video isn't conclusive."

Sean stared at the screen. "The toxicology report is probably going to show us that Billy was roofied."

"It's still a stretch between Billy getting roofied and somebody murdering him in the parking lot with an overdose." Mac set down his notepad and picked up his sandwich.

"We need to find out if the guy put something into Billy's drink. The tox report will tell us if there was something that made Billy more pliable or would knock him out completely in a short time." Sean set down his coffee. "Make note of the timestamp and take a screenshot of this. I'm going to want several screenshots of our mystery man, too. We'll need those when we talk to the casino staff to help jog their memories. Let's keep working until lunch. After that, I'm going to need to stretch my legs and clear my head. Be thinking about what you want for lunch. It'll be my treat."

———

Ray sat in his car, chewing on a homemade ham sandwich while studying Jimmy Morgan and his useless life. It took a while to research what had happened to Jimmy during Ray's imprisonment. He finally found out where Jimmy lived and how he supported himself. He wasn't surprised to discover that Jimmy was only slightly less useless than Billy Spellman. *It's amazing the amount of information you can find out about a person if you know where to look.* Learning where to look was one of the many things he had studied while still in prison.

————

Declan Bishop had pulled him aside one day and asked him what crime had gotten him locked up. After he told the story, Declan had sent him away. They didn't speak for several weeks. One afternoon, when he was lying on his bunk reading a spy novel, Declan entered his space and started talking.

"I've been thinking about your situation." He started pacing the length of Ray's bunk. "You don't belong here. All the other men in my group committed the crimes that landed them in prison. Many of them committed far more crimes, but they were never charged with them. But you, you're here because someone wanted something that you had. One of the Ten Commandments is 'Thou shalt not covet'. Your so-called friend coveted and was willing to destroy your life to get what was yours."

Declan stopped pacing and looked him in the eyes. "The Bible also teaches something else: revenge, an eye for an eye and a tooth for a tooth. You need to think about what you are going to do when you're released. My other men will go back to doing what they did before and hopefully be better at their particular specialty and not get caught again. You are a convicted felon even though you didn't commit the crime. That will stick with you forever. Your friend never paid the price for what he did to you. He needs to and so do all the people in the system that let it happen. I want you to think about your situation and what you plan to do about it. We'll talk again in a few weeks." Declan left him, and he spent the rest of the day staring at the ceiling, thinking.

————

Ray picked up his soda from the cup holder. Jimmy was mowing the grass around the landscape berm of a shopping center parking lot. The mower was one of those professional models that the operator stood on and guided over the grass. The company Jimmy worked for had landscaping contracts for quite a few professional buildings and shopping centers in town. They also worked on the landscaping of some private homes, but only the ones in high end neighborhoods. Jimmy worked the heavier equipment like this mower, loaders, or excavators. The company's website said they did snow removal, as well. Most likely, Jimmy operated one of their plows in the winter months.

Ray put his soda back in the cup holder and picked up his binoculars. Jimmy was wearing a sleeveless T-shirt with the company's logo on it and a pair of tan cargo shorts. His skin was tanned and reflected how much time he spent out in the sun. Ray snorted. When they were younger, Jimmy wanted to be a plumber and start his own business. Neither one of them got what they wanted.

Ray checked his watch. Jimmy had another hour of work left. Soon he'd be loading up his truck and driving back to the company's headquarters, a large steel building that held the company's equipment, supplies, and a small office. It was on the corner of two rural back roads, a hayfield and trees on the remaining two sides. Jimmy's usual evening regiment was to drop off the company truck and drive his old beat-up Ford to one of the local bars where he would have a few rounds with a couple of his friends. After that, he would swing through a fast-food restaurant before heading home, where he would eat his food and finish a sixpack of beer before going to bed.

Ray shook his head. Jimmy really wasn't much better than Billy Spellman. It was a sad observation, really. Both men had so much potential when they were young, but had squandered everything with bad choices. There's an old saying about how the things you do in your youth will haunt you in your old age. That was true for both of them. Their bad choices led to the same conclusion. Death in their 30s.

MORE INFORMATION

S usan peeked around the corner of the event planner's truck to check on the size of the crowd. There were at least forty people gathered in front of the dais. The entire event was being held at the far end of the fairgrounds parking lot next to the sheriff's office and the jail. Location didn't make an awful lot a sense, but at least the weather was nice and there was plenty of parking.

Tom Oliver wandered out front talking to people in the crowd. Susan recognized Jeff Olsen, the *Moose Droppings* reporter. Channel 6 News drove up in their van, and behind them, more cars were arriving. She ducked behind the truck and nearly knocked her mother over.

"Stephanie better hurry and get here. It does not look good for her to be late to her brother's announcement." Mrs. Webb furrowed her brow.

"Mom, I already told you. Stephanie is not coming."

Her dad came over and asked the same question. "Where is your sister?"

Susan threw up her hands. "How many times do I have to tell you? Stephanie is not coming."

Mr. Webb scowled. "Dennis is announcing his campaign, and his entire family should be here."

"Well, she probably would've been if you hadn't called her a traitor to the family for talking to the detective at the sports bar." Susan shook her head.

"Her loyalty needs to be to this family. She said she moved back here to be closer to all of us. This is her opportunity to be closer and support us." Mr. Webb put his hands on his hips.

"Dad, being closer to the family and supporting each other is a two-way street. You expect her to be here for all of us, and yet you continue to ignore her and refused to support what she's doing." Susan sighed. "Honestly, she's your child just as much as the rest of us are, and yet you treat her like she's some kind of burden. I hope things work out with her and the detective because if they don't, she's probably going to move away again, this time for good."

Their conversation was interrupted when Tom Oliver strode around the corner. "Okay, I think it's time for Mr. and Mrs. Webb to go out and join the crowd. Dennis and I will step out as soon as we settle your parents out front."

Mrs. Webb nodded. Mr. Webb spoke. "Tom, can you explain why we're holding this announcement at the end of the fairgrounds parking lot instead of on the courthouse steps or in front of the sheriff's office?"

Tom laughed. "We didn't want to hold it on the courthouse steps because that's where the detective made his announcement. When we asked the sheriff's department if we could hold the announcement in the parking lot, apparently sheriff Sparks had a fit about it. He threatened to have us all arrested if we did anything on the property. So, we hit on the idea of holding it here. We were going to have to rent the sound system anyway, so we rented the platform with a podium to go with it. From the television camera angle, you'll be able to see Dennis with the sheriff's building in the background. It was the only way we could do an end run around the sheriff."

"Where did all these people come from?" Mrs. Webb grabbed her husband's arm.

"They are a mixture of supporters, prominent community people, and friends of our law firm. We wanted to make sure Dennis had a good crowd for his announcement." He took a step back. "Now we really need to get you out front in the crowd. As soon as the TV crew is set up, I'll bring Dennis out, and we'll start the program."

"Thank you, Tom. Come on, Susan, let's go out front." Mr. Webb reached for his daughter's arm.

"No. I need Susan and Douglas to stay back here. Normally, we would bring out the candidate's wife and children after he made the announcement, but since Dennis isn't married, we thought we would have his brother and sister stand beside him. Anyway, we need to get going. The TV crew is probably finished setting up." He stretched out his arm to point them in the direction he wanted them to go. They walked away, holding hands.

Dennis and Douglas left their spot near the back of the truck and stood beside Tom. "There's a good crowd out front, and we have the press. You practiced your speech all week. The weather is cooperative. This will be a good launch. Are you ready, Dennis?"

Dennis took a deep breath. "Okay, let's do this."

———

Mac parked the car in an empty slot toward the back of the casino parking lot. They were actually only a few feet away from the camera someone had disabled the night of Billy Spellman's murder. The parking lot was full of cars.

Sean looked around. "It's a Wednesday afternoon, and all

these people are drinking and gambling? Doesn't anybody go to work anymore?"

Mac chuckled. "You watched the videotapes. Most of these places are filled with retirees."

Sean snorted. "When I retire, I plan to do something more useful than staring at a slot machine."

Mac laughed. "Yes, I can see you now, sitting outside in the garden, trying to determine which insect is eating your tomatoes. Or maybe planning a garden offensive to stop the deer from breaching the fence."

Sean chuckled. "Well, it still beats wasting hours gambling away my savings." He got out of the car. "I hope we don't have any problem with the casino security or the tribal police. I want to question each of the women separately and with only us in the room."

Mac locked the car. "I'm pretty sure the others have questioned both ladies thoroughly already."

"That's what I'm afraid of. We need to get an accurate account of what each woman saw and didn't see. I hope the others didn't try to influence the women's memories." Sean pulled out his badge and placed it in his jacket pocket.

"When we're finished with our questioning, do you want to have lunch here?" Mac also pulled out his badge.

"No. I don't want to get dragged into a conversation about the case. I want to form my own conclusions." Sean grabbed the door. "We can get lunch at a different place. My treat."

The casino was as packed as the parking lot. They wove their way through the slot machines and people until they reached the security office. John Halperin, the head of security, greeted them.

"We set aside an office for you to conduct your interviews. The two ladies are waiting in a room near the receptionist area. We'll bring them in one at a time. I'll be walking the floor while you're doing your questioning. When you're finished, just text me. I'll come back here to escort the first one out and bring the second one in. Do you need anything like water or coffee?"

"No, thank you." Sean pulled out his notebook and a pen.

"Which of the ladies would you like to see first?"

"Please bring in the one who served Mr. Spellman his first three drinks." Sean opened his notebook.

"Are you sure? She really didn't see anything." Halperin looked confused.

"Yes, I'm sure."

When Halperin left the room, Mac turned to Sean. "Why do you want to see that one first?"

"Because she saw Billy before the incident. I want to know what his mood was like. Was he annoyed? Was he nervous, like he was expecting someone? Was he angry?" Sean sat down behind a desk. "Move that guest chair around to the side of the desk and sit there. I don't want her to have to stare at both of us across the desk. I want her to be as relaxed as possible in this situation."

Mac did as Sean suggested. "I told you they thoroughly questioned the ladies already. You caught his comment that she didn't see anything."

"Yes. That's another reason I want to question her first." He flipped through the pages of his notebook. "I grabbed the wrong notebook. This one is blank. What was the lady's name again?"

Mac flipped through his notebook. "Her name is Jeannie Kirk. She's worked at the casino for three years. She's married and has two kids."

Sean nodded. "Thank you."

A few minutes later, Halperin came in, followed by Jeannie Kirk. She was a small

woman with a pleasant face and short brown hair. She wore a green blouse, a black sweater, black slacks and tennis shoes. Halperin nodded at Sean. "Text me if you need anything." He left the room, closing the door behind him.

Sean motioned towards the guest chair. "Have a seat, Mrs. Kirk. My name is Detective Sean Landers, and this is my partner, Detective Joseph Mackenzie. We are with the County Sheriff's Department. The tribal police have asked us to assist them with the investigation of the death of William Spellman." He pulled a picture out of his pocket. It was an enlargement of Billy Spellman's driver's license photo. "Mrs. Kirk, do you recognize this man?"

Jeannie reached into the pocket of her sweater and pulled out a pair of glasses. She looked at the photo for a moment then nodded. "I remember him. He was a regular here. He never played anything except the slot machines. He always ordered the same drink, too, white Russians. He was a decent tipper but didn't talk much. He usually came in around the same time. I don't know how long he stayed. My shift always ended around two hours after he got here. I really don't know anything more about him."

Sean glanced at Mac. "You seem to remember him quite well. Do you normally remember the people you serve?"

"The regulars I do. Especially the ones who tip well. My husband and I are saving up to buy a house, and the tips really help." She took off her glasses and folded them up in her hand.

"You said he didn't talk much. When he did speak, what did he talk about?"

"He usually just ordered his drink. Sometimes he'd complain about the machines if he wasn't winning, but most of the time he just ordered his drink and thanked me when I brought it." She shifted her position in her chair.

"What kind of mood was he in that night?"

"He seemed rather happy. He was having a good night at the machines."

"Did he normally play the same machine or sit in the same area of the casino?"

"He always played the same machine. That was handy.

It's nice when I can find the good tippers easily." She fidgeted in her chair again.

"One more question, Mrs. Kirk. Did he ever come here with someone or perhaps meet someone here?"

"No. I never saw him with anyone else. He would just come in and sit down at his machine. If somebody else was playing it when he got here, he would sit at a machine close by and play it until the person left. Then he'd go back to his usual spot." She glanced around the room.

"Thank you, Mrs. Kirk. You've been most helpful." Sean pulled out his phone and texted Halperin. The man must have been standing outside the door because he entered the room almost immediately.

"I'm finished with Mrs. Kirk."

Halperin nodded and led her out of the office, closing the door behind him.

Sean turned to Mac. "What was your impression?"

"Just like I said, she's been thoroughly questioned by the others. She remembered an awful lot of details. More details than I would have expected a server in a casino to remember. What did you think?"

"I got the same impression you did. She's been questioned too many times. I wish we could've questioned her first, but we're only here to assist. It's actually their case." He jotted a few things in his notebook. "The most important information we got from her was that Billy Spellman was a creature of habit. He always ordered the same drink, and he always tried to sit in the same place. If someone was targeting him, he made it very easy for them." He jotted down a few more notes. "Who's the next waitress?"

Mac consulted his notebook again. "Her name is Lynelle Hickman. She's divorced with one child. She's worked here for just over a year."

When the door opened, Halperin came in with the second waitress. Lynelle was tall, slender, with thick red hair. She wore a white V-necked tee shirt with lace trimming, a short denim jacket, matching tight-fitting jeans with ankle-high boots.

Halperin nodded at Sean and left the room.

"Good morning, Ms. Hickman. Please have a seat." Sean pointed to the guest chair. He pulled out a picture of Billy Spellman and showed it to her. "Do you recognize this man?"

"Yes, he's one of the regulars."

"What can you tell me about the man who was with him and bought him a drink?"

"He wasn't a regular, but I have seen him here a few times. I've never served him before. That night was the first time. When I did see him, he was playing a slot machine and looking around the room. He always had a beer, but he never ordered one during my shift." She crossed her legs.

"Can you describe him to me?"

"He was good looking with a pleasant voice. He had a mustache, a thick one. His hair was stuffed under a ball cap. It was short. He was polite when he spoke to me, and he gave me a good tip." She adjusted her position chair.

"Is there anything else you can tell me about him?"

"Not really. After he paid me for the drink, I didn't see him again."

"So, you're saying that he left right after he bought the drink?" Sean jotted in his notebook.

"Well, he left that area of the casino. Whether he left the building, I don't know."

Sean glanced at Mac before turning back to the woman. "Ms. Hickman, one more question. What happened with the towel that you brought along with the drink?"

"The towel? I'm not sure. Nobody else asked me that question. Let me think for a minute." She frowned.

Sean glanced back at Mac, who looked confused.

"Now I remember. When I walked back to that area again collecting empty glasses and taking orders, it was sitting on the counter next to his empty glass." She wrinkled her forehead. "He seemed a little off."

Sean straightened up in his chair. "What you mean by off?"

"He wasn't really drunk, but he was definitely feeling buzzed. He also wasn't as focused on the machine. A lot of gamblers form a rhythm when they play the slots, tapping the machine at regular intervals. He had a lot more breaks in his tapping. When I picked up the towel, he actually smiled at me. He'd never done that before. I asked if he wanted another drink, but he said no. I collected his glass and towel. By the time I made the rounds again, he was gone."

Sean was frantically jotting in his notebook. "Thank you, Ms. Hickman. You've been very helpful." He pulled out his phone and texted Halperin. It took him a few minutes to arrive this time.

"Thank you, Mr. Halperin. My partner and I are finished here for now. We will contact you if we have any further questions."

Halperin nodded and escorted Ms. Hickman out the door.

"Come on, Mac. Let's make a quick escape. You can tell me in the car where you've decided you want to have lunch."

PROBLEMS

Sean stood in front of the mirror in his bathroom, shaving with his electric razor. His shower was heating up, and the mirror was fogging. The sound of French horns came from his cell phone. *This is not going to be good.* He reached over and picked up the phone. It showed a text message from Mac.

> Mac: Get to the office ASAP. Don't stop for food.

"Wonderful. Now what hit the fan?" He checked his face again in the mirror. His shaving job would have to do. A quick shower and he could get dressed and get on his way.

———

Sean parked his car in the lot. He barely got the car door open when Mac walked up.

"No need for you to go into the office. I grabbed all the mail, reports and your notebooks. I already checked out a unit. We need to get out of here as quickly as possible. I'll spring for breakfast." Mac handed him a large envelope and two smaller letters.

"What is going on?"

"Little Bonaparte is announcing his reelection out in the parking lot this morning. He's going through the building checking to see who's here and who isn't. Rumor has it he's making notes on who will not be standing next to him in the parking lot when the news cameras start rolling. Lots of folks in the office are in panic mode, think the Titanic after hitting the iceberg. Everybody is searching for a lifeboat, and by that, I mean an excuse to get out of the building before the news crews show up."

Twenty minutes later, they were sitting in a booth in a local breakfast house, enjoying food and coffee and going over their reports.

"How did you know what was going on at the office this morning?" Sean picked up a slice of toast.

"Believe it or not, I got a phone call from Burt Tolliver this morning giving me the heads up on what was going on." Mac picked up his coffee cup.

"Tolliver called you? Is the undersheriff trying to stab his boss in the back?" Sean took a bite of his toast.

"No. He was actually trying to save the sheriff from himself. Coercing his employees to stand beside him during his reelection announcement would've caused all kinds of political problems. Of course, little Bonaparte wouldn't be thinking that far ahead. Tolliver was giving all of us a way out if we wanted one to avoid a stink that might hit the papers later." Mac took a sip of his coffee, set it down, then grabbed another packet of sugar.

"You know, Tolliver should actually run for the position. I mean, except for that ridiculousness with the SWAT team, he runs everything else anyway. Things would go a lot smoother if he was officially at the helm instead of Sparks." Sean picked up his fork.

"Really. I was under the impression that the most qualified person for the job was one of the detectives." Mac opened the sugar packet and dumped it into his coffee.

"I want to run for the position. I want to fix the problems we're having. Little Bonaparte is nothing but a media whore. The moment a camera comes into a room, his face is in front of it. Everything he does is to get publicity and his name in the papers. That's not how you seriously manage a law enforcement department. You need to look at the needs of the community and the resources you have to meet those needs. He just wants to do the things that bring glory or look good on the evening news. If the things he does accidentally make law enforcement become more efficient, well, that's an unexpected bonus. His idea of running the department is completely ass backwards."

"You should jot that down. Those are excellent points to make in a debate. Now, we should probably open the envelope with our reports and the copies I made of the emails that came in this morning. You also got a letter. I grabbed it from your in box." Mac finished his coffee.

Sean set the large envelope on the table and opened the LA letter. He read it and nodded. "I wondered when I'd be hearing from them."

Mac looked up from his meal. "Hear from whom?"

"It's a retrial from an old case of mine. The first one ended in a mistrial. Now they are finally going back to court. I'm going to get subpoenaed to testify again." He folded the letter and put it back in its envelope.

"When will this happen?" Mac took another bite of toast.

"I'm not sure, but it should be some time in the next two months." He finished his coffee.

Sean emptied the large envelope out on the table and started sorting everything according to the case it referred to. The waitress strolled up and refilled their coffees.

"Good. There are results here from the Mercer case and

the Spellman case. There is also information here about a couple of our burglaries from last month." He handed the burglary papers to Mac and began reading the Mercer case.

They sat for a while in silence, both of them studying the reports while eating their breakfast. Sean finished first and set his fork on his plate before moving it aside.

"Okay, the hair found at the scene matches the hair found in the stocking cap across the street. Stephanie was right. That's where our perpetrator parked before going into the Mercer house. So, in that case, we've narrowed down the suspect pool." He picked up his coffee cup.

"I'm not surprised Stephanie was right. She seems to have a trained eye for detail. How are things going with her, by the way?"

"Things are actually going well. We've seen each other several times since I took her out for that fancy dinner. I really like her. She's very easy to get along with. She's not a fancy or pampered person. I feel very comfortable with her." Sean placed the Mercer report back into the envelope.

"Easy to get along with? Comfortable? Sounds like you're describing a golden retriever, not a girlfriend." Mac set down his paperwork.

"Mac, you know I don't enjoy discussing my personal life, past or present. I like her very much, but we are still getting to know each other."

"Are you doing anything with her this week?"

"Not until Saturday. She's in Boise and Pocatello until Friday. They have some sort of internal lab inspection going on. She left Monday morning and was supposed to inspect the Pocatello lab first. I talked to her last night. She was back in Boise. She's supposed to inspect their lab today, and then she has a training class that runs all day Thursday and finishes up some time Friday morning. She should be back here late Friday night. On Saturday, we're going to spend the day out on Lake Coeur d'Alene. I borrowed Dean Cope's boat for the day. We're bringing food and drinks, and we'll have a nice relaxing day on the water."

"Oh, you're going to have a great time. I've seen Dean's boat. It is really nice. Do you have any experience with boats?"

"Yes. I had a boat when I lived in LA. We spent a lot of time on the ocean on our days off." He quickly reached for his coffee cup. Thoughts of Peggy still hurt.

"Is Dean going to give you a tutorial on his? It's got a lot of bells and whistles." Mac reached for his own coffee.

"I'm meeting him at the marina on Friday at 6:00. He's going to walk me through all the features. I understand it actually has a grill and sink on the swim platform." Sean set down his coffee.

"Yes. Sharon's family is quite wealthy. Her dad loves to fish but has some health issues, so he really can't go alone. I think he helped pay for the boat. This way, he has a built-in captain to keep him company and take him to the best fishing spots on the lake."

"That's good thinking."

"I should borrow the boat sometime and take Karen and the kids out on the lake. What information does the Spellman report have?" Mac finished his last piece of toast and pushed his plate to the edge of the table.

"It's the analysis of the stuff found in Billy Spellman's car. Most of it was trash from fast-food places. The only thing of interest was the bag of pills Stephanie found in the glove compartment. It contained alprazolam and hydrocodone. Well, clearly Billy Spellman still had a drug problem, despite making two trips through rehab."

"Do you think that makes his overdose more or less likely?" Mac grabbed his coffee again.

"I'm not sure. We're assuming the man in the casino spiked Billy's drink. We know he was found later, dead in his car with a needle still in his arm. Did he inject himself or did the casino man do it? Was the heroin dose a lethal one, or was it laced with something in order to kill him? I need the tox report in order to answer those questions." Sean slid the reports into the envelope.

"I think we should check the local pawn shops for some of these burglary items. I'm not exactly sure what time Sparks is making his announcement, but I don't think it's safe to return until after lunch." Mac handed him the burglary reports.

"That works for me." Sean slid out of the booth.

———

Ray parked his car in his assigned spot of his apartment's carport. The sun would be up in an hour, and he was completely exhausted. Between his regular work hours and the amount of surveillance time he was putting in, he'd be lucky if he got undressed before collapsing on his bed. He got out of the car and locked it before walking around the side of the building to his basement apartment. The reason he chose to rent this place, besides the fact that it had the lowest rent in the area, was its hidden entrance. Like everything else in this poorly maintained apartment complex, nobody bothered to really take care of the landscaping. One tenant had a kid who cut the grass on occasions, but nobody ever bothered trimming the shrubbery. The walkway and steps leading to his apartment door were hidden behind some tall, thick bushes. His comings and goings couldn't be seen by his neighbors, a situation that suited him nicely, especially on nights like this.

He'd been away from his apartment since Thursday. He'd packed a bag before leaving to go to work that day and spent the last two nights in his car parked near Jimmy's home. Surveillance took a lot of patience. Declan Bishop had warned him many times when he spoke about his plans for revenge. "When you're casing a mark, make sure you do it multiple times and during different hours of the day. Get to know their schedule as well as you know your own. Don't leave anything to chance." Declan's advice had worked well for the first two incidents, so he would keep following it for the next two.

There were only a few weeks left to prepare the last details for his vengeance against Jimmy. This one was the hardest to plan. Jimmy was the reason for all the tragedy in his life. If it wasn't for Jimmy, he'd never have met the prosecutor or his so-called defense attorney. He could have helped his mother and maybe the outcome of her disease would have been different. This killing was personal. This killing was not about taking away something dear to someone else. This killing was payback for the man who'd stolen everything from him. This killing would not be quick.

He jiggled his key in the sticky lock to get it to release. He'd have to remember to pick up some WD-40 at the hardware store tomorrow before the lock stopped working altogether.

The scent hit him as soon as he opened the door. "Shit." He dropped his bag and lunch pail on the floor and ran to the fridge. He nearly choked when he got it open from the stench of sour milk. The stupid machine must have died sometime in the last two days. He opened the freezer door. The TV dinners in the front were all soft and wet when he picked them up. His samples in the back were swimming. "Shit." He only had a few weeks to secure replacement stock before August 5th. There wasn't enough time to do a full background check on another corpse. He slammed the fridge door shut. *Bloody, cheap piece of crap. All that time spent following Jimmy, finding just the right time and place to nab him and get him to his final destination.* He grabbed one of the cushions on the couch and slammed it against the wall. "Three more weeks? The bloody fridge couldn't last three more weeks."

Okay, how can this be salvaged? The abduction date couldn't be changed. There were too many moving parts, and he wouldn't let Jimmy escape his punishment. He buried his face in his hands. He had to get some sleep in order to think clearly. What had Declan said? "When a good plan goes to shit, look at each step and see if anything can be done to move around the problem and get you to your objective." That would be the first thing he did in the morning. Right now, the samples needed to be dumped and the management company called about a replacement fridge. He closed his eyes and rolled his neck to release some of the stiffness from sitting in the car for hours. He yawned, nearly breaking his jaw. Stumbling toward the sofa, he pulled out his cell phone and dialed the management company. Ten minutes later, he was standing in front of the fridge with a large trash bag, throwing out his spoiled food and samples.

THE LAKE

Stephanie placed the bottle of suntan lotion in her small bag. They'd be out on the water all day, and she wanted to make sure she wasn't turned into a lobster by the time they headed back to shore. Thank heavens the boat had its own bathroom. She'd be mortified if she had to ask Sean to head for the shore every two or three hours.

Her large bag sat open on the coffee table. It contained two changes of clothes: her shorts and tank top, in case the weather got very warm, along with jeans, a long sleeve shirt, and a thick sweatshirt with a hood, in case the wind picked up.

It had been years since she'd been out on the lake with her parents and siblings. Warm days on the water were easy to handle. You could always go swimming if you got too hot. But there were times when the wind picked up and the temperature dropped quickly. She vividly remembered sitting and freezing on the deck, wrapped in a towel or anything else she could find. She had no idea how big the boat was or what other amenities it had besides the bathroom. All she could do was pack for all contingencies and hope it was enough. She even put two rolls of toilet paper in her bag. "Well, it's better to be safe than sorry."

She wore dark blue palazzo pants and a summer blouse, along with tennis shoes and a light sweater. Her hair was scooped up and held in place by clips. Once she got out on the water, she could let her hair down if the wind would allow it. At least she was leaving the house looking well groomed. Under her clothes, she wore her bathing suit. Again, since she didn't know anything about the boat, it seemed an easier way to prepare for swimming or sunbathing.

She zipped up her large bag and walked over to the small one to do a last-minute check. There were breath mints, dental floss, hair scrunchies, hand lotion, and towelettes. It also held her wallet, brush, and comb. The only things left to pack were her towels. She had bought a special waterproof bag in Boise to take along on this trip. It would hold her dry towels for now and anything wet after they went swimming. When she finished packing, she set the three down by the door and frowned. "Sean is going to think I've packed for a weeklong vacation."

When the doorbell rang, she quickly checked her face in the mirror next to the door. *Please, God, let us have a wonderful time together and don't let me do anything embarrassing or stupid.* She took a deep breath and opened the door.

Sean stood there, smiling at her. He looked her up and down. "You look very nice. Are you ready for a great day on the water?"

She smiled. "Yes, I am."

———

Sean walked along the boardwalk, carrying her large bag and towel bag. On one shoulder hung a backpack. That was all he'd brought. Stephanie's cheeks grew warm. *He must think I'm ridiculous for bringing all this stuff.*

Sean stopped in front of a white boat with wood accents. The name on the back read *The Kelpie*. The boat was large, beautiful, and obviously expensive. "Well, I think we'll be very comfortable for the day." He stepped on to the extended swim platform and set down his burdens. He reached out his hand and helped Stephanie aboard.

"Sean, this boat is amazing. Dean actually let you borrow it?"

"Yes, he owed me a favor. I used to own a boat when I lived in Los Angeles. I thought about getting one here, but I haven't really had the time to look for one. I know I can't afford one this fancy." He opened the steel and Plexiglas doorway that led to the cockpit. It had an L-shaped bench seat set around the table. Further in, was the helm station. "Have a seat while I bring in the luggage." He laughed.

"Please don't embarrass me more than I already am. I didn't know how big the boat was, so I packed everything I thought I might need in case of changes in the weather. I can see now I won't need half of it, but it's better to be over prepared then under prepared."

He came back in and set the bags on the bench seat and the table. "There's storage here under the seat cushions. We can hide the stuff away until we need it."

"Do we need to stop somewhere to pick up food and drinks?" She laid her hands on the table.

"No, we're fully loaded. I picked up everything this morning and stocked the boat before I drove to your place. There are drinks in the small refrigerator up here and more food and drinks in the big refrigerator downstairs." He picked up her large bag and tucked it away under the bench. She watched as he put the rest of the luggage away in other drawers and cubbyholes. When he finished, he turned to her. "Follow me. I'll show you the downstairs cabin."

Four steps led down to the cabin floor. She was completely stunned by the comfort and style of the place. There was a large angular bed tucked under the bow of the ship. It had a superb view of the flat screen TV mounted on the wall. Another bench seat that could convert to a bed along one side and another set of beds down the other side. Sean opened a door and revealed the bathroom. There was a toilet and a small sink with a portal over it. On the other side of the sink was a small shower with a Plexiglas door.

"Oh my, I never expected this. You can actually live on a boat like this. How many does it sleep?"

"Dean says it sleeps six comfortably. His father-in-law helped him buy it, and he and his in-laws are frequently out on the lake. His father-in-law loves to fish but has some health problems, so he needs to have someone with him when he's out on the water. I don't think Dean could have afforded a boat like this without his father-in-law's help." He closed the bathroom door.

"They were willing to let us use the boat today? If I had a boat like this, I'd be in it every weekend as long as the weather was good."

"They had some family get together today in Spokane, so they weren't using it. I got lucky with the timing." He grinned. "Shall we go upstairs and cast off? There are over 109 miles of shoreline around Lake Coeur d'Alene, and I want to take a spin around the lake to find the perfect spot to park the boat and swim."

She lifted her hand and gave him a salute. "Aye, Aye, Captain, lead the way."

———

Sean parked the boat in a small cove. There were no other boats around them or homes along the shore. It was a great private spot. He went downstairs to change into his swim trunks while Stephanie slipped out of her clothes to reveal her own swimsuit. It was a black and white tankini with a pleated skirt. This was the reason she wore the palazzo pants. They hid the tankini.

Sean came up the stairs carrying a large beach towel. His swim trunks were a bright red with white trim around the waist and the bottom of the legs. There were two exterior pockets with Velcro closures. He looked very relaxed and incredibly handsome.

Stephanie smiled at him to cover what she was really feeling. *How did a guy like him ever notice me?*

"You look great. Do you want to sunbathe on the bow first before we go swimming? The sun will warm us up, and the water will cool us down. After we dry off, I'll cook lunch." He gave her a big smile.

"That sounds wonderful. What's for lunch, anyway?" She went over to the drawer where he placed her bag of towels and pulled it out. She also grabbed her suntan lotion.

"I'm going to grill kebabs and corn. This thing has a built-in grill and sink next to the swimming platform."

"You're kidding. This boat is amazing."

"Yes, and I want to take full advantage of all its amenities while we have it."

They both laughed as Sean led the way around the helm to the front deck. There were special mats laid out for sunbathing. They lay down with their feet pointing toward the bow. "These mats adjust so you can sit up as well as lie down."

"Oh, I'd like that. How does it work?"

After he'd adjusted her mat. He adjusted his own.

She felt her face grow warm. "Ah, Sean, would you mind putting some lotion on my back and shoulders? I tend to burn easily if I don't put some on when I'm in direct sunlight."

"Of course, I'd be happy to." He grinned at her as she handed him the bottle. A moment later, his warm hands were spreading the smooth lotion on her skin. His touch sent electric tingles through her muscles. Sitting here alone with him, his simple touch felt erotic. When he finished, he handed her the bottle. "My turn."

He turned his back to her. She slowly rubbed the lotion into his skin. Running her hands over his muscled shoulders and back increased the feeling of intimacy. A shiver of excitement ran down her spine. When she'd finished, he turned and smiled at her. "Thank you. You have a very gentle touch." He moved away and held out his hand. "Can I have the bottle for a moment?"

When she handed it to him, he placed some lotion on his chest and each of his thighs before handing the bottle back. She smiled at him. He had muscles in all the right places.

She finished her own chest and legs before stretching out on the mat.

They relaxed in the sun while Sean told her about his progress on the Mercer and Spellman murders. She told him about her trip to Boise. After a while, it was too warm to stay in the sun. They went back to the cockpit and got sodas out of the fridge.

The water was cool and felt great after their time on the deck. Around 2 o'clock, they got out of the water and dried off on the swim platform.

"Why don't you go below and take a quick shower to wash off the lake while I get lunch set up. When you come back up, I'll take a quick shower, too."

"Thank you. I'd like that." She retrieved her bag with her spare clothes and the small one with her sundries in it. When she came back up, she was wearing her shorts, a tank top and sandals. A large hair clip kept her wet hair off her back.

Sean had extended the canopy over the cockpit to keep the sun off the bench and table. There were plates and flatware sitting on placemats. Smaller bowls of sliced eggs, shredded cheese, and croutons surrounded a large green salad in a plastic bowl. There was also a bottle of ranch dressing. A plate of sliced French bread, two wineglasses, and a bottle of Pinot Noir finished the table setting.

Sean stood on the swim platform checking out the grill. He looked up and smiled at her. "I approve. That's a perfect outfit for a comfortable lunch on the water. I'll get cleaned up and be back shortly. Help yourself if you're hungry." He pulled his backpack out of a drawer and went below.

Stephanie sat on the bench and looked out at the lake and shoreline. This really was a beautiful area. It was surprising that no other boaters had come close to them. There were lots of people out on the lake, but they were much further out in the water.

Sean was true to his word. He returned faster than she expected. Well, he was faster at getting cleaned up than she had been. He wore navy colored cargo shorts, a light blue T-shirt, and flip-flops. He carried a large platter that held four kebabs and two ears of corn and headed straight for the grill. A few minutes later, the smell of roasting meat wafted through the cockpit. Stephanie's mouth watered.

"How do you like your kebabs cooked?"

She smiled. When her father was grilling, he never asked her how she wanted her food. He served it the way he liked it, medium rare. "I'd like mine well done, please."

When he finished grilling the food, he asked her to bring out the plates. The meal was absolutely delicious. "Sean, this meal was perfect. I'm completely stuffed." She leaned back against the cushions.

"We have dessert, too, you know. I picked up an Oreo ice cream cake yesterday. It's downstairs in the freezer. We can have it later, after we've relaxed for a bit." He leaned back and stretched his legs under the table.

"I love this area. It's so beautiful, and there are so many outdoor things to do." She closed her eyes as the cool breeze blew over her face.

"Yes, that was one of the reasons I accepted the job up here. After living in a big city with smog and so many people, it's very appealing to be someplace with lakes, mountains, and lots of pine trees." He shifted his position and slid a little closer to her along the bench. "You know, about a week after I moved here, I saw my first moose up close. I was driving over to Mac's house. The thing was just walking along the road. I never realized how big they are. I gave it a wide berth, but it still turned and looked at me as I drove past. Even though there are about 180,000 people in the county, it still feels very rural, with the wild animals like the turkeys and the deer that wander over people's lawns."

"I know. I grew up here and remember when there were fewer people and a lot more animals wandering around." She opened her eyes and looked at him.

He slid along the bench until he sat next to her. He reached out and pulled the clip out of her hair. It tumbled down onto her shoulders. After tossing the clip onto the table, he reached out and stroked her cheek. "Thank you for coming out here with me today. It's been a long time since I had someone I cared about, someone I could enjoy a warm sunny afternoon with." He reached up with his other hand and cupped her face,

Her breath stalled in her chest.

He leaned in and kissed her.

Her body absolutely tingled from his kiss. She leaned into him and wrapped her arms around his neck.

He deepened the kiss.

Her nerves sang.

He kissed her several more times before moving to her neck.

When she leaned back to give him better access, a moan escaped her lips. When he started nibbling on her earlobe, she almost jumped off the bench. Waves of passion moved through her body. He knew exactly what to do to light her fire. The world around her disappeared. The only thing of importance was Sean.

The boat suddenly lurched to one side as it was struck by the wake created when a speedboat containing four teenagers turned too close to their boat. They broke apart as the other boat slowed down and came around. The boy at the wheel was laughing while his friend was making wolf whistles. The two bikini-clad girls in the back of the boat were also laughing as a boat sped off.

Stephanie's cheeks were flushed from passion and embarrassment. Sean was furious. "Those two clowns better hope they never cross my path when I'm working. I will not be merciful." He turned to Stephanie. "Are you all right?"

"Yes, just a bit embarrassed. What time is it?"

He scooted around the bench and stood up. There was a clock on the console of the helm. He walked over to it. "It's 4:15. I'm afraid we need to head back to the marina. I have to make sure that we leave the boat as clean as we found it."

Stephanie stood up and joined him at the helm. She slipped her arms around his waist and looked up at him. "I had a lovely time today."

He smiled at her. "Did you now. So did I." He brushed her hair from the side of her face, leaned down and kissed her before starting the engines.

JIMMY

Ray groaned as he turned off the alarm on his phone. The work calendar had him scheduled for 7:30. The funeral home had been unusually busy for the last two weeks. Normally, he would welcome the overtime and the chance to collect more samples. Unfortunately, none of the people coming in for embalming were viable candidates. They had processed two gang members involved in the turf dispute. One man with two prior DUIs had driven drunk and crashed his car into a tree. A man with prior convictions had been shot while trying to rob a bank. And finally, two young men with a history of drug abuse were dead from fentanyl poisoning.

During his time in prison, while he planned out his vengeance, he did a study of forensics. The main reason he had to do research on the people whose samples he collected was to ensure that none of them had any kind of criminal record. There was too great a risk that their DNA samples were logged into the CODIS database. CODIS is the acronym for the Combined DNA Index System and is the generic term used to describe the FBI's program of support for criminal justice DNA databases. The purpose of his leaving DNA evidence at his crime scenes was to give the police clues that led nowhere. Unless they could match a sample collected at the scene to a sample that existed in some database, it wouldn't link to a suspect.

Ray lay back and stared at the ceiling. The anniversary of his mother's death was coming up soon, and he was running out of time. He clenched his fists. It had to work out. Everything was in place except for the samples. It took two days for the management company to replace his refrigerator. They brought in another used model, probably removed from one of their other rental properties. *I wonder how long that piece of crap is going to last*? When he'd settled his final two scores, it would be time to move away from this place, somewhere with a milder winter, Arizona, perhaps, or maybe Florida. *Time to get up. Can't afford to be late for work.*

He started the coffeepot on his way to the shower. He finished drying in the kitchen while microwaving a couple of breakfast sandwiches. He'd packed a lunch the night before and set the lunch pail on the counter next to the coffeepot before getting dressed.

Armed with his lunch and a thermos of coffee, Ray headed for his car. He was almost at the corner of the building when he heard the voices.

"My sister said she's having the surgery in about two weeks. I'm just waiting for the confirmation of the date. I'll fly there two days before so I can learn about her kid's schedules and get a little settled in before she has the surgery. I should be gone for three to four weeks. I'll leave you enough food for Sammy. You need to make sure his food and water bowls are clean and full. His cage should be cleaned every other day. I have a stack of newspapers I will leave with you. Thank you so much, Helen, for taking care of him when I'm gone. My sister really needs me, and I can't take Sammy with me."

"It's no problem, Linda. I like birds. Are you driving your car to the airport?"

"No. I'm getting a ride with one of the airport taxi services. It's too expensive to park my car at the airport for that long. It's better off here."

He waited until the two women's voices grew fainter before turning the corner and getting into his car.

When he arrived at work, he found the rest of the members of the staff inside the chapel, talking to a small group of people. A couple of women in the group were crying. Clearly, someone else had passed away, and these were the friends and family members. He went into the embalming room and began preparing the table for the new arrival.

Forty-five minutes later, he found out who had passed. Mountain Street Baptist Church was one of the bigger churches in the city of Spokane. It ran a community outreach program that helped feed the poor, sheltered battered women and conducted an after-school activities program for at-risk children. The director of their community outreach program was an injured war veteran named Wyatt Hardecker, a devout member of the church and much loved by the staff and clients of their outreach program. Wyatt was severely wounded in Afghanistan and nearly died from his injuries. It took several surgeries to save his life and left him with a bad limp that required the use of a cane. He was a very trusted employee and actually lived on their outreach campus.

When he didn't show up to help with the morning breakfast service, the pastor, Philip Moreland, grew concerned and went to check on him. He found him dead in his room, still in his bed. Apparently, his injuries had left him susceptible to blood clots, and one went into his lung. He died of a pulmonary embolism. His actual funeral service would be held at the church building. The congregation members took up a collection to pay for his coffin and other funeral expenses. They wanted an open casket service to be held on Saturday. Open casket services took longer because of all the extra things that needed to be done to make the deceased look presentable.

Ray needed to start his part of the embalming process this morning before the assistant mortician could do his portion. The last element of the process after the body was prepared was to apply makeup to give the illusion that the deceased was sleeping and get him dressed in the clothes provided by the family.

As he worked with the corpse, Ray felt guilty about his sense of relief. It was a sad occasion for the people who knew and loved this man, but for Ray, it was divine Providence. As a wounded war hero and devout church member, this man was the perfect candidate to provide the samples that he needed.

―――――

Mac pulled their car into the designated parking slot. "Is it just my imagination, or do we seem to have more robberies than usual?"

"No. You're not imagining it. That's our third one in as many days." Sean opened the car door and stepped out. He looked at his watch. "We have another hour before we can clock out. That should be enough time to put a decent dent in today's paperwork."

"That's assuming we don't get any more calls today. I need to get home on time this evening. With all this nice weather, Karen wants me to barbecue chicken tonight. She'll have all the trimmings prepared, and we'll have a picnic in the backyard. I love it when the sun doesn't go down until 9:30. Makes me feel like I have a lot more free time than I do in the winter. I know that sounds silly. We actually have the same amount of time. It's just when it gets dark around 4 o'clock, it feels like we get less than 24 hours in the day."

When they reached their office, there was a large envelope

in Sean's in basket. "I hope it's something we've really been waiting for." He turned on his computer before opening it and dumping the contents next to his keyboard. He frowned. "It's just some insurance reports on the jewelry stolen from that home invasion in Hayden Lake. These are some excellent pictures of the missing pieces. I don't think we're going to find them in any pawnshop. They're too nice and would raise too many red flags."

A few taps on his keyboard brought up his emails. He scrolled through them and stopped at the one from the coroner's office. "Bingo. We got the toxicology report for Billy Spellman."

"What did they find?"

Sean skimmed through the results. "Definitely alcohol, along with Alprazolam. There was also heroin and fentanyl in the system. There wasn't enough heroin to give him an overdose. I'm pretty sure the fentanyl killed him. None of this proves murder, unfortunately, especially since he had the alprazolam in his glove compartment. The only thing that makes his death suspicious is that disabled camera. We need to find out who bumped into him at the casino. That's the only contact he really had with someone other than the waitresses. Damn. I was hoping we'd get more answers."

———

Ray waited in some bushes near the corner of the landscaping company parking lot. It was far enough from the main entrance of the company building to go unnoticed by anyone going in or out but had a perfect view of the parking slot Jimmy always used for his company vehicle.

He'd parked his own car two miles from the building and hid it in a clump of trees and bushes on a dirt side road. Three weeks ago, he brought home an old three speed bicycle from a garage sale. This morning he placed the bike in the back of his car, being careful to clean it first to make sure it had no fingerprints and then touching it only with gloves on. It was funny. A man walking along the road caused suspicion. However, the same man on a bicycle didn't get a second look. The bike now lay on the ground behind the back of the building.

From weeks of observing the habits of Jimmy and his coworkers, he'd learned the gate was open at 7 o'clock, the arrival time of most employees, and at 5 o'clock, the departure time of the office staff. The rest of the time, the gate remained locked. An employee who returned early with equipment had to use the keypad to open the gate. From the inside, the gate opened any time a car pulled up to the sensor. Jimmy was traditionally the last one to return with his truck. He planned to wait until Jimmy opened the gate and then slip through before it closed. He'd show up on the surveillance video, of course, but that would be long after his business was concluded.

Jimmy's routine was always the same. He parked his truck and got out with a handful of papers. He had his own key to enter the building. He'd come out a few minutes later and leave in his car.

Ray checked his watch. Jimmy was even later than usual. He sat there in the bushes with his duffel bag full of the supplies he needed. He was getting nervous. He'd waited so long for this day. Fifteen minutes went by, but there was still no sign of Jimmy. What if he went somewhere else in the truck? What if he had engine trouble or a flat tire? What if he was not alone when he returned? All this planning and it might be for nothing.

Everything I went through for the past 12 years, losing my mother, losing my freedom, the beatings in prison, and my future destroyed. Jimmy was the cause for all of it. His hands shook. He had to calm himself. It would work out. The first two revenge acts were successful. Jimmy would be, too. Karma was on his side.

He heard an engine in the distance. A few moments later, Jimmy's truck came into view. He closed his eyes and took a deep breath before slipping on his ski mask and a lightweight jacket two sizes too large for him with the gun hidden in the pocket. There were two cameras mounted on the building. One overlooked the parking lot, and the other one focused on the door. His jeans, gloves, tennis shoes, and tee shirt didn't look suspicious while riding the bicycle. In his duffel bag, he'd carried the ski mask and the loose-fitting jacket, among other things. It wasn't a great disguise, but would distort his image and proportions on the videotape. He crept out of his hiding place and worked his way toward the gate, slipping inside before it closed. Removing the gun from his pocket, he held it securely in his gloved hand. He waited until Jimmy was unlocking the building's door, then he ran up behind him and stuck the gun in his back.

"Do as you're told, and you won't get hurt."

"Hey, man, I don't have much money on me, but you can take it."

"I'm not here for your money. I want what's in the office. If you do as you're told, you won't get hurt. I'll be in and out of here in 15 minutes. Now, get inside."

Jimmy walked through the door with Ray close behind him. There was an old metal chair with armrests sitting up against a support post. "I want you to sit down in that chair."

Jimmy quickly sat down. Ray reached into his other pocket and pulled out several heavy-duty zip ties. "Tie your legs to the legs of the chair."

"Hey, man, this isn't necessary. I won't bother you. You can steal whatever you want from this place. I don't care." Jimmy was sweating.

"I said do as you're told, and you won't get hurt. I want you tied in this chair so I can get what I came for."

Jimmy grabbed one of the zip ties and hooked his right ankle to the chair leg.

"Now put another one around your calf."

Jimmy obliged.

"Now tie the other leg the same way."

Next, Ray told him to tie his right wrist to the chair. Jimmy was right-handed. When he was finished, Ray grabbed a zip tie and tied his left wrist, then put another zip tie on each arm just below the elbow. With Jimmy secured to the chair, he pulled off his ski mask. "Hello, Jimmy. Remember how you took away my life because you wanted my girlfriend? Well, it's payback time." Ray pulled out a knife.

Jimmy's eyes went wide. He started screaming.

Ray put the knife to Jimmy's chest and sliced.

Jimmy's screams echoed through the rafters.

THE THIRD VICTIM

Sean rinsed the shampoo out of his hair while his cell phone rang and danced around on the counter. "Oh, crap, now what's gone wrong?" He rinsed the rest of his body and grabbed the towel draped over the top of the shower door. Mornings that started with a call or text interrupting his usual routine signified nothing good. He quickly dried himself off. He checked the phone. He had a message. He tapped the button for playback.

"Sean. It's Burt Toliver. Call me back as soon as you get this message."

"Great. Now I know it's bad." He tapped the button to return the call. Burt answered on the first ring.

"Hey, Burt. What hit the fan?"

"Thanks for calling back so quickly. There's been another murder. This one is really bloody. Get here as quickly as you can. I've already called Mac. I've assigned you the usual car. Don't bother coming in the building. Go straight to the crime scene. I'll text you the address." He hung up without saying goodbye.

Sean shook his head. He hadn't been to a really bloody murder scene since he left Los Angeles. When rival gangs went after each other, it wasn't unusual to find a bloody body of a gang member who was captured by the opposition. He dried his hair and got dressed. No point having breakfast. If the scene was as bad as some he'd experienced before, there was a good chance he wouldn't be able to hang onto his food, anyway.

He arrived in the parking lot to find Mac already in the driver's seat of their car. Mac lived closer to the office than he did. He quickly parked his car and got in the car with his partner.

"You know where we're going?"

"Yeah, it's rural but not too far from here." Mac put the car in gear.

————

Jeff Olsen parked his car along the side of the road, several yards from the police roadblock. He'd gone into work early this morning hoping to talk the editor into giving him a different assignment than covering this morning's county Commissioner meeting. He was getting sick and tired of hearing the debate about the proposed bus transfer site. There had to be something more interesting to cover this morning. Five minutes later, he heard the call over the police scanner about a body found in a local business warehouse. He ran out the door. He would text his editor when he got to the scene. They could send somebody else to the commissioners' meeting.

The police were stopping anyone along the road. A few people were being allowed into the business parking lot, but he was sure he wouldn't be one of them. He pulled out his camera with a telephoto lens and walked closer to the building. While he was still 100 feet from the sheriff's deputy, a car pulled up, and he recognized Joseph Mackenzie and Sean

Landers. That was interesting. The sheriff seemed to send these two out to investigate every homicide.

––––––––

As soon as they topped the hill, they could see the crime location in the distance. Sheriff's officers had blocked off the north and south ends of the road, as well as the road coming in from the west to stop everyone approaching the crime scene. They were allowing some civilian cars through their blockade. These must be the employees of the business arriving for work. They wouldn't be getting any work done today, but they would all have to be questioned.

Their car passed a man holding a camera with a telephoto lens. Mac snorted. "That *Moose Droppings* guy is already here."

"We're bound to get a lot more press. As long as they don't let any of them close to the scene, we'll be fine. Crime scenes are much easier to work when they're inside a building away from prying eyes. Of course, all of that changes when little Bonaparte shows up and holds a press conference."

"Sparks is going to the commissioners' meeting this morning. Toliver told me he was sending the sheriff to the meeting to discuss the security needed for the proposed bus transfer site. He didn't mention the murder to Sparks, and the man never listens to the scanner. We should be safe, at least until lunchtime." Mac slowed down the car.

The sheriff's deputy guarding their road was Paul Clark. Mac stopped the car and rolled down the window. "What are we walking into, Paul?"

"I'm glad you two are here. It's a bad one. Deputy Murphy got here first, took one look at the crime scene, ran out of the building and lost his breakfast. We're gathering the employees at the far corner of the parking lot so you can talk to them. They're all really upset."

Sean leaned toward Mac's side of the car. "Paul, do you know who's gone into the crime scene and looked around?"

"Only Murphy, as far as I know. After his reaction, they're keeping everyone out so the crime scene doesn't get contaminated. I'm glad I'm out here on traffic duty. I don't want to go in there and see it." He straightened up and stepped away from the car. Mac nodded at him and moved the car to the entrance of the company parking lot.

Sean and Mac each put on gloves before heading over to the door. One officer stood three feet in front of the open door. He nodded at them and stepped aside as they continued forward. After two steps, Sean knew exactly why the man was standing so far from the door. The stench of blood filled the air. Sean turned to Mac. "Brace yourself."

The lights were on in the building. The walls were lined with shelving units containing various gardening tools and parts for lawnmowers, weed whackers, and other landscaping equipment. Someone had knocked over a smaller shelving unit, leaving its contents scattered over the floor. In the center of the building near one of the support posts, a man was strapped to a chair lying on its side. The man was covered in blood, and so was the surrounding floor.

Mac froze. "Oh God." He turned his head away.

Sean took a few steps closer. Someone had sliced this man to ribbons. There was a knife on the floor not too far from the body. He took a few steps closer, careful not to step in any of the blood. He squatted down to get a better look at the knife. It was large. The style was called a Tactical Folder. He stood up, closed his eyes, and steadied himself. He was having a Déjà vu experience of his last gang war in LA. "I need still shots and video of the entire area before anyone else comes in here. Mac, make sure the crime lab has been called out, and also notify the coroner. I need to speak to the owner of the company. Come find me when you've ensured the others are coming."

Mac nodded. "Do you want Tim to come in to do measurements?"

"Yes. Let's get out of here. The smell is getting to me, too."

Sean walked over to the group of employees the sheriff's department had gathered in the far corner of the parking lot. There were two women and nine men. The two ladies appeared to be in their late 40s or early 50s. The men were in their 20s and 30s, with one exception. *That's got to be the owner*. The man appeared to be in his 60s, heavyset, clean-shaven with thinning hair. Sean pulled out his badge. "I'm Detective Sean Landers with the County Sheriff's Department. I'd like to speak to the person who found the body."

A man wearing the company polo shirt, jeans, and a baseball cap stepped forward. "I found him." When he came closer, Sean noted the man was in shock. His gait was stiff, and he was shaking.

"Can you come over here with me? I have a few questions for you." Sean led the man away from the group until they were out of earshot.

"What is your name, sir?"

"I'm Peter S s-s-heppard," the man stuttered.

"Peter, are you normally the first one here in the morning?"

"Yes. I'm the manager. I usually open up the building and give all the landscapers their work assignments for the day." The man jammed his hands under his armpits while he stood there.

"I'm sorry, Mr. Shepherd, but I need to ask you what you did after you opened the door and exactly what you saw." Sean pulled out his notebook and pen.

"I… ahh… The smell hit me as soon as I opened the door. I thought maybe an animal had gotten into the building. When I t-t-turned on the lights, I s-s-saw Jimmy." Peter's hand shot up to his face and his body jerked like he was about to be sick.

"Did you touch anything other than the light switch?"

Peter shook his head but kept his hand clamped over his mouth.

"What did you do after you saw Jimmy?"

Peter closed his eyes, visibly trying to get control of himself. After a minute or so, he answered. "I ran out of the building. I needed to get to fresh air." His voice quivered as he spoke. "I called 911, and then I called Howard."

"Who is Howard?"

"Howard Pritchard owns the company." Peter was still shaking.

"Peter, one last question. Did you go back into the building after you left?"

"No." Peter actually looked angry at the question.

"Thank you, Peter. Why don't you have a seat over there on that truck bumper. I'll come find you if I have any more questions."

After Peter, Sean questioned the owner. When he finished, he walked across the parking lot to speak to Mac.

He found Mac leaning against the landscaping truck, unwrapping a piece of nicotine gum.

"I'm glad only one company person and a sheriff's deputy saw the crime scene. Otherwise, we'd have to call the paramedics out here to deal with everyone's trauma."

Mac closed his eyes and took a deep breath. "Don't be so sure. The way I feel, we may have to call them, anyway."

Sean nodded. "Did you call in the cavalry?"

"Yes. Everyone will be here shortly. What did you find out?"

"The man who found the body is the manager, Peter Sheppard. He's pretty shaken up. Our victim is James Morgan, but everyone called him Jimmy. I spoke to the owner, Howard Pritchard. He said that Jimmy was with the company for about seven years. He didn't want to hire Jimmy at first because he thought the guy was nothing but trouble. He lost his last job because he showed up drunk at work and he was in the middle of a divorce. Apparently, Mrs. Pritchard was good friends with Jimmy's mother and persuaded her husband to hire him. Jimmy turned out to be a good employee. He came to work on time, hardly ever missed a day, and did good work. There were no complaints against him from any of the clients." Sean turned the page on his notebook.

"I'll bite. Why is Jimmy strapped to a chair lying in a pool of his own blood?"

"While he was a good employee at work, after work hours, he wasn't such a good boy. He drank a lot and got into a lot of fights. His wages are being garnished for child support, and he had some less than savory friends."

"You think one of his less than savory friends decided to take him out? I mean, this is a good isolated place for a murder. I've got some officers canvassing houses to see if anyone saw anything or perhaps had video cameras pointed toward the road, but I'm not optimistic. Why would you put a business out here, anyway?" Mac scratched his nose.

"Apparently, this isn't as isolated as you think. The owner's house is on the other side of that hayfield behind the building along the west road. He owns all this property up to that fence over there. He said he didn't want his house and his business to have the same street address. So, he built a shop and the parking lot on the north-south road."

"Okay, I can understand that." Mac looked around. "I'm sure this incident isn't going to do much for his property values."

"Probably not." Sean checked his watch. "It's going to take a while to process the scene. Everyone should be getting here soon."

"You and your girlfriend meet up at the worst places."

"Stephanie is out of town. She'll be disappointed that she missed this." Sean closed his notebook and stuffed it in his pocket, along with his pen.

"Where is Stephanie?"

"She's been out-of-town all week at the North West meeting. It's some sort of forensic scientist convention. She's in Portland and won't get home until late Friday night."

Mac raised his eyebrows. "Does that mean poor Cliff has to work the scene by himself?"

"Probably. There really isn't much for them to collect. The main thing I'm interested in is the knife. With a knife like that, there's a good chance that the killer may have cut himself and we could have a sample of his blood on the blade or the handle." Sean turned and looked from the building to employees in the parking lot. "We better interview those people and clear them out a here. As the day warms up, the smell of the building is going to get worse. I don't want to have fainting people to deal with." The sound of a car drew his attention to the road. The two cameramen, Billy and Sid, arrived at the scene. "Mac, why don't you go interview those people. I'll deal with the others when they get here and set them on their tasks."

Mac nodded and headed across the parking lot.

A BREAK

Sean set his coffee and Danish down on his desk before hanging his coat over the back of the chair. The voice mail light blinked on his phone, but he ignored it. He'd return calls after he finished his first coffee. The computer hummed when he turned it on. He took a bite of the Danish while waiting for the login to appear on the monitor.

An officer came up to the desk and handed him an envelope. "This came in from the lab," he said before leaving the room.

Sean opened the envelope and pulled out a lab report. His eyes ran down the list of all the items that had no match in the system, another murder with no leads. Wonderful. None of this made any sense. The county hadn't seen a murder in five years. Now suddenly there were three in the space of five months. He turned to the last page of the report and nearly fell off his chair. A sample of blood that Cliff had collected came up as a match to a twelve-year-old rape case in Spokane. Finally, somewhere to look. He leaned back in his chair and checked his watch. Mac would be here in about twenty minutes. Not a lot of time but enough to find out who worked the case and see if he could get more information.

———

Mac maneuvered the car onto the street. "What's the name of the detective we're seeing?"

Sean took a sip of his coffee before putting it into the holder. "Stephen Oliver, he was the junior detective on the case. The senior guy retired to Arizona last year."

"Arizona, that's too hot for me. I wouldn't want to live running from air conditioning to air conditioning. Besides, I'd miss having snow for Christmas." He turned onto Highway 95 and headed for the freeway.

Sean laughed. "You'd miss the icy roads, freezing cold, and shoveling your driveway?"

"Of course not, I'd stay indoors, have everything delivered, and hire the kid next door to do the shoveling. I just like standing next to my Christmas tree, looking out the window when it's snowing." He maneuvered the car onto the freeway on ramp, heading toward Spokane.

Sean shook his head. "I imagine Karen would rather sit in a lawn chair, sunbathing in front of the swimming pool with Christmas lights wrapped around a nearby cactus." He opened the file on his lap.

"You're probably right." Mac sighed and was silent.

Sean read through the file again. *The victim had been fighting with her boyfriend at a party and left by herself. Three blocks from home, she was pulled into the yard of an abandoned house, beaten and raped. Neighbors didn't hear anything and a thick hedge blocked the view of any passing cars. The man wore a mask and latex gloves. After stumbling down the street to a house with lights on, she knocked on the door and the occupant called 9-1-1. They did a rape kit at the hospital and DNA testing at the state lab.*

We found no match in any criminal data base and the crime remains unsolved.

He closed the file and looked out at the passing landscape. "They didn't find any match to their DNA sample in a criminal data base until our brutal murder. How does that happen? A guy goes out and rapes a woman, is an upstanding citizen for twelve years and then butchers a guy? It doesn't make any sense. We are missing something that's crucial, and I can't figure it out." He punched the dashboard, then tried to shake the pain from his hand.

"Sean, we'll figure it out. The officer may have interviewed someone or have something in his notes that ties all of this together." They rode the rest of the way in silence, with Mac concentrating on driving and Sean brooding in the passenger seat.

Mac turned into the visitor parking area of the Spokane City police department and parked. Sean grabbed the file and got out of the car. "You ask the first round of questions. I want to hear the officer's answers before I ask my own."

Mac nodded, and they entered the building. It took them a few minutes to get their visitors passes from the desk officer and a few more minutes before Stephen Oliver came out to meet them. He was a thin man, medium height, with wispy blond hair. "Good morning, gentlemen. I have the files you wanted to see set up in a conference room. If you'll follow me, we can get started."

The conference room was rather small and close to the lobby. The table was round with six chairs. In the center sat a carafe of coffee, a pitcher of water, foam cups, along with sugar packets and nondairy creamer. Sean chuckled. At his department, they'd be having this meeting in the hall rather than a room with coffee.

Mac pulled out a chair and sat down, setting his notebook on the table. Sean picked a chair opposite him and Stephen sat closest to the door.

Stephen cleared his throat. "This rape was my first case after being hired by the department. Henry, my partner, said the case never made sense. You read the report. In twelve years, we've never had a DNA match until you called me." He opened up one of the file folders on the table. "We didn't have any suspects. The girl never saw her attacker's face because of the black ski mask he wore."

Sean and Mac glanced at each other.

"We found three men within a six-block radius of the crime. They were each questioned and listed as persons of interest. An officer stopped one man about two blocks from the crime scene. The officer talked to him and filled out a Field Interview card." Stephen pulled it out of the file and set it on the table. "The man's name was Wyatt Hardecker, a soldier on leave visiting his parents. He claimed to be walking home from seeing a movie. He had a movie ticket stub in his pocket." Stephen pulled out two more cards. "Another officer stopped two men five streets away. They had been to a local bar. Both men smelled of alcohol. One man was named Gerald Innes, and the other one was Peter Simpson. This is where the case stopped, with no credible leads. Over time, there were other rape cases, but nothing that matched the MO and, of course, no DNA matches in semen, blood, or any other body fluid."

Sean looked over the cards for anything that struck a chord. He slid the file over to Mac, who took down the names and last known addresses of the field interviews. Sean leaned back in his chair. "Is there anything else you remember about the case that may not have made it into the file?"

Stephen scratched his chin. "On my own, I followed up on what happened to the victim. I have a sister who was nearly raped, and I... well, I wanted to make sure the victim would be okay. She left the area about six months after the incident and went to college in Montana. Her family lived here for another five years then moved to Oregon. I wasn't able to find out any more than that, but I know neither she nor her family have returned to the area."

Mac continued taking notes. Sean shifted his position and reached for the file again. "Thank you for your help. We'll follow up on the three men and see if any of them are tied to our case." He turned to his partner. "Are you ready, Mac?"

Mac closed his notebook and stuck it along with his pen back into his coat pocket. "Yes, I'm ready."

Stephen led them back to the lobby. "Let me know if there is anything else I can help you with. If you solve your case, you might also solve mine."

Sean nodded, then turned and left the building.

———

Sean rubbed his chin. He'd been on the phone and computer for hours tracking down Wyatt Hardecker. Mac came into the office and dropped into his chair. "I'm not getting very far with Innis and Simpson. I can track them for four years after the police talked to them, but after that, they each moved out of the area. I can't find out where they are. How are you doing with Hardecker?"

Sean leaned back in his chair. "I made some progress. Two weeks after the police questioned him, Hardecker's unit was deployed to Afghanistan. During one of their missions moving equipment, his unit was attacked, and he was seriously injured. He spent three weeks in a hospital in Germany. He nearly died during the initial surgery to save his life. He lost the ability to have kids and almost lost a leg. They sent him back to the States for another surgery and physical therapy. Somewhere along the way, he had a religious conversion, and after his medical release from the military, he started working with churches and different charity programs. According to the state employment records, he works for Hands of the Angels missionary program. They work with families in poverty, the homeless, single mothers and at-risk youth. I plan to go over there this afternoon and see if I can talk to him."

"Good luck. I have to be in court this afternoon on that burglary case I worked last year." He sat up straighter. "I'd better grab some lunch before I head over to the courthouse. If you find out anything important, call me tonight." He stood.

Sean sighed. "I'm not very hopeful. This doesn't sound like our man, but I'll let you know."

Mac tapped his hand on the table and nodded before leaving the room.

Sean closed his eyes. This case was draining him. Too many questions and things that didn't add up and too few clues to follow. He closed his eyes. He needed to step back from it. *It's odd. This was the first time since I moved here that I can't find peace.*

He picked up his phone and called Stephanie. "Hi, sweety. I really needed to hear your voice…"

————

Ray sat in his car on the road behind one of the local veterinary clinics. It had taken a while to track down his former girlfriend, Amber Ricci, but he finally found her. He had expected her to take her maiden name back after she divorced Jimmy. He was quite surprised that she hadn't. Of course, she and Jimmy had had a daughter. The little girl looked to be around 10 years old and luckily took after her mother.

Amber had always wanted to work with animals. Her original ambition was to go to veterinary school and open her own practice. Somehow, that dream got derailed. Another lost opportunity, thanks to Jimmy. He couldn't be sure what happened. Maybe she dropped out of school after his arrest due to all the drama. At least his ego hoped that was the reason. However, it was more likely she dropped out when she got pregnant. Judging by the age of the little girl and the record of their marriage at the courthouse, Amber was about four months pregnant when she walked down the aisle.

The veterinary clinic's website listed her as a veterinarian's assistant and said she'd been associated with the business for six years. She must've gone back to school right after her divorce.

The first time he saw her pick up her little girl at school, he wanted to punch his fist through his windshield. He had loved her. He had planned to marry her when he finished school. They were supposed to grow old together. That little girl should have been his. Jimmy had destroyed so much because of his selfish desire. Well, he had paid for it finally, in full.

Of all the people on his revenge list, Amber would be the most difficult. He debated whether to put her on the list at all, but Declan Bishop had assured him it was necessary. "The woman betrayed you when she married your friend. And it wasn't that long after they sent you to prison. Maybe there was something going on between the two of them before you were arrested? Are you sure she didn't know about the boxed meth lab that got planted in your car? She never came to visit you while you were in the county jail or showed up for your trial. You won't find peace until you deal with all the people who wronged you. That means she has to be on your list."

He checked his watch. Amber would be off work in a few minutes. He would follow her again today to find out where she went after work. It was important to know her patterns and habits. It was the only way he could find out the times when she would be alone.

He leaned back into the car seat. *A few more weeks, and it will all be over.*

HANDS OF THE ANGELS

Sean arrived at the Hands of the Angels Center; a large steel building behind the Mountain Street Baptist church. Inside the building, the Hands of the Angels charity performed three of its primary missions. The first to feed the poor, which they accomplished by providing three meals per day to the people who showed up, an oatmeal breakfast with fruit and coffee, soup and a sandwich for lunch, with meat, potatoes and a vegetable for dinner. It was just after 1:00, and there were a surprising number of people still lined up to get in to today's lunch service.

Their second mission was to run a shelter for the homeless, consisting of thirty beds for men down on their luck. They housed battered women and children at a different location.

Their third mission was to help at-risk children. This program was comprised of after-school activities and sports divided by age groups. Altogether, this was a very large and impressive community outreach program.

Sean parked his car in an open parking slot and turned off the engine. He pulled the notebook out of his pocket and checked the name again. He needed to speak to a Reverend

Philip Moreland, lead pastor of the church and head of their charity programs. Speaking to the man's employer would be the fastest way to find out more about Wyatt Hardecker. He also hoped to arrange a private meeting with Mr. Hardecker. The man didn't fit the profile of their perpetrator, but he had no other leads to follow.

He got out of the car and made his way along the sidewalk. More people had walked up to the soup kitchen line, and it now stretched the length of the building. Carefully moving past the people in line, he slipped through the door and entered the building. It looked like a large high school cafeteria. He walked to the other side of the room and opened the door. He stood in a hallway that ran the length of the building. Half way down on the right side hung a sign that said office. Hopefully, he would find Moreland there.

The door opened before he reached it, and a short, bald-headed man stepped out and locked the door. The man turned toward him and jumped in surprise.

"I'm sorry. Are you Reverend Moreland?" Sean pulled out his shield and credentials.

"Yes, I am. I'm sorry, officer…"

Sean interrupted him. "I'm a detective."

"Oh, detective, well, you've caught me at a bad time. We are a couple of volunteers short today, so our lunch service is running behind. I'm headed down there to help." He looked anxious to get moving.

"I only have a few questions about one of your employees. It won't take long. We can talk while we walk back to the cafeteria." Sean pulled out his notebook and a pen.

"All right, if we can do it while we are walking. Which employee are you interested in?" The man slipped his keys into his pocket.

"I'd like to ask you about Wyatt Hardecker." He looked at his notebook as he walked. It took him a moment to realize that the Reverend wasn't walking with him. He stopped and looked around. The Reverend stood in the hall with a stunned look on his face. Sean frowned. "What's wrong, Reverend?"

"Why on earth would you ask questions about Wyatt Hardecker?" The man looked genuinely puzzled.

"It's related to a case I'm working." He wrinkled his forehead.

"Wyatt was a remarkable man, a kind and gentle soul who truly wanted to help his fellow man." The Reverend pulled out a handkerchief.

"What do you mean was?" Sean scratched something in his notebook.

"He died almost two months ago." The man dabbed his eyes.

Sean's eyes went wide. "Ahh… I'm sorry. I didn't know. Ahh… may I ask what happened?" Sean's mind started racing. The guy had died before the Jimmy Morgan murder.

"Wyatt came to us a few years ago. He was a broken young man with a need to help others. He was a member of the United States military who served in the Middle East. His convoy was attacked, and he was seriously injured. He nearly died in the field, but the medics were able to stabilize him enough to get him to the hospital. After an emergency surgery, they sent him to Germany for yet another surgery. They thought he'd never walk again, but with excellent medical help and a lot of physical therapy, he did walk with the help of a brace and a cane. He found the Lord while in the hospital. Since he was raised in Spokane, he came to us wanting to help with our mission. We were thrilled to have him. He helped in the kitchen with our meal program. Wyatt rearranged our at-risk youth program and made it a lot more fun for the children by adding art and music. He got local artists and art teachers to volunteer a few hours a month to work with the kids. He did the same thing with the music program."

The Reverend rubbed his eyes with his sleeve. "He was a

wonderful, giving young man who loved working with people. He showed up every day, despite his disabilities."

They reached the cafeteria. The line was a little shorter, but not much. The Reverend went straight to the kitchen and spoke to one of the cooks.

"We seem to have a lot more people today than usual. Do we have enough food?"

The woman kept stirring the soup. "Yes, I got a call this morning from Father Brenner at St. Benedict's. There was a busload of migrants arriving, and we should expect additional people for the next few days. He sent someone over with a donation to help with the cost. Their facility isn't ready yet. They are still waiting on the arrival of two refrigerators and the final health inspection."

"That was nice of them. Where do you need me to help?" He reached over to a rack and pulled off a clean apron.

"If you could help with filling up the soup bowls, that would speed things up. Don't forget to put on the plastic gloves." She pointed to the glove box.

Sean was champing at the bit. He made an impromptu decision. He needed to ask more questions and if he had to wait for the Reverend to finish the lunch rush, he might as well make himself useful. "If I put on some gloves, can I help, too?"

"Are you sure, detective?" Reverend Moreland looked surprised.

"Sure. What do you want me to do?" He reached for a pair of plastic gloves from the box.

The cook smiled. "If you could help hand out the drinks, that would be great. Just ask the person if they want bottled water or orange juice."

Sean nodded. "I can do that." He walked over to the serving area and slipped into the island between the two tables. Now there were enough people they could speed up the service by having two lines. People came in and picked up a plastic food tray and walked down the line as the volunteers placed wrapped sandwiches, a bowl of soup, and a piece of fruit into the different slots on the tray. The drink was the last thing to be added. It took about forty-five minutes to serve all the people who were still in line or just arriving. At the conclusion of lunch, Sean followed the Reverend back to his office.

"You were telling me about Wyatt and what a wonderful help he was to your work here. If you don't mind my asking, how did he pass away?" They reached the office door. When Moreland unlocked it, they went inside.

The office was not fancy. It had an old government issue metal desk along with several dented filing cabinets. The only nice pieces of furniture were the chairs. The desk had a fine leather executive chair and there were two leather guest chairs on the other side. Moreland sat down behind his desk while Sean chose one of the guest chairs.

The Reverend was silent for a moment then looked up at Sean. "I found the body. Wyatt stayed here on campus and looked after the place at night. It worked out well. We couldn't afford to pay him much, but by supplementing his salary with room and board, we were able to keep him with us. Like I said before, he was well liked by our clients and loved by the rest of the staff, a true godly man." Moreland took a deep breath before continuing. "The doctors said it was a blood clot. He… he didn't show up to help with the breakfast, so I went looking for him. I found him still in his bed. They said he'd been dead for hours." He grabbed some tissues from a dispenser on his desk and rubbed his eyes.

Sean shifted uncomfortably in his chair. "I'm sorry for your loss.

Moreland took a deep breath and composed himself. "It was a loss for our organization and for myself. My wife and I never had children, and Wyatt became sort of like a son to me. I know I should clean out his room. We could use the space, but I just don't have the heart to go in there and go through his things."

"Sir, I know this is a painful request, but would you mind if I looked at his room?"

Moreland frowned. "Why exactly are you interested in Wyatt?"

Sean cleared his throat. He wasn't really prepared for this. He thought he'd be asking Wyatt Hardecker questions, not speaking to his grieving friend and employer. "Well, my partner and I are working on a murder case that happened a month ago. There is some evidence that we found that matched something from a Spokane case from twelve years ago. The officers who worked the case spoke to three men they found out on the streets within a few blocks of the crime. We are following up on the three men."

Moreland looked even less happy. "And you're telling me that Wyatt was one of those men?"

"Yes, they found him two blocks from the crime scene and asked him some questions. They were satisfied with his answers and let him go." Sean shifted in the chair.

"What type of crime was it?" Moreland placed his hands on the table.

Sean leaned forward in the chair. "Reverend Moreland, it was rape."

Moreland shook his head. "I will never believe that Wyatt was capable of something like that. He was a good man."

"Reverend, I'm not saying he did anything, only that he was simply a few streets away from where a crime was committed. I came here to talk to him and ask a few questions. I didn't know that he had passed away." Sean leaned back in his chair. He wanted to see the room where Wyatt lived. He had to be very careful if he wanted to get permission from this man. "I need to get back to my office." He stood up while Moreland kept staring at his desk. "Would it be possible to see his room before I leave?"

Moreland looked up. His eyes met Sean's like he was looking for something. He must have found it. "I suppose I should look at the room. I have to hire another director, and we'll need it either as his quarters or another office." He looked down at his hands and folded them together. "At least he is in heaven with the angels. He is finally free from the pain of his injuries." He stood up. "Follow me."

When they left the room, they turned in the opposite direction in the hallway from the lunch area. At the end of the hall, he turned left and walked about halfway down the new hall before stopping in front of a door. He fumbled in his pocket for his keys and went through the group before finding the one he wanted.

Moreland swung the door open. There was a smell in the room, body odor and stale air. It had a small window with heavy curtains that obviously hadn't been opened since Wyatt passed away. The room was a bit of a contrast. On one side was a small single bed with the end of the blankets and sheets still neatly tucked in and folded, a witness to the occupant's military training. On the other side of the room was a small six drawer dresser covered with all kinds of things from unwashed socks to books. There was an old wingback chair in the corner with a handmade patchwork quilt wadded up and lying on the seat. Both items look like they had been salvaged from the church's donation center. A rickety floor lamp stood next to the chair, along with a small table. On the table was a small radio that plugged into the wall and a box of tissues. As Sean looked around the room, he noticed there was no television. The only thing on the walls was a flat piece of wood with Matthew 18:8-9 carved in it. Sean frowned and pulled out his pen and notebook, jotting down the Bible verse.

Wyatt had lived very much like a monk in this place. There were two doors at the back of the room. One led to a small closet with a few clothes, one jacket, and two pairs of shoes. The other door led to a small washroom that contained a toilet and a sink with a mirrored medicine cabinet above it. On the space at the back of the sink was a bottle of liquid soap, a half-used tube of toothpaste and a toothbrush sitting in a cup. Someone had carelessly draped a hand towel over the towel rack. Sean made an impromptu decision. While Moreland was distracted looking at the things on the dresser, he pulled a small evidence envelope out of one jacket pocket and his handkerchief out of the other. Using the handkerchief, he grabbed the toothbrush and slipped it into the evidence bag. He stuffed everything back into his pocket before leaving the washroom. There would be DNA on the toothbrush, and he could have the lab run it. Since Hardecker was already dead, it wouldn't make any difference in the old rape case, but it might give him some clue about the blood found at the scene of Jimmy Morgan's murder. He didn't have a warrant, so he could get into a lot of trouble, but his gut told him this was important.

"I need to get back to my office. Thank you, Reverend, for your time. And I am truly sorry for your loss."

Moreland rubbed a tear from his cheek. "Would you mind seeing yourself out? I would like to spend a few more minutes in this room alone."

Sean nodded. "I understand." He turned and left the room.

DINNER

Susan hesitated to knock on Stephanie's door. They hadn't spoken since her sister had dropped out of their brother's campaign. There were many times when she picked up her phone to call Stephanie and see if they could meet for coffee or something, but she never dialed. She wanted to mend their relationship, if it was even possible. The rest of the family might write Stephanie out of their lives, but Steph was her little sister, and she loved her.

This is ridiculous. You came over here specifically to talk to her, so knock on the door and talk to her. She lifted her hand, ready to knock on the door, but stopped. *What if she's not alone? What if the detective is with her?* She lowered her hand. *Would he make the situation better or worse?* She thought for a moment. *He'll probably make the situation better. She won't slam the door in my face with him standing there.* She lifted her hand again and knocked on the door.

It took a few minutes before Stephanie answered. She looked completely stunned to see her sister standing on her doorstep. "Susan? Is everything all right with the family? Is somebody hurt?"

She wanted to throw her arms around Stephanie and kiss

her. Even after the way they had all treated her, it was obvious she still cared about them. "Everyone is fine. I wanted to see you. I miss you."

Stephanie stepped forward and threw her arms around her sister. "I missed you, too."

They stood there hugging on the threshold for a few minutes before Stephanie stepped away. "Come in, please. Can I offer you some coffee?"

Susan wiped the tears from her eyes. "I'd love some coffee." She stepped inside and closed the door behind her.

Stephanie motioned to her dining table. "Have a seat. I just finished brewing a pot. I'll grab you a cup. I can even offer you a muffin to go with it. I picked up a large pack at the store yesterday. Sean absolutely loves baked snacks." She moved around the kitchen, gathering the different items.

Susan watched her with a smile. She couldn't remember the last time she'd seen her sister this happy. "So, you're still seeing the detective?"

Stephanie walked to the table and set down a platter with a variety of muffins. "Oh, yes, as often as I can. It's been a little difficult the last couple of weeks with our work schedules. I was gone for an entire week for a forensic conference in Portland, and he's been very busy working on the three murders we had in the county. On top of all that, he's had to attend several events for his campaign." She went back into the kitchen and returned with a tray that had two coffee cups, a small pitcher of cream, and a bowl of sugar.

"Well, at least you get to see him at his political events."

"I don't go to any campaign events with him. I'm staying completely neutral in the sheriff's race. I told Mom I would, even though she didn't believe me."

Susan couldn't miss the bitter tone in her sister's voice. "That's part of the reason I'm here. This ridiculous fight over a stupid political office is not worth destroying the family. You had no idea that your boyfriend was running for office when you first started seeing him. And Dennis didn't consult with anyone in the family when he decided to run. I found out when he asked me to be his volunteer coordinator. But that was after the campaign was already organized."

Stephanie went to the kitchen again and returned with the coffeepot. "I agree that it's not something worth breaking a family apart over. But since I've never really been recognized as a member of the family, I suppose nothing has changed."

"Steph, that's not true. You're my sister. You know I love you. If the detective is someone who makes you happy, then you have my support." Susan took one of the coffee cups.

"Susan, our father called me a traitor to the family. I knew eventually you and our brothers would start talking to me again. But Dad never will and Mother follows dad's lead." Stephanie grabbed a napkin and a muffin.

"Steph, I promise you I am going to fix the situation. Dad is being unreasonable. He's treating the sheriff's race like it's a championship game."

"Yes. And he's acting like I'm a cheerleader for the other team. I said I would remain neutral, and I meant it. Sean is actually at a fundraiser right now. I won't see him until tonight. He's coming over for dinner. I'm making him Grandma's double smoked salmon recipe." She grabbed a coffee cup and the coffeepot. "I'll pour you some coffee."

"You're going through all that trouble for him. You two must be getting serious. How often do you get to see him?"

"We try to see each other a couple times a week. Lately, it's been only meeting for the occasional lunch. We're both been so busy. Last month, he borrowed a friend's boat, and we spent the whole day out on the lake. It was wonderful."

Susan looked at her sister. *Well, I think I've met my future brother-in-law.* "I'm so glad you've met him. He seems like a really nice guy."

"He is, and I love him." She got a dreamy look on her face and smiled at her muffin. Have you been seeing anyone?" She poured herself a cup of coffee then added some cream and sugar.

"I still see Ben on occasions, but he's not a keeper. He's more like a good friend to hang out with."

"I'm sorry, Susan. I thought you and he were a good match." Stephanie took a bite of her muffin.

"No. I haven't found my true love yet. I have hope he's out there." She sighed. "I'm thrilled for you, though." Susan glanced at her watch. "I better get going. Dennis has a campaign event that I need to help with. Plus, I remember how long it takes to make Grandma's signature dish. I'm also sure that's not the only thing you're serving him. You clearly want to make an impression. I hope your cooking skills have improved since the last time you cooked for the family."

"I was 16 years old, and Mom barely let me do anything in the kitchen."

"Yes. And after that, you got to do even less. I'll never forget the look on Dennis and Douglas' faces. The noodles in mac & cheese are not supposed to be crunchy." She laughed and stood up.

"Thank you for dropping by, Susan. You're always the one I was closest to in the family. I'm glad at least the two of us can still be friends." Stephanie got up from her chair.

"I mean it, Steph. I'm going to heal the breach in this family. Please, give me some time to get it done. I love you, little sister. I'll see myself out. Goodbye." She waved when she got to the door and then closed it behind her.

———

Stephanie checked her hair and makeup in the mirror. Sean would be here any moment. She'd picked a new outfit for this occasion, a summer dress with a floral pattern on a white background. She wanted everything to be perfect.

The table was set for dinner. She'd bought a fine linen

tablecloth with lace trimming. She didn't own any fine China, but she had a nice set of ironstone dishes with trees on them. She had very nice water and wine glasses. There was even a basket of bread rolls on the table. The setting wasn't as fancy as the restaurant he took her to on their first date, but the table looked nice.

The knock on the door made her heart speed up. *Relax. It's going to be a lovely evening.* She took a deep breath and walked to the door. The smile on Sean's face when she opened the door made her heart beat even faster.

"You look lovely." He sniffed the air. "Dinner smells amazing." He held up a bouquet of mixed flowers. "I seem to remember you saying a spring bouquet was your favorite. Did I get it right?"

She stepped forward and kissed him. When they broke apart, he laughed. "I'll take that as a yes."

"Please come in."

When he stepped over the threshold, she closed and locked the door behind him. He handed her the flowers, and she sniffed them.

"I need to put these in water. Can you open the wine? The Riesling is in the refrigerator. I read it's supposed to be a little cooler than room temperature when you serve it." She strolled off to the kitchen, with him following her.

While Stephanie got a vase from one of her cabinets, Sean pulled the wine out of the refrigerator. He was about to ask her where the wine bottle opener was but noticed one lying on the counter. "This wine looks good. Dinner smells amazing. Are you going to tell me what we're having, or do you want to surprise me?"

She laughed. "It's double smoked salmon. It's my grandmother's special recipe. She always made it for family occasions. We are also having roasted Parmesan and rosemary potatoes, lemon butter broccoli, and honey glazed carrots. I didn't bake the bread, though. I bought it at the local bakery."

She grinned at him before putting water in the vase. After she had arranged the flowers, she took the vase into the dining area and placed it on the table. "These flowers are perfect. Thank you, Sean."

He came in with the wine bottle and set it on the table. "I love to see you smile. Makes me forget about all the other problems I've got to deal with." He stepped closer to her and pulled her into his arms. "I'm so glad I met you." He leaned down and kissed her.

A buzzer in the kitchen interrupted them.

"Oh, the salmon is ready."

"Do you need any help?"

"No. Why don't you pour the wine while I bring the food?" She disappeared into the kitchen. One by one, she placed the dishes on the table. When she set down the last one, she stopped and examined the display. "Okay, I hope you like it."

"It looks delicious, and I'm hungry."

She sat down as Sean scooped up potatoes and put them on his plate.

Stephanie grabbed a bread roll. "How are things going with your latest case?"

They talked about work and his campaign. She told him about her sister's visit.

"Do you think Susan will persuade your parents? I really hate the thought that I'm the reason your family is refusing to speak to you."

"You have done nothing wrong. They are being completely ridiculous and unreasonable. My father gave me a choice, and I chose you. I hope Susan can fix it, but I'm not holding my breath. My father can be stubborn as an ox. I will not let him stand in the way of my happiness." She reached across the table and took his hand. She looked up at his eyes and smiled at him.

He squeezed her hand. "I love you."

"I love you, too." She let go of his hand and rubbed a tear from her eye. "There's still more food. Would you like seconds or maybe dessert? I have a peach pie. You said that was your favorite. I didn't bake it. I got it from the same place as the bread rolls." She stood up and picked up her plate and flatware.

Sean got up and walked around the table. He took the plate and silverware from her hands and set them back on the table. "I would like dessert but not peach pie." He pulled her close, leaned down, and kissed her. He kept kissing her as he slowly led her to the bedroom.

CONNECTIONS

Sean briskly walked down the hallway to his office. He didn't make eye contact with anyone and kept his mouth tightly shut. The Novocain was wearing off, and his cheek felt like it was sliding off his face. The last thing he wanted was to smile at someone with only half of his mouth and look like an idiot. He really didn't have time to go to the dentist's office today, but he lost a filling, so he didn't have any choice. Tonight was another fundraiser, and he couldn't risk being in pain while meeting new donors and supporters.

When he finally reached the safety of his office, he found Mac going through the murder book from one of their cases.

"What are you doing?"

Mac looked up and laughed at him. "You look like you spent your lunch hour with a bottle of Jack Daniels."

"It's nice to know that you always have my back."

"That's what partners are for." Mac stood up and grabbed the book. He pushed his chair over to Sean's desk and set the book down. "Your instincts were spot on. We got the report back on your toothbrush, and it's a match for the blood sample at the Morgan murder."

Sean's sour mood lifted immediately. "So, the church program coordinator was a rapist many years ago." He pulled out his desk chair and sat down.

"Okay, so how did a dead man's blood wind up in our murder scene?"

"That, Mr. Mackenzie, is the mystery we have to solve, since Hardecker died before Morgan, and I've never heard of a ghost murdering someone and bleeding at the crime scene. It's clear someone planted the blood there."

"Could it have been the rapist knife the killer used?" Mac opened the murder book binder and turned to the page with the still shot of Jimmy Morgan tied to his chair, lying in a pool of his own blood.

Sean got up and started pacing. "Not likely. The blood would've looked old and dried on the knife, but this looked fresh. I'd say it was placed on the knife after Morgan was already dead. Why does someone want to lead us to Wyatt Hardecker? Where did they get a sample of his blood? Did he voluntarily give it to them? If not, where did it come from? Was it from a blood draw at a medical facility?"

"Well, I guess we're going to have to take a very close look at Mr. Hardecker. Are you going to tell Stephen Oliver in Spokane that we solved his rape case?" Mac closed the murder book.

"I can't. I didn't have permission to take the toothbrush. It's questionable evidence, and I can get into a lot of trouble for submitting something from a man who died before our murder victim and tying it to our case. We have to keep this evidence between us for now and be quiet about our investigation of Mr. Hardecker. This is an important clue in our case that will hopefully point us toward a suspect. We're going to have to find other evidence that also leads us to the same suspect in order to make a case that will hold up in court. We should start looking into Mr. Hardecker by reading his obituary and seeing where that takes us." Sean sat down at his desk and turned on his computer. Two hours later, they had a lot more information about Wyatt Hardecker.

"Well, we have a timeline for his life and his death. We already knew he was much loved by the people of the church. His parents are dead, and he has a sister who lives in West Virginia. He was cremated and his ashes sent to her. None of this brings us any closer to finding out how someone got hold of his blood or how that blood ended up at our crime scene. We've got to be missing something." Sean leaned back in his chair and stretched his back.

"Did you ever figure out what that Bible verse was in his room?" Mac scratched his chin.

"No. I suppose I can look it up now." Sean typed on his keyboard. "Here it is, *and if your hand or your foot causes you to stumble, cut it off and throw it from you; it is better for you to enter life crippled or lame, than having two hands or two feet, to be cast into the eternal fire. And if your eye causes you to stumble, pluck it out, and throw it from you. It is better for you to enter life with one eye, than having two eyes to be cast into the hell of fire.*"

"Wow. That's a cheerful verse to have hanging on your wall. Why would anyone want... wait a minute? Do you think his war injuries left him incapable of...?"

Sean nodded. "That actually makes sense. He rapes a woman while on leave from his military unit. We don't know if that was his only victim. He is severely injured in the war and has a religious conversion in the hospital. Maybe he considered it punishment for his past sins and spent the rest of his life trying to atone."

"Well, that's food for thought. I think we need to talk to someone at the VA. They handled his medical treatments. We can find out the last time he had his blood drawn for tests. We can also find out the process of how they handle blood samples. Have any of them ever gone missing?" Mac shrugged his stiff shoulders and rolled his neck, which made a cracking noise.

"There's not enough time for me to go to Spokane and make it back for my fundraiser." Sean frowned.

"If I leave now, I can make it to the VA and get home on time for dinner. I'll let you know in the morning what I found. Good luck tonight. I hope you raise a lot of money."

"Thanks, Mac. I'll see you tomorrow."

———

Sean shook hands with Sheldon Dwyer, the host of his fundraiser. It was a warm evening, so the two men stood on the front step of Dwyer's large, expensive house along the Spokane River.

"Thank you, Mr. Dwyer, for opening your lovely home this evening for my fundraiser and inviting all the people. I greatly appreciate your help and your support."

"It's my pleasure, Detective. I am eager to have someone competent in the sheriff's position. Walter Sparks has been a disaster. He's placed too much emphasis on fancy equipment and not enough on recruiting more deputies to stop the rising crime in the area." Dwyer took a step back toward his door.

"I totally agree, sir. As you know, that is the main reason I'm running. Well, I best get going. It's late, and I'm sure you're ready to call it a night. Thank you again for your generosity." Sean gave the man a nod, then turned and headed toward his car in the driveway.

He placed his phone in its cradle then pushed the buttons to call Stephanie while he started the car. She answered on the first ring.

"I was hoping you would call. Did it go well?"

He laughed as he backed out of the driveway. "This was the best fundraiser I've had to date. You should've seen these people's house. It was amazing. Their property goes right up to the river, and they have their own boat dock. They have a huge partially covered deck, and the whole place was lit up with those big string lights. Sam said there were seventy-eight people in attendance, and they were very generous with their money."

"That's wonderful. It really ran late, didn't it? Did you have to talk to many people after your speech?"

He maneuvered the car along the narrow road, heading for the Greensferry Bridge. "Yes. A lot of them questioned me about crime in the county while they were handing me checks. It always makes me feel awkward when they do that, like they're paying me for extra protection of their neighborhoods or something."

"Welcome to the world of politics. You will make a great sheriff. Any movement on your murder cases?"

"No. Mac went to the VA this afternoon to check on how they handle their blood samples. I'll find out in the morning if that idea pans out."

"Do you mind if I make a suggestion?"

"Of course. I always want to hear what you think."

"Thank you, Sean. I can't tell you how much it means to me to have someone who listens to me and values what I have to say."

He smiled. "That's because I love you. Now, what is your suggestion?"

"I've been thinking about what you told me earlier this evening about the blood in the Morgan case. The last place someone would've had access to that man's blood was the mortuary while they prepared his body for the funeral."

Sean raised his eyebrows. "That's a good idea. I hadn't thought of that. I'll have to check it out tomorrow." He stopped at the stop sign before turning onto the main road.

"I should let you go. It's late, and I don't want you to get in an accident while you're driving. Will you text me when you're home safe?"

"Of course I will. You have a good night's sleep. I look

forward to dinner with you again tomorrow night. Good night. I love you."

"I'm looking forward to dinner and the dessert." She laughed.

"Oh, you are a wicked temptress, aren't you."

"You'll find out tomorrow night. And I love you, too. Good night."

"Good night."

Sean grinned all the way home.

————

Sean strolled into the office and set down the tray with two coffees and the bag of donuts on his desk. It was his turn to swing through the coffee shop this morning. He wanted to get his computer up and running before Mac got there. He could've used another hour or two of sleep this morning, but had no such luck. When the door to the office opened, he expected to see Mac coming in, but it was Officer Clark.

"This was delivered in the early morning mail. I thought you'd want to see it as quickly as possible." He handed Sean an official-looking envelope from the Los Angeles County criminal court.

"Thanks, Paul. I've been expecting this." Sean set the envelope down and turned on his computer.

The door opened again. This time it was Mac. "Good morning. Hello, Paul. What are you doing here?"

"Just making a delivery before I head out on patrol. Have a good day, guys." He left the room.

"Oh, thank heavens there's coffee. One of the kids wasn't feeling well, so I didn't have a very good night's sleep. Which one is mine?"

Sean pointed to a cup and opened the bag of donuts. "Here, take this with you. I don't want to end up with jelly all over my desk."

"Hey, it was only the one time."

"Okay, what did you find out at the VA?" Sean sat down and took a sip of his coffee.

"Basically, when the VA does a blood draw, they hang onto the blood until they've finished their testing, then it's disposed of. The only people who actually handle the blood are the phlebotomist who drew it and the lab technicians. The last time Hardecker had blood work done was in November." Mac took a bite out of his donut.

"So, you think the blood for our crime scene came from the VA?"

"No. I mean, it is possible that it came from there, but it's highly improbable. Someone would have to be selling or giving away the blood samples for the specific use of throwing police off the scent at crime scenes. Other people's blood would've shown up as blood evidence at other crime scenes. Plus, that's a long time to hang onto a blood sample. They get fresh samples every day. If someone was selling them for that purpose, they would've sold something more freshly drawn than seven months ago." Mac drank some of his coffee.

"Stephanie said something interesting last night when I called her after the fundraiser. She said the last people who had access to Hardecker's blood would've been the mortuary that handled his body." Sean bit into his donut.

"That's an interesting thought. The blood sample would be a lot fresher than his last medical draw. Do we know which mortuary did the work?"

Sean turned to his computer and tapped on the keyboard, bringing up Hardecker's obituary. "It's listed right here at the bottom of the article. You ready for a road trip to Spokane?"

"Only if we can swing through another coffee shop on the way. I'm going to need more caffeine to stay awake today."

ANSWERS

"All right. Thank you. We'll be there shortly." Sean ended the call. "The owner of the Ever Peace Funeral Home will see us. They have a funeral this afternoon, but he has about half an hour of free time this morning."

"Good. I'm glad you didn't make me go through all this traffic for nothing." Mac had to step on the brakes for another traffic slowdown. "Do they ever stop working on the freeways in Spokane? Every time I have to make the trip into this town, half of the lanes are blocked for some reason or other."

"Come on. You've lived here a lot longer than I have. You know the winter takes a toll on these roads, and they have a limited amount of time to fix everything before winter comes again."

Mac grunted. "I may have lived in the area longer, but I try to avoid going into Spokane if at all possible. I don't like traffic, and the sales tax in Washington is too high."

Sean snorted. "You'd never survive LA traffic. Their roads are congested like this year-round, no matter how many lanes they have." He sighed. "I'm not looking forward to going back there to testify, but the case was a bad one. It was gang related killings, and this defendant is a sadistic son of a bitch. I think he should get the death penalty, but I will settle for life in prison. Hopefully, my testimony will help make that happen." Sean checked the instructions on his phone. "Get off the freeway at the next exit, then turn left at the light. The funeral home is four streets down and on the right side."

Mac pulled into the parking lot and parked the car in a slot closest to the front door. They both got out.

"I hope this leads somewhere. Otherwise, I have no clue about how Hardecker's blood ended up at our crime scene." Sean opened the front door and held it for Mac.

———

Ray pushed the large dry mop across the floor of the entry hall. With a funeral scheduled in the chapel for this afternoon, it was important that the building was as clean as possible when the mourners arrived. He turned, ready to run the dry mop up the other side when he saw them. He recognized them instantly, the two detectives assigned to his murders. He froze. *How did they figure everything out so quickly*? He'd been so careful. He blinked. *It had to be Jimmy.* That was the only killing where he didn't research his planted evidence. He wanted to break the mop handle. How could he have been so stupid, insisting on using his mother's death date as the day for Jimmy to meet justice. Declan Bishop had warned him about that. "Never get hung up on a specific date to commit a crime. Always be prepared to walk away if the preparations or conditions are not perfect."

He had to get out of here. If they didn't have the complete story yet, they would in the next 24 to 48 hours. He hurried down the hall, heading back to the workroom.

He found Luke, the assistant mortician, and told him he was feeling sick. He grabbed his personal things, clocked out, and went to his car. He had to get home as quickly as possible. The only way to stay ahead of the law and finish what he started was to disappear now.

————

Sean stepped over the threshold. "There's supposed to be a sign that says office."

Mac pointed to the end of the hall. "It's over there."

They were halfway to the office when the door opened and a man stepped out. He was in his 60s with thick white hair. He wore a black suit, white shirt, and a wide black tie. Sean smiled. If he passed this man on the street, he would've instantly pegged him for an undertaker. "Are you Mr. Matthews?"

"Yes. You must be the detectives. Let's speak in my office." He turned and went back inside the room.

The office looked very plush and comfortable. The walls were covered with oak paneling. There was a large walnut credenza along the back wall with a matching desk and a black leather chair sitting in front of it. There were two very comfortable-looking leather guest chairs in front of the desk, with a third one in the back corner of the room. Mr. Matthews pointed to the guest chairs and went to his chair behind the desk. "How can I help you, gentleman?"

Sean pulled out his notebook. "We have a case. We need to know which of your employees was on duty while Wyatt Hardecker's body was here."

Mr. Matthews looked alarmed. "Was there something wrong with our services?"

"Not that we are aware of. We simply need to know the names of your employees who were on duty while the body was here and the work that they performed." Sean kept his voice very calm and even. He didn't want the man to become over concerned to the point where he would demand a warrant.

Matthews frowned and remained quiet. After a minute, he spoke. "I will need to pull my records. It will take a few minutes."

"Thank you, sir."

———

Ray rushed around his apartment, grabbing clothes, papers, and anything else of importance. He had a couple of cardboard banker's boxes sitting in the bottom of his closet. He loaded them up and set them by the door. He loaded everything of value into his duffle bag.

There wasn't much food in the refrigerator, but he took it all. He also took his sample materials out of the freezer and carefully placed them in a plastic zip-lock bag. The only samples he had were from Wyatt Hardecker. Once they got his name from his boss, it wouldn't be long before the detectives found out about his felony conviction. One glance at the court report would supply the missing pieces to connect their murder investigations. He needed to be at his hiding place long before that happened. He couldn't take his car like he'd originally planned. They would put out an alert for his car and license plate. He needed another form of transportation fast. Luckily, the answer to his problem was only a few feet from his own vehicle. The neighbor who would be gone for a few weeks helping a relative. He walked over to his duffel bag and pulled out a slim Jim, a special tool used for breaking into cars.

It took three trips to bring all his stuff to the carport and load it into the trunk and backseat of his new getaway car. It took a few more minutes to hot-wire the vehicle. He was on the road quickly. With all his observations of his fickle ex-girlfriend, Amber, he figured out the perfect place to take her once he kidnapped her. All those years ago, when they were dating, they would sometimes sneak off to her family's small cabin near Chilco Lake. It was called a lake, but he always thought it was more like an overlarge pond. The cabin was neatly tucked in a clump of trees with a long front lawn and a small beach. There were other homes around, but because of the shape of the lake and the location of the foliage, it couldn't be seen by the neighbors. It also had a private road leading up to the place.

———

Sean stirred the noodles in his bowl. "Dean was right. This Ramen restaurant food is excellent."

Mac nodded while chewing a mouthful of noodles.

Sean reached for the letter from LA. "I need to book my flight today. I should call them to see if they have any idea how long I will need to be there. I have the first election debate coming up, and I can't miss it."

"When do they need you?" Mac reached for his soda.

"I'm supposed to be there on the 6th. The debate is on the 14th. I'm really annoyed that I have to be gone over the weekend. I'd like to take advantage of the wonderful weather while it lasts and take Stephanie out on the lake again." Sean set the letter down.

"How many names did the mortician give us?" Mac finished his Ramen and set down the bowl.

Sean pulled out his notebook and removed the time-clock readout Mr. Matthews gave him. "There are seven names on the list. We have eight persons of interest because Matthews was there but does not punch the time-clock."

"Okay. I'll take the top four, and you take the bottom four." Mac reached for the list.

Sean finished his lunch while Mac copied down the names. "We'd better head back."

Checking out these names was a good idea, but he didn't hold out much hope that they would lead anywhere. It wasn't until he researched the last name on his list that he hit pay dirt. "Mac, Ray Tisdale, the embalming intern, has a felony record."

"I didn't know you could work in a funeral parlor as a convicted felon." Mac got up and moved his chair over to Sean's desk.

"Apparently you can. The guy's worked there for almost a year."

"Maybe it depends on the crime. What did he get arrested for?"

Sean tapped a few more keys. "It was a drug offense. Apparently, the guy had a boxed meth lab in his car when he was pulled over. Let's take a look at the court record." A few more keystrokes and the record appeared. "Okay. This was a little over 12 years ago. He was convicted and sent to prison for 10 years. He was released a little over a year ago. He must've studied for that position online and got hired shortly after he got out. Well, at least he got an education while he was inside."

"Sean, look at the name of the prosecuting attorney."

When he did, his eyes went wide. "The prosecuting attorney was David Turner? Who was his defense attorney?" He scrolled the page.

Mac whistled. "Son of a bitch, it was Curtis Spellman."

"Look who testified as one of the witnesses."

Mac stood there with his mouth open. He blinked a few times before he spoke. "Remember what you said was your first reaction at the Mercer scene?

"Yeah. Step one."

"Well, partner, here is a list of the steps."

Sean got up from his chair. "We need to get moving. Write down his current address. I have to talk to Burt. We're going to need some backup for this."

———

They arrived at the apartment complex along with three other sheriff's units. They did not arrive with lights or sirens, so they wouldn't warn their suspect. They spread out around the apartment building.

Officer Clark called over the radio. "The car registered to the suspect is in the parking garage."

Another officer went to the door of the apartment. Sean, Mac, and the third officer acted as backup. When knocks on the door went unanswered, the third officer came up with a battering ram and forced the door open. A quick examination of the room made it clear the occupant had gathered up some possessions and fled.

Sean slapped his thigh. "Somehow, this guy knew we were coming." He turned to Officer Clark. "Paul, I want you to knock on doors in this complex and ask if anyone saw him leave. Also, see if any of his neighbors might know where he could've gone."

Mac shook his head. "I wonder if he was watching while we worked at one of his crime scenes? He might know what we look like. If that's the case, he could've seen us arrive at the funeral parlor."

"Mac, this isn't going to go well. We need more information about this guy. Didn't Jimmy Morgan have an ex-wife? She may have known our perp. I think you and I should question her."

––––––

Ray sat drinking a soda in his stolen car. Amber rented one unit of a two unit duplex that sat up against a bend in the freeway. Interstate 90 was much higher than the house, so the backyard ended with a high berm that led up to the road. The duplex was the only unit on the short leg of an L shaped road. It sat on the corner of the L and a cul-de-sac.

Ray was parked on the street on the long leg of the L. He

had a perfect view of the house but was far enough away that his presence wasn't obvious. *Tomorrow is the day.* On Tuesday and Thursday, a neighbor picked up Amber's daughter and took her to school. He planned to go up to the door after the neighbor left, armed with a cloth drenched in chloroform.

He took another drink from his soda can and nearly choked as a familiar car pulled up in Amber's driveway. When the two detectives got out, he wanted to snap the steering wheel in half.

AMBER

Mac pulled out his badge and hung it from his pocket. Sean kept his in his hand. He glanced at Mac, who nodded back before Sean knocked on the door. When the door opened, he had to look down. A little girl with wide green eyes and long brown hair stood in front of him.

"Hello, is your mother home?"

"Lucy, is someone at the door?" A woman came out of what must have been a bedroom. She was tall and slim with hair the same color as the little girl's. She looked rather nervous at the sight of two men on her doorstep. "Can I help you?"

Sean held up his badge. "I hope so. Are you Amber Morgan?"

She nodded. "Yes."

"Ms. Morgan, we would like to talk to you about your ex-husband, James."

Sean looked at the little girl who stood a few feet away watching their conversation.

Amber turned to see what he was looking at. "Lucy, go into your room and play."

The little girl left immediately. Amber called after her. "Shut your door."

When he heard the door close, Sean spoke. "My name is Detective Landers, and this is my partner, Detective Mackenzie. First, we'd like to extend our condolences for your loss."

"Thank you. Jimmy and I didn't speak much after the divorce, but we stayed civil because of Lucy." She walked over to a chair and sat down. She motioned for them to sit on the sofa.

Sean started his questioning. "When was the last time you saw your ex-husband?"

"It was on July 4th. Jimmy's mother wanted to see Lucy. The family was having a large barbecue at their house, and their other grandkids would be there, too. Lucy doesn't get to see her cousins very often. If Jimmy had been by himself, I would've said no, but Lucy is the only granddaughter, and Jimmy's mother just adores her. I knew she'd be safe, no matter what the men got up to." Amber twisted the end of her blouse into a knot.

"You didn't like your ex being alone with his daughter?"

"Oh, don't get me wrong, he would never purposely hurt Lucy. It's just that he drinks too much. When he gets drunk, he loses track of her. I know he loves her, but his family values sons, not daughters."

"Did your ex-husband have any serious enemies? Anyone who wanted to see him dead?"

"He had a lot of drinking buddies and some people he owed money to, but nothing that was serious enough to have him killed. I honestly have no idea who would've done it." She picked the knot out of her shirt.

"Ma'am, do you by any chance know a man by the name of Raymond Tisdale?"

"Ray? What does Ray have to do with this?"

Sean and Mac exchanged a glance. "Do you know why Mr. Tisdale was arrested all those years ago?"

She snorted. "I didn't understand what happened then, but I know the truth now."

"What you mean by that?" Sean pulled out his notebook and pen.

"Ray and I were an item back then. We were pretty serious about each other. We had a lot of plans. Ray was going to go to electronic school. He was very good with computers. He wanted to get his IT certificate first and then learn how to program. He told me he'd finally found a way to pay for school. His mom worked hard to take care of them, but she didn't earn enough to send him to college. I was going to go to school to learn how to become a veterinarian. We had such hopes and dreams. Ray was supposed to pick me up from work, but he never showed. I found out later from Jimmy that he'd been arrested for having a meth manufacturing kit in the back of his car. It didn't make any sense to me. Ray never did drugs. It was Jimmy's older brother Vince, who was in the drug scene. Vince had a friend, Les Wyler, who was a very unsavory character. I'm sure he dealt drugs. None of it made any sense to me. Jimmy convinced me that Ray decided to do something in the drug trade in order to raise the money for school. I should've known that was a lie, but I was so shocked, and Ray hadn't told me how he planned to get the money for school. I found out later that he'd gotten a job." She ran a hand over her eyes to wipe away the tears.

"After the incident, my parents wouldn't allow me to see Ray anymore. I wasn't even allowed to go to court or testify as a character witness. Ray was convicted and sent to prison. Jimmy kept coming by. He was so nice and consoling. I was still in shock and lonely. After a while, we started dating. I got pregnant with Lucy and we got married." She rubbed her eyes again.

"It was obvious very early on that the marriage was a mistake. I should've left him before she was born, but I was afraid. My parents never forgave me for being pregnant before marriage. They refused to financially support me. I had no choice but to stay with him. Jimmy started drinking even more, and things kept getting worse." She rubbed her eyes again.

Mac got up and grabbed a tissue box sitting on the kitchen counter. He handed her the box and returned to the couch.

"Thank you." She wiped her eyes and blew her nose. "I'm sorry, but this is not a very happy story for me." She wiped her eyes again.

"You said you didn't know the truth then, but you know the truth now. What do you mean by that?" Sean wrote some notes in his book.

"One day, while Jimmy was at work, one of the many jobs he had while we were married... He never kept them for long because of the drinking. Anyway, Les Wyler showed up at the door. I really didn't want to let him in, but he said he had something important to tell me. That's when I found out Jimmy asked to have some drugs planted in Ray's car to get him in trouble with the law. He knew my parents would never allow me to see Ray again, and this was his way of breaking us up. Les explained how he didn't have any drugs at the time, but he had a box of meth stuff and put that in Ray's car instead. He apologized for his part of the whole thing, but I didn't want to hear it. I threw him out of the house. I was so angry. Knowing what Jimmy had done to Ray and to me finally gave me enough strength to leave him. I stayed with a friend until I could get financially on my feet. I filed for divorce as soon as I could. I wanted to contact Ray, but I really didn't know what to say to him. After all, I'd married the man who'd betrayed him. I didn't think he would understand or forgive me, especially when his mother got sick. He and his mom were close. I visited her several times and tried to help her, but I had Lucy to take care of, too, so I couldn't see her as much as I wanted to. I did attend her funeral. Ray didn't deserve any of the things that happened to him. Everything was Jimmy's fault."

Sean took a deep breath. No wonder Ray snapped. His friend had destroyed his entire life. Revenge was never an answer, but Sean could see how Ray would consider it justice. "Ms. Morgan, did you know that Ray was out of prison?"

"No. When did he get out?" She set the box of tissue down on the floor.

"A little over a year ago. Have you…"

"Mommy." Lucy was calling out from the bedroom.

"Excuse me for a minute." Amber got up and went to her daughter.

As soon as she was out of earshot, Sean leaned over to Mac. "I've got a bad feeling about her being alone here. Did he know it wasn't her fault? She had nothing to do with what happened to him? Her comment about not knowing what to say to Ray and marrying the man who betrayed him, well, that set off warning bells for me. I think we need to get her into protective custody. After that crime scene at the landscaping company, I'd rather have her and her daughter sequestered in a hotel until we find this guy than get called out to another bloody murder scene. What's your opinion?"

"I'm with you. We don't know what happened to this guy in prison, but he's clearly out for revenge." Mac got up from the couch. "I'll call Burt and make the arrangements. You need to convince her to come with us." Mac walked out the front door.

Amber came back into the room. "What happened to your partner?"

"Ms. Morgan, there are some things about your husband's murder that we cannot discuss yet, but I have a feeling that you and your daughter are in danger. My partner is calling the Sheriff's department to make arrangements to put you and your daughter into protective custody. I'm not sure for how long, but we will contact your employer to explain your absence. You need to leave here with us." Sean tucked his notebook and pen in his pocket.

"Detective, you are scaring me. Do you truly feel this is necessary?" Amber turned to the bedroom where her daughter was playing.

"Ma'am, please, trust me. I'm not making this decision lightly. I have good reason to believe that you and possibly your daughter are in danger. If you could quickly pack a bag with a couple of days of clothes and some toys for your daughter, my partner and I will take you down to the sheriff's office. From there, you will be placed somewhere for your protection."

Amber started to cry again.

"I'm sorry, ma'am. I know this is frightening. I believe this is important for your safety and your daughter's. Do you have a suitcase?"

She bent over and picked up the tissue box. "Yes. I have a suitcase that will hold our clothes. I've got a smaller bag that I'll give Lucy for her toys."

"Thank you, ma'am. I'm going to go outside and talk to my partner while you pack. Let me know if I can help carry anything."

She nodded and walked to the bedroom.

When Sean got outside, Mac had just hung up the phone. "Burt is getting everything prepared on his end. Did she put up much of an argument?"

"No. She's pretty scared. She's packing now. We should be out of here in about half an hour."

They stayed in the front yard until Amber and Lucy came to the door.

"Let me get that." Sean took the suitcase from her.

She readjusted her purse on her shoulder and took her daughter's hand. "Come

on, Lucy. We're going to take a little trip."

It took a couple of minutes to put the bags in the car and

get the two of them settled in the backseat. Sean breathed a sigh of relief when they pulled out of the driveway and drove off.

————

Ray wanted to scream. All the planning, all the work he'd gone through and that stupid detective was ruining everything with only a few hours left to go. How was this man figuring everything out so quickly? Declan Bishop had always said if you planned out everything carefully, you'd be done with everything before the police figured out what was going on. He slammed his fist against the dashboard. This was his revenge. He'd almost completed it. There was only one person left who betrayed him who still needed to pay, and he'd just watched her drive off in the custody of that detective. He wasn't going to sit still for this. If that detective wanted to add his name to the list of people who wronged him, then so be it. He sat for a moment, trying to get his breathing under control. He wasn't stupid enough to kill a cop. That was an unnecessary step that would bring down too much heat. No. He had to be clever about this. He looked in the rearview mirror and smiled. Everything was already in place. He nodded at his reflection. The detective would pay for his interference the exact same way that Turner and Spellman had.

MISSING

A WEEK LATER.

"Has anyone heard from Stephanie yet?" Cliff walked to the office area of the forensics lab. People either answered no or shook their heads. He didn't like that at all. She was always punctual. If something happened and she was going to be late or she was sick, she always called in. It was 10:30 in the morning and nobody had seen or heard from her. He walked into the reception area where Evelyn was typing on her computer.

"I think I'm going to call the Sheriff's office and ask to speak to Sean Landers. Maybe he knows where she is." Cliff frowned and bit his lip.

"Do you need the phone number?" Evelyn stopped her typing.

"I know I have it somewhere in my desk drawer, but I'm really worried. Would you mind calling over there? I'm going to try her cell phone one more time." He looked up to see Evelyn punching in a phone number.

"I'll be in my office. If you get him, transfer him to my phone. Thanks Evelyn."

She nodded, then turned to face the phone.

He called Stephanie again as he walked to his office. It went straight to voicemail, just like his four previous calls had. Something was wrong. Evelyn's voice came over the intercom in his office.

"Detective Landers isn't back yet, but his partner, Detective Mackenzie, wants to talk to you."

"Thanks, Evelyn. What line is he on?"

"Line 3."

Cliff answer the phone. "Mac, I thought Sean would be back by now."

"If his plane left on time this morning, he should land in Spokane about now. I expect him at the office as soon as he can drive here. Why do you need him? Is there a problem?"

Cliff scratched his chin. "Stephanie hasn't shown up to work yet, and she's not answering her cell."

"Has she ever done anything like that before?"

Cliff sat down in his chair. "No, never, she's always on time. And she always calls in if there is a problem. Mac, I don't like this. I've got a bad feeling."

"I'll have a deputy drive to her house and do a wellness check. What kind of car does she drive?"

Cliff rubbed his face. "She has a blue RAV4."

"Okay. I'll call you as soon as I hear something from the officer. I expect Sean to call as soon as he's out of the airport and back in his car. I'll have him contact you."

"Thanks, Mac."

———

Mac hung up the phone and rubbed his chest. He was having a bit of trouble breathing, and he felt a little nauseous. *I must be trying to catch the same thing the kids have.* He loved his children dearly, but they were constantly coming home with colds and other illnesses. Like all families, it wasn't long before he and his wife ended up with the same sickness. He needed to be here today. Sean was coming back and needed to be filled in on the latest information. The fact that no one could reach Stephanie was troubling. Maybe she was ill, too, and had taken something to help her sleep. Or perhaps she was at one of the local emergency clinics being seen by a doctor and getting some medication for whatever ailed her. Anyway, he needed to make a call to request a wellness check.

He had just requested an officer check up on Stephanie when his cell phone rang. He answered on the second ring. "I hope you're in the airport parking lot."

"Yes, and I didn't think I was going to make it here. We ended up flying through some turbulence, and things got a bit rocky. The guy in the seat next to me was suffering from a severe case of motion sickness, which, of course, made the trip even more special. Plus, I've been cramming debate questions for the last two days. Sam emailed me and insisted I spend every moment that I wasn't on the stand going over the questions and coming up with intelligent answers."

"Before we continue with this fascinating conversation about your riveting adventures, when was the last time you spoke to Stephanie?"

"Last night, why?"

"Because I talked to Cliff Bowman about 10 minutes ago. He requested we do a wellness check. She never arrived at work this morning, and she's not answering her cell."

There was dead silence on the other end of the line. Mac could practically hear the thoughts racing through Sean's head. "I just tried calling her before I called you, and it went straight to voicemail. I thought she might be busy with something at work and couldn't answer the phone. Mac, I'm going to leave right now and go straight to her house. If you hear from whoever is doing the wellness check, call me immediately."

"I will. I have the same bad feeling you do." Mac hung up his phone and leaned back in his chair. The room seemed warmer, and he was starting to sweat.

A deputy came in with an envelope. "This came in from the fingerprint section." The man set the envelope down on the desk. "Are you all right, Mac? You look a little pale."

Mac started breathing faster. He wasn't getting enough air. "I... I'm not feeling very well." He grabbed his chest and went limp as a rag doll.

———

"Oh, come on." Sean shouted at the traffic on I 90. The memory of Mac's comments about the road construction when they were on their way to the funeral home played in his mind. Neither the traffic nor the repairs had improved since that day. He had been sitting in the same spot for the last 10 minutes. Traffic was at a complete standstill. Whether the problem was because of the road crews running some piece of equipment blocking the traffic across the lanes or someone had gotten upset and caused an accident, he didn't know. He was anxious and in a hurry, and stuck in an unmoving group of cars.

If I was in the department's vehicle, I'd put the blue light on the roof and drive through the center space between East and West bound lanes.

The car in front of him finally moved, and he was able to travel about 5 feet. "Wow. The scenery really has improved. What happened to the flying cars they promised us? It really doesn't matter. If everyone got a flying car, we'd most likely have some other problems, like birds or clouds, that would limit the flow of traffic."

His cell phone rang. The screen showed the caller was from the sheriff's office. "Any updates, Mac?"

"Sean, it's Burt Toliver."

"Oh, sorry. I was expecting Mac to call me back."

"Sean, I've got bad news."

Sean froze. Had they found Stephanie? Was she hurt?

"Mac is in the hospital. He had an apparent heart attack. I don't know his condition."

Sean's chest tightened. The blood drained from his face. "But I just talked to him about 45 minutes ago." Traffic started moving again, but he didn't notice until the driver behind him honked his horn.

"Sean, when Mac requested the wellness check for the lady from the crime lab, he said you were going to go to her house straight from the airport. I want you to do that and meet up with Deputy Hart. Let me know if there is anything that you need."

He shook his head to help clean out the fog. "Yes. Thank you, Burt. I'll get there as soon as traffic allows."

"Good. I'm sorry about Mac. I'll let you know if I get any news, but I suspect his wife will call you before she calls me."

"Thanks, Burt." He ended the call.

———

By the time he arrived at Stephanie's apartment, there were two patrol cars and a detective unit on scene. The time it took him to get here had allowed him to calm down and think rationally about the situations. There was nothing he could do about Mac. His partner's fate was in the hands of God and the physicians who worked on him. Stephanie was another matter. She'd been kidnapped. It was the only logical explanation for her disappearance.

Dean and Frank were standing on the lawn talking to deputies Clark and Hart. Dean walked up as soon as Sean parked his car.

"Sean, Burt doesn't know about you and Stephanie. I'm sure he wouldn't have allowed you to be here if he knew.

Frank and I have a light caseload, so we are here to help and give cover, if necessary. Also, I'm sorry about Mac. Has Karen called you yet? We haven't heard any news since the ambulance took him to the hospital."

"No. Karen won't call until she knows something definitive. The fact that we haven't heard anything means they are either still treating him or doing testing. I don't expect to hear from Karen for a while. Now, have you looked at the scene here?"

"Yes. Alan Hart found her car still in the carport with her purse, keys, and lunch on the passenger seat. Alan and Paul talked to the neighbors who were home, but no one saw or heard anything. I'd say she was kidnapped, but we haven't a clue who did it or why."

"I do."

"What?"

"We're looking for Raymond Tisdale. There's already a BOLO out for him. I need some officers to go to his apartment complex and talk to the neighbors again. He didn't take Stephanie's car, and he left his own at his apartment, which means he stole one. Check and see if any of his neighbors are missing a vehicle. He had to get a car from somewhere, and his apartment complex would be the easiest and fastest."

Dean made notes while Sean gave him the address for Ray's apartment. They walked over to Stephanie's car. When Sean looked inside, his stomach clenched. He couldn't lose her. He'd barely survived the loss of Peggy. If Stephanie was gone, too… Well, that would break him.

"Dean, I need you and Frank to oversee the gathering of evidence from Stephanie's car and keep track of the officers doing the apartment search."

Dean nodded. "What are you going to do?"

"I need to talk to the only person who might have an idea where Ray took Stephanie."

Dean frowned. "Who is that?"

"The ex-wife of Ray's last victim, Amber Morgan."

————

Sean arrived at the safe house where they were keeping Amber and her daughter Lucy. It was a small ranch-style house on a rural road in Hayden. It had a long driveway and was hidden by trees and bushes. It had a high solid fenced backyard where Amber and Lucy and the officers guarding her could relax outside unseen. He'd called ahead, so they were expecting him. When he entered the house, he found Amber sitting at the dining table with Deputy Garcia, while Lucy was outside playing croquet with Deputy Meyer.

"Hello, Ms. Morgan. I need to ask you a few questions."

"Okay." She looked at the officer next to her. "The deputy told me that Ray had kidnapped someone. How can I help?"

"When you and Ray were dating, was there any special place you liked to go? By the lake or perhaps one of the parks in the area. Someplace that's private and secluded."

"Why are you looking for a place like that?"

"We're pretty sure he was going to kidnap you and take you somewhere. It looks like he was trying to get even with everyone he thought had wronged him all those years ago. You said it yourself. You married the man who betrayed him." Sean pulled out a chair and sat at the table.

"Okay, but I still don't understand why you're looking for a place like that?"

"Everything he's done so far was well planned out. He would've had a specific place picked out to take you, I'm guessing someplace that would've meant something to you and him. We interrupted his plans, and now he's lashed out and taken someone that we know. He wouldn't have had enough time to find another location to take her. I'm guessing he's taken her to the same place he was going to take you. I'm hoping you have some idea of where that place could be."

Sean ran his fingers through his hair. It was a longshot, and he knew it, but it made sense. It fit the profile.

"The only place that I can think of is my parents' cabin on Chilco Lake. It's not a big place, but it is tucked away in the trees. You can't see the neighbors on either side or across the lake. We used to go swimming there sometimes and have picnics. When my parents were going to be gone for several hours, I'd take the keys and we'd go up there. My parents never would've approved of the two of us going there unchaperoned. We were lucky they never found out about it."

He could've kissed her. The place sounded perfect, connected to their past and secluded. *The perfect place for another murder.* "I need the address and directions on how to get there."

RESCUE

Sean parked his car behind some bushes on the side of the dirt road leading up to the Ricci family cabin. He had no idea if his guess was right, but he didn't want someone to spot the car and call the police. *Ray might have a police scanner to follow law enforcement movements while he committed his crimes.* With Stephanie's life at stake, he wasn't going to leave anything to chance.

He put on a dark green jacket and stuffed his phone and small binoculars into the pockets. The weather was still warm, but the jacket would help protect his arms from the thick brush and foliage around the property.

He stuck to the dirt road until he could see the outline of the house through the trees. After that, he worked his way through the underbrush until he was close enough to see the house and its windows. There was a lean-to on the right side of the house big enough to hold a car. It was currently occupied, and he quickly pulled out his cell phone and binoculars before making a note of the license plate number.

No one had bothered to do any landscaping on this side of the house. It just had some grass and weeds that led up to the small sidewalk which ran from the carport to the front door.

There was one small window on the downstairs side of the cabin. The glass was opaque, so he assumed this was the downstairs bathroom. There were three small windows on the second floor. These were for each of the bedrooms. Amber had drawn him a crude map of the cabin's layout. All the large windows were on the other side of the house, facing the lake. He would have to sneak around the house through the foliage and face the house in order to get a view of the interior.

The lake side of the cabin was very nice. There were large glass French doors with windows on either side in the downstairs living room and a smaller kitchen window. Upstairs, windows appeared to run along the hallway. They all gave a spectacular view of Chilco Lake. It wasn't a large lake, but it was beautiful.

He moved through the foliage until he could see into the living room. A branch snapped behind him. He spun around, expecting to find Ray standing behind him with a weapon. Instead, he found a deer about four feet away, staring at him. It never failed to astonish him how local wildlife wasn't terrified of humans. They weren't tame enough that you could pet them, but they got a lot closer than expected.

After taking a few deep breaths to slow his racing heart, he pulled out his binoculars again. What he saw made him want to pull out his gun and storm the house. Stephanie sat on a wooden dining chair in the middle of the living room, held in place by what appeared to be rope and duct tape.

He searched the other windows for a glimpse of Ray, but had no luck. Was the man out searching the perimeter? He had to be in the house or somewhere close by. After all, there was a car in the carport, and this place wasn't within walking distance of anything.

He pulled out his cell phone. With eyes on Stephanie, he could positively confirm her location and get Burt Tolliver to bring in the cavalry. Damn. There was no signal where he was. Amber had told him there was cell phone coverage at the house. He could feel his blood pressure rising. He did not want to take his eyes off of her, but as one man, he couldn't just charge the house. He had no idea where Ray actually was. The man could be hiding anywhere. He also didn't know what type of weaponry the man had with him. *Ray could easily kill Stephanie before I reach her.* He had to call for backup and pray it wouldn't arrive too late.

He slowly worked his way back through the foliage, checking every few feet for a cell phone signal. He was parallel with the house before one bar finally appeared on his phone. That still didn't solve his problem. He had a signal, but he was only 6 feet from the building in thick brush. If any of the windows were open, Ray could hear his voice. He needed to get out of earshot, but stay within cell phone range. All he could think of as he worked his way through more foliage was Stephanie strapped to that chair. He wanted to tear Ray apart with his bare hands for taking her.

After several yards, he reached the sweet spot, out of earshot but within cell phone coverage. "This is Detective Sean Landers. I need to speak with Burt Tolliver ASAP." By the time Burt got on the line, Sean was practically climbing the trees.

"Sean, I spoke with Dean and Frank. They said you know who kidnapped her. How is that possible?"

"I don't have time to explain all the details. She's currently tied to a chair and being held by the man who murdered David Turner's mistress, Curtis Spellman's son, and the landscaping guy. I need backup. I need it fast before he kills her." He wanted to get back to the front of the house and see what was going on. Everything felt like it was going in slow motion.

"Are you telling me you've actually been chasing down a serial killer?"

"Burt, I will show you all the evidence and all the details

when this is over. Right now, I need the SWAT team, especially the sniper. Please hurry. They can approach with lights until they reach the dirt road to the house. Do not use sirens. I don't want to tip this guy off that we're coming, so you need to phone the team members. I'm not sure, but he may possess a scanner. I'm texting you the address. It's a cabin on Chilco Lake. There's limited cell phone coverage out here. I have to get back to my observation spot, but there is no signal there. I'll be in the foliage with a line of sight to the lakefront side of the house. Tell everyone to use extreme caution and remain hidden from the view of the house. We don't know what weapons he has with him. Since he is a known killer, he will kill his hostage if he thinks we're closing in."

"Okay. I'll send the cavalry. Be careful."

When Sean arrived back at his hiding place, he breathed a sigh of relief. Stephanie was still alive and tied to the chair. She did not appear to be injured as far as he could tell. Now it was a waiting game. If Ray made a move against her before the SWAT team arrived, he'd have no choice but to rush in and try to save her. Even if that decision proved fatal to both of them, he knew he had to try. He could never live with himself if he watched her die and did nothing.

———

Jeff Olsen took another sip of his cold coffee and stared at his computer screen. He was supposed to write an article about the upcoming openings of the three six-year terms on the planning and zoning commission for tomorrow's edition of the paper, but the words weren't coming. There were some days that he really hated his job. He'd love to work on a big city paper, but he been here so long the thought of actual change, not to mention the cost of moving, made the idea only a pipedream. He scooted his chair back, intending to go to the break room to refresh his coffee when his cell phone rang. He glanced at the name. It was his source in the law enforcement community. He answered the call. "What have you got for me?"

"There is something big going down at Chilco Lake. You need to get down there right away. Here is the address…"

Jeff wrote it down on the back of an envelope before grabbing his camera and heading out the door.

———

Stephanie shifted her position in the chair. She had an itch on her leg, and the strap on her left arm was too tight. The duct tape over her mouth prevented her from talking. All she remembered was loading up her car and walking around to the driver's side and opening the door. A man grabbed her and pinned her to his chest and put a smelly rag over her face. The lights went out until she woke up tied to this chair. She'd never seen the man before. He looked terrible, like he hadn't slept well for several nights. It wasn't until he asked how Sean had figured out so quickly that he was the one who killed the landscaping guy that she realized who he was. Of course, Sean had told her about making the connection between all three murders after discovering a convicted felon worked for the funeral parlor. When he removed the duct tape over her mouth she played dumb, telling the man she did not know what he was talking about. Lab technicians only analyze evidence. It's up to law enforcement to put all the pieces together and figure who did it and catch the perpetrator. After that brief conversation, he put the duct tape back over her mouth.

She looked out of the French doors, hoping to see the police arriving with Sean. In the meantime, she was banking on the idea that the less of a threat she was to this man, the less likely he was to hurt her.

———

Sean froze when he saw movement through the foliage to his right. He reached down and pulled his gun out of his holster. A moment later, Paul Clark came into view. He'd never been so happy to see the officer in his life. He hastily put his gun back in his holster before whispering. "Are the others here, too?"

"Yes. Everyone is getting into position. The sniper team is setting up on the other side of that narrow part of the lake. After studying the map, everyone agreed that would be the best place for them to locate." He handed Sean a radio with an earpiece. "Here. Now you can follow along with what's happening."

———

Ray came out of the kitchen holding a ham sandwich and a beer. He was careful not to lock eyes with the forensic lady. Killing was easier if you didn't think of the victim as human. He walked behind her and sat down on the couch to finish his meal. The house was getting a little stuffy, but he didn't want to open any of the windows on the front or sides of the house. Just in case the clever detective got lucky and figured out where they were, he didn't want anyone to sneak into the house without him noticing. He set the empty plate and beer can down on the coffee table and walked to the French doors. When he opened them, a pleasant breeze blew into the house.

He turned around and saw Stephanie squirming in her chair. "I know that's uncomfortable, but it's necessary to make sure you don't escape. I'm just waiting until it gets dark, then I can leave the area with less chance of being caught. I'm sorry you got mixed up in all of this. You can blame your boyfriend for that. If he'd left everything alone and let me take Amber, well, she'd be sitting here instead of you. She was the last one on my list. After I took care of her, then everything would be complete. Everyone who ruined my life would've paid the price they owed me. Now I have to go make a life somewhere else with that one loose end haunting me forever. It's unfair. I didn't deserve what happened. Two people who could have stopped it, well, they were too busy with their own plans to give justice to an innocent man." He started pacing the room.

"I really am sorry you got mixed up in this. I promise I will make it as quick and painless as possible. In the meantime, enjoy the view and the sunset. This really is a beautiful place to spend your last hours."

He turned and looked out the French doors. The sunlight glimmered on the water, and the view from the house showed only trees and thick foliage around the edge of the lake. That's when he saw it. Movement in the greenery, slightly to the left of the water. They were here. Damn that man for being so clever. He ran to his duffel bag sitting on the floor next to the sofa. He pulled out a pistol. This is not how things were supposed to go. He wasn't going to go back to prison, no matter what. Before they killed him, he was going to get one last piece of revenge against the man who denied him what he wanted. He walked over to Stephanie. She turned to face him, and her eyes went wide. He held up the gun. A shot rang out.

FAMILY

The large meeting room at the city library had a standing room only crowd. There were three podiums set up on the dais, each with its own microphone. In front of the dais was a long table with three chairs, one for the moderator and the other two for the questioners.

Susan stood beside her brother Dennis while he was receiving last-minute instructions from Tom Oliver. They'd been practicing in the law firm's board room for this debate for the last three days. She and Douglas sat at the far end of the table, firing questions at Dennis while Tom Oliver took notes and offered suggestions on how to give a better answer.

She kept glancing around the room, looking for Sean Landers and hoping that Stephanie stuck to her word about remaining neutral in this contest. If there was any hope of healing the family, she needed to be absent from this debate.

On the other side of the room, Walter Sparks was talking to several members of the public. The room was quite noisy with everyone in private conversations. Still, Susan expected to see the detective somewhere in the crowd, but there was no sign of him. She had an uncomfortable feeling about the man's absence.

"Okay, they're about ready to start. Douglas, you and Susan need to take your seats. I assume your parents are saving them for you?"

Susan nodded at Tom while Douglas gave Dennis a pat on the shoulder and wished him luck.

A man in a light gray business suit got up on the dais and went to the center podium. "Ladies and gentlemen, if you would please take your seats, we are ready to begin this evening's debate for the office of County Sheriff. I've been informed there will only be two candidates debating this evening. The first candidate is our incumbent sheriff, Walter Sparks."

Sparks climbed the steps to the dais and waved to the applauding crowd.

"Our second candidate is his opponent, attorney Dennis Webb."

Dennis stepped up to the podium, smiling and waving to the crowd. There was much more enthusiastic applause for Dennis than for the sheriff.

"The third candidate who was supposed to be here tonight, Detective Sean Landers, has dropped out of the race. Gentlemen, the format for this evening is as follows…"

———

Sean leaned back on Stephanie's couch with his feet resting on her coffee table next to a copy of the newspaper. The entire front-page article was about Ray and his quest for revenge. The *Moose Droppings* guy had done a very accurate and thorough job of telling the story, including Stephanie's kidnapping and rescue.

Sean's cell phone was in speaker mode on the armrest next to him.

Mac's voice sounded a little raspy. "So how is Stephanie doing?"

"She's still in shock. They shot the guy while he was standing next to her, pointing a gun at her. She had his blood on her face and clothes. They took her to the hospital. She didn't have any injuries except for bruises from the rope, zip ties, and duct tape. I've been with her all night."

"Was she able to get some sleep?"

"She woke up several times screaming and crying. I finally made her take some sleeping pills. That seemed to settle her down and let her sleep. She woke up about an hour ago. I made her take a hot shower while I ordered takeout for lunch. It should be here any minute." Sean glanced at his watch.

"Can you order me some takeout food? The crap they serve at the hospital isn't fit for human consumption."

"Aren't your bad eating habits part of the reason you're in there?"

"You're beginning to sound like Karen. So, everything yesterday went according to plan?"

"No, Mac, it really didn't, but it worked out in the end. Thank God. I wish you were there to see it. I mean, I stood there, watching Ray aim the gun at her head. I thought she was going to die right before my eyes. Then I heard the rifle shot. The sniper team took him out just in time."

"You got very lucky, Sean. It could easily have gone the other way. That was fast thinking to figure out that he would use the same location when he abducted Stephanie that he planned to use for Amber. I'm sorry I wasn't there to help."

"Mac, you need to get better. Even though this won't go to court now that Ray is dead, we still have an awful lot of mop up paperwork to do."

"Are you going into the office tomorrow?"

"No. I'm taking a few days off. I don't want Stephanie to be alone. I want her to know she's safe."

There was a knock at the door. Stephanie strolled out of

the bedroom with wet hair, dressed in sweatpants and a T-shirt. "I'll get it." She yelled at Sean's phone. "Hello, Mac. I'm glad you are going to be all right."

Mac hollered back. "Hello, Stephanie. I'm glad you're okay, too."

Stephanie pulled her wallet out of her purse, which was sitting on the shelf of the entertainment center. She answered the door and paid for the meal.

Sean continued the conversation. "Seriously, Mac, when do you think you'll be back?"

"Well, partner, that's a rather sticky question. Karen and I have been talking, and I don't think I'm coming back. This heart attack was a close call. I was really lucky that it happened in a building where almost everyone knows how to give some emergency medical care. If they hadn't started CPR immediately, I might not have made it. The doctors are going to send me to a nutritionist to put me on a restrictive diet. I also have to see a specialist to help me with my nicotine problem. It's going to take me a while to heal, and it's probably better for me to do it at home rather than go back to work. Karen has a degree in accounting, so she shouldn't have too much trouble finding a job. I'm going to stay home and be Mr. Mom for a while. Don't worry. I'm just retiring, not disappearing off the face of the earth."

"Still, the department isn't going to be the same without you."

"Hey, I need to go. Karen just arrived with the kids. I'll talk to you later. Keep an eye on Stephanie. It's going to take her a while to get over this. She's going to need you to help her get through it."

"I know. Thanks for everything, Mac. Say hi to Karen for me. Later."

"Yeah, later."

The line went dead.

Stephanie walked up to him, holding two delivery bags.

"Do you want to eat at the table or here in front of the television?"

———

Sean was back in his usual corner of Stephanie's couch. Stephanie snuggled against his shoulder, and he had his arm around her to keep her close. Even though the evening was comfortably warm, she had put on a hoodie that matched her sweatpants. The anchor on the evening news explained the story of the three murders and Stephanie's kidnapping, complete with video footage and still shots from each crime scene. The reporter was giving Sean far more credit than he thought he deserved. If Ray hadn't made the mistake of planting Wyatt Hardecker's blood at the Morgan murder scene, they never would've made the connections. When a picture of Ray came on the screen, Stephanie buried her face in his chest.

"Hey, it's all right. He can't hurt you or anyone else." He brought his other arm around and hugged her tight.

Stephanie moved and looked up at him. "I know he can't hurt anyone anymore. I just don't understand how he could kill those innocent people just to get revenge."

"I don't understand it, either. Prison changes people. If he had tried to get his case reopened and hired a competent lawyer, he probably would've gotten the entire conviction overturned and dismissed. Instead of pursuing justice, he chose to pursue vengeance. That never goes well."

"You should have stayed in the sheriff's race. You understand how the department should work."

"Anyone with good organizational skills can be sheriff. It's an administrative position, not a law enforcement one. I don't want to spend the time that campaigning requires. You are my priority, your safety and comfort. I love you." He kissed her.

A knock on the door interrupted their conversation. "I'll get it. You stay here. I don't want you bothered by any well-wishers or curious neighbors."

When Sean opened the door, it surprised him to see five people standing out front. A moment later, Susan threw her arms around his neck and hugged him.

"Thank you for saving my sister."

He took a half step back, not knowing how to handle the situation.

Stephanie got up from the couch. "Mom? Dad? What is everyone doing here?"

Susan let go of Sean and ran to Stephanie. "Oh, sis, I'm so glad you're safe."

Sean stood there and blinked a few times before stepping back and opening the door wider, inviting everyone in with the wave of his hand. When everyone was inside, he closed and locked the door.

There was another awkward moment while everyone just stood there waiting for the sisters to finish their embrace. When they did, both of them were crying. Stephanie walked over to Sean and took his hand before looking at her parents. "Mom, dad, this is Detective Sean Landers. Sean, these are my parents, Harold and Doris Webb. And these two are my twin brothers, Dennis and Douglas."

Sean held out his hand to Stephanie's father. "I'm pleased to meet you, sir."

Her father looked at it for a second before taking it. "I, ahh, I want to thank you for saving my daughter. The paper said you were the one who figured out where that monster had taken Stephanie. Thank you." Doris stood beside him, nodding and crying.

Stephanie stepped in to save Sean. "Please, everyone, sit down. Would anyone like something to drink? I have wine, beer, soft drinks, or I can make coffee."

That broke the ice. Her parents sat down on the couch,

while the twins and Sean grabbed the dining room chairs and arranged them around the coffee table. Susan helped Stephanie gather drinks and glasses in the kitchen and arrange a platter of muffins.

In the living room, the twins were questioning Sean about the case while Stephanie's parents listened intently.

Susan whispered to Stephanie. "You have a good man there. He'll make a fine addition to the family."

CONNECT WITH AUGUSTINA

You can stay up-to-date on upcoming releases and sales by joining my newsletter.

https://augustinavanhoven.com/join-newsletter/